I, FATTY

I, FATTY

a novel

JERRY STAHL

BLOOMSBURY

Published by Bloomsbury, New York and London Distributed to the trade by Holtzbrinck Publishers

All papers used by Bloomsbury are natural, recyclable products made from wood grown in well-managed forests. The manufacturing processes conform to the environmental regulations of the country of origin.

Library of Congress Cataloging-in-Publication Data

Stahl, Jerry.
  I, Fatty : a novel / Jerry Stahl.—1st ed.
    p. cm.
  ISBN 1-58234-247-4
  1. Arbuckle, Roscoe, 1887–1933—Fiction. 2. Motion picture actors and actresses—Fiction. 3. Hollywood (Los Angeles, Calif.)—Fiction. 4. Motion picture industry—Fiction. 5. San Francisco (Calif.)—Fiction. 6. Trials (Murder)—Fiction. 7. Comedians—Fiction. I. Title.

PS3569.T3125I15 2004
813'.54—dc22
                        2003028011

First U.S. Edition 2004

1 3 5 7 9 10 8 6 4 2

Typeset by Hewer Text Ltd, Edinburgh
Printed in the United States of America by
Quebecor World Fairfield

For Stella Jane Stahl and Chris Calhoun

There is nothing funnier than unhappiness.
—Samuel Beckett

Introduction

I WAS ONCE picked up by the police on Fatty Arbuckle's front lawn. Of course, by then Fatty—who preferred to be called Roscoe—had moved on. Arbuckle died in 1933. And this was the mid-eighties, before the dawn of the Crack Era. Street dealers dotted that no-longer-upscale strip of Adams Boulevard, near downtown Los Angeles, flagging down white kids in cars to sell them loads, a potent combo of Doredin and Codeine 4. Dors-'n'-4s offered a slow-motion rush that lasted half an hour, with a residual opiate buzz that kept you scratching your nose and not moving your bowels for days at a time. Looking to deeply wound legions of much-loathed punks—core consumers for the narcotic combo described above—a cabal of LAPD, DEA, and two mysterious men named Leon from Compton made Doredins disappear, forcing an entire community to jump to junk.

Fatty's pad, by the time your author landed facedown in front of it, had already been converted to a stately outpost of Christ called Amat House. Amat served as home base for a batch of Vincentian priests, a sect devoted to chaste men doing charitable works. These, apparently, did not include rushing out to aid drug-crazed strangers in moments of distress—though I do recall a couple of startled white faces peering from a pushed-aside curtain as an officer bade me lie "lips down" on the sidewalk. I was not, technically, on the Catholic brothers' lawn; my face was pressed between the prongs of the metal fence that surrounded their grass. Still, I remember savoring the dank, naturey smell of steer manure, pretending that I was on a farm, napping with my face in the dirt, the way farmers do.

All of which would mean absolutely nothing if not for the fact that three-quarters of a century earlier, in 1916, a fetus-faced five-foot-seven, 375-pound millionaire was shooting heroin and contemplating his ruin in the very chamber from which the strange white faces stared down at my own. Who knows but that Arbuckle, nodding in some bygone era, closed his eyes and heard the cries of drug abusers three generations unconceived stumbling down the sidewalk of the house he occupied?

At the time of his needle ride, 29-year-old Roscoe "Fatty" Arbuckle was more popular than Charlie Chaplin. And, on that particular August day, at the screaming height of World War I, in an upscale corner of the cow town packed with transplanted White Trash, first-generation Euro-escape artists, marginal theatrical types, and native Mexicans, the colossal, nodding Arbuckle could claim to be the most loved movie star waddling the earth—if not the most clean-living.

Hooked by an incompetent intern who botched a boil-lancing procedure and prescribed heroin to ease the agony, Arbuckle was left with an on-again, off-again habit on top of his already rampant alcoholism. Attending to his special "needs" was a Japanese manservant named Okie, a combination valet, handyman, and gofer whose status in Arbuckle's life presages the "personal assistant," now a virtual prerequisite for Hollywood status holders.

Okie stuck with his master through three marriages, an arrest for murder and rape, three trials, and an overnight fall from massive stardom to object of mass hate—a spiral that stripped him of millions and left him in financial ruin. It was the financial ruin that got Okie worried.

As rumor has it, Okie worked for free when Arbuckle lost his fortune due to legal bills. He stayed on, earning nothing, in what many of Arbuckle's friends considered an act of supreme employee devotion. The darker truth is that Okie—real name Tomokita Ito—knew he had nowhere to go. Who would hire a manservant whose last man was a fat rapist and sex murderer? It behooved the cagey valet to have a plan B—which he did. If you so choose, you're about to read it.

From the time of his employer's first surgical mishap—when pain drove Fatty the actor to become Fatty the addict—Okie controlled the drugs. He knew how much to dispense, and when to stop dispensing it. But at the end, when it was clear the man whose fate determined his own was never going to win back more than a sliver of his former status—or earning power—Okie took matters into his own hands. In a series of "no story, no medicine" sessions, the determined servant withheld narcotics to his employer until, facing the throes of withdrawal, the big man told his story. Bit by tragicomic bit.

Okie'd boosted one of those newfangled Dictaphones from the back of Adolph Zukor's Pierce-Arrow and learned how to use it. They scheduled sessions wherein Arbuckle would dredge up his life as best he could, and when he began sweating too badly to focus, Okie would give him his shot.

Roscoe's last wife, Addie McPhail, knew that her husband was overworked. Sustaining a career was hard enough, but the pressure of staging a comeback was *crushing*. Sometimes Roscoe's leg hurt so badly he could not get off the divan without an injection. Happily—for us—Addie never questioned his occasional disappearances to his "study" with Okie in tow. Roscoe always returned chatty and affectionate, if a little glassy-eyed.

The apocryphal version of *I, Fatty* is that Arbuckle finished spilling his proverbial beans—eyes on Okie's fingers around that loaded syringe as he poured his life out—on the very day, maybe at the very minute, he expired. (The way the book landed in my hands is a saga in itself and would require another tome.) Suffice it to say, the reality of how the manuscript came to exist at all can never be known for certain. As to the truth of the document you're about to read, the jury's out on that, too.

Not that a jury's version of reality has much to do with anything. One lesson Roscoe learned—the way one does after surviving three murder trials, worldwide vilification, jail, and pie fights—is that what people are willing to believe about a man, and what a man believes about himself, tend to be wildly divergent enterprises.

Roscoe "Fatty" Arbuckle stood out as the O.J. of his day. The difference—aside from niggling matters of race, guilt, and innocence—is that, for his "crimes," not only was Roscoe hounded from the top of the Hollywood food chain to the bottom, but the furor over his alleged behavior left Hollywood itself nearly hounded out of existence, victim of a morally indignant, rabidly fascinated, tabloid-fed public.

Of course, that very public's appetite for the sordid details of Arbuckle's "crime" gave rise to an entire industry of celebrity-obsessed, and celeb-baiting, journalism that persists to this day. As do the church-based fundamentalist moralizers who blamed Fatty for all the family-threatening ills of a society they believed to be straying from right-living into moral decay. Bad enough the millionaire butterball was a degenerate perv—*he worked for Jews!* And Jews, as every fundamentalist knows, want nothing better than to corrupt the heart of the heartland.

The tale of Arbuckle's rise, fall, and double-edged redemption is here filtered through the sometimes bilious, sometimes anguished, oddly lighthearted soul of the man himself. As narrator—and male lead—Roscoe stands out as funny as he is tormented. A simple Kafka in a fat-suit. He was massively candid, given the circumstances. Which were pretty extreme. But who knows?

As the somewhat portly Dr. Johnson liked to remind his admirers, "Seldom any splendid story is wholly true."

PART 1

Daddy Was a Custer Man

DADDY REFERRED to my mother's reproductive organs as "her little flower."

In my earliest baby-boy memories, the man's either looming and glum—not drunk enough—or bug-eyed and stubbly after a three-day bender, so liquored up he tilts when he leans down to snatch me off the burlap rags my brothers and sisters piled on the floor of our Kansas shack and called our "sleepy blankets." I'd blink awake in the air, shaking cold, my face so close to Daddy's the rye fumes burned my eyeballs. He'd rattle me till my teeth clacked, then start ranting in that high, Hoosier whine he only got when he was blotto and wanted to hurt something.

"*You broke her little flower, pig boy!*"

—WHACK!—

"*Sixteen pounds of baby? That's just wrong!*"

—SLAP PUNCH SLAP—

If, against my better judgment, I'd speak up—"*Ouch, Daddy, please . . . I'm sorry!*"—it only made him more furious. He'd drop me outright—one blessing of fat, it's good padding—and strike a pose like John L. Sullivan, whom he liked to think he resembled.

"*I'll show you sorry, Jumbo! You broke Mama's little flower squeezing your sideshow keister out of her . . . If you'd never been born, she wouldn't have gotten sick!*"

That was Daddy. Willie Arbuckle. Born in Indiana, died in Kansas, California, Mexico, and anywhere else he tried his luck. In the magazines, I always called him a "gentleman farmer." The real article was a professional boozehound, gifted at going belly up in five languages. He married a church-going lovely, beat her senseless, then embarked on a life of leaving for glory and crawling home broke.

Daddy liked to say that his fondest wish was to have "gone with Custer." The general had perished four years before Dad moved to Smith Center—which, in 1880, was the geographical center of the continental United States. *"The boys in the Seventh U.S. Cavalry found glory at the hands of savages—and all I've ever done is pass out in Kansas."*

Just a Big Little Boy

I was born three days ahead of schedule—always eager to get to the next date—so Mama had to make do without a midwife. When Daddy got word, he barreled in from the fields, took in my girth and my mortally exhausted mother, and let out a yowl. According to my sister Norah, who was bringing in boiled sheets, Daddy threw Mama's Bible against the wall and cursed. *"Goddamm it, Dee, that can't be mine. It's got the haunches of a hog!"*

He hated me on sight. Which does something to a boy. Knowing I caused so much distress for my mother and father by just *being me* made me want to eat. The more I ate, the more Daddy went Hun on me for how fat and stupid I was. I topped 100 at 5. When my mother died, Daddy told me I killed her. The old man got whirly drunk, belt-whipped me, and locked me in a steamer trunk for a week. I was 12. He kept screaming that after I was born, my mother "stopped being a wife." I had ruined her womanhood.

Ladies and their little flowers pretty much scared me from then on. Because you could break them without knowing it. Or somebody could say you did.

"*Jesus didn't need a penis!*" Mama liked to remind me. For as long as I can remember, she would quote the Bible to show me that sex was wrong. As I grew older, it seemed worse than wrong. It seemed impossible. After I married and suffered a droopy honeymoon, a doctor in Los Angeles said that my girth had left me with a weakened nuptial muscle. "Heft problems. Nothing to be ashamed of," he explained. "Eat more blood-meats."

Easier to just say I'd been drinking. Easier to just drink. . . . I knew how to be affectionate, and relished a cuddle. But it didn't come up that often.

A Curious Parallel

A funny thing—well not funny, but *funny:* when that DA accused me of forcing myself on poor, demented Virginia Rappe in San Francisco, I felt the same way I did when Dad used to stagger in drunk and beat the molasses out of me. I knew I was innocent, but I knew it didn't matter. Truth was whatever the person hitting you with a belt buckle needed to believe. Underneath the shock and heartbreak at how fast everybody chose to assume the worst—from Bigger Than Chaplin to Señor Dogmeat in less time than the Red Line took from Hollywood to Glendale—there was this feeling, too: *Dad was right.* I could almost see his sneering face floating just over mine, "*You broke that poor girl like you broke your mama.*"

Even if I never touched Virginia Rappe, or any other female, people had their reasons for believing. For wanting to believe I'd done something worth hating me for. I hated the name Fatty, and I made a career out of being that name. (Buster Keaton said that to get people to love me, I became what I loathed the most. Buster was the one pal who stood by me through it all.)

So, before we really get going here, I just have to say this: Something strange happens when you lose everything. Something strange happened to me. All those years of being lucky, being successful—first comic actor to direct his own movies, first to make a million a year—I never felt comfortable. I had to pay a bootlegger to feel even half-good, and after that, a croaker, for narcotics.

Once all my money—and all my luck—was used up, I could relax. I wanted to die, but at least the feeling was *familiar*. Does this make sense? Before the court lynched me, I was as big a success as Daddy was a failure, and I needed the hooch more than he did. Sometimes more. After the St. Francis fiasco, I didn't need the drink. I mean, I did, but not the same way. Thanks to Virginia Rappe, I had an excuse to feel the way I had always felt, but could never explain when things were aces.

But there I go, rushing the gag. . . .

Hell on the Prairie and Santa Ana

We—Dad, when he was sober and at home, my ailing mother, and a ragtag quartet of siblings—occupied a drafty one-room cabin with a sod roof. If Daddy hit me too hard, I'd bang off a wall and chunks of sod would fall off, which made him madder.

"If you hadn't been born, Mama wouldn't've got sick, and your brothers and sisters wouldn't be huddled like pack wolves on the floor of a one-room shack in Kansas . . . ."

Like I say, that's all I heard as a young pudge. Daddy believed that every failure he suffered was on account of me. It was my fault he'd ended up some washed-up souse of a farmer and prospector. When he was really plastered, he'd even tell me that I wasn't his, and beat me harder, while Mom just shut her eyes and recited Bible quotes. If he was tired of punching, he'd drag me outside and make me haul wood off the ground until I had enough for a fire. He'd beat me in the head with branches, then start a fire and threaten to toss me in. *"Time for sucklin' pig!"* he'd chuckle. It was the only joke he ever made. And he made it over and over.

When I was 5, Dad up and moved the family to Santa Ana, this broke-down cowboy town in California. (Though from what I could tell, every town in California was broke-down, and drowning in cowboys.) "Santa Ana is heaven for kids," Mom said. "Lots of open fields and space."

We were going to have a new life. Which we did. Except the new life had less money in it than the old one. Daddy couldn't find work, so he drank more while all us kids got jobs. Thanks to my bulk, I looked older than 5, so I was able to get a job doing cleaning up and light delivery for a grocery. Anything was better than being in our house, which was dark and damp, even with the sun scorching the ground outside. Then Mom enrolled me in school and things got bad.

School nearly destroyed me. I'd never been around anybody but my own family, so I couldn't talk to other kids. They'd call me Fatty and I'd get the clam-ups. So in second grade I just kind of dropped out. But I had to go *somewhere*, so every morning I'd ditch my brothers and sisters and duck into whatever theater left their stage door open. Right from the first, the theater was an escape from life. It was life, but better.

Santa Ana was what they called a low-end stop on the vaudeville circuit. There were lots of stock companies floating around. Back then, actors were pretty much nomads. Normal people saw them as whores and hoboes who couldn't get honest work. All these troupes would float through—like the first one I weaseled my way into, the Frank Bacon Stock Company.

I was always sneaking into theaters. I loved sniffing around backstage, eyeballing the costumes, running my fingers through the makeup dust on the battered trunks. What I loved most was eavesdropping on the performers. Off the boards they seemed even more exotic than on. Pirates and Gypsies rolling cigarettes and reading the funny papers.

If the manager didn't throw me out, I'd hide in the wings and watch the show. All that clapping! The first time you hear clapping, it's like firecrackers. A room full of firecrackers, all going off for some little shnip with a big Adam's apple doing Hymie dialect. Or for a couple of hoofers. Or a Chinee plate-spinner. Nobody could spin a plate like the Chinee.

When their run was over, I'd stay to watch the troupes pack up and march off to their next glamorous marquee performance. Everybody stared at them when they sauntered up Main Street to the train station. Shopkeepers came out and sneered. If a little kid threw a rock at an actor, his Dad would chuck him under the chin. If he hit one, he probably got a penny.

But the actors didn't seem to mind. Maybe it wouldn't be so bad, being stared at, if you weren't the only one. Daddy used to tell me I should work in a sideshow, 'cause then I'd be surrounded by people just like me. Geeks and deform-os. Gosh knows I knew a little something about being gawk-fodder.

Daddy-Fetchin'

Mostly, what I tried to do with my young life was not go home. My older brother and sister had moved out, and Mom was pretty much sick all the time. "Bedridden" is what my sister Norah called it. "Mama's bedridden, so don't be a strain." All I wanted was to help her. But I hated having to Daddy-fetch.

If Daddy was home, and he was drunk, he would "show me what a belt is for"—which was better than showing me "what a branch is for." Though not exactly a cupcake picnic either. Daddy'd see the welts next morning and apologize with tears in his eyes. Sometimes he would beg me to hit him in the face, and when I didn't—I couldn't—that would set him off all over again.

But I was talkin' about fetchin', wasn't I? See, if he wasn't home, it meant he was drunk somewhere else, and I was dispatched to get him before he landed in a ditch. "Roscoe, your father hath strayed again," Mom would croak from her daybed. Mother quoted the Bible all the time, and as her condition got worse, she even talked biblical.

I hated Daddy-fetch duty, as the activity was known in the family. With my older brother and sister gone, it fell to me to scour the bars. The worst part was, in public, my father would act like he didn't know me. I knew this, but I always thought if I just slicked my hair back, if I sucked in my gut enough, if I made a joke or sang the right ditty, he would look up and smile and tell everybody I was his boy. He might even call me Roscoe instead of Fatty. But it never happened that way. Boo-hoo and blubber just naturally go together.

When I spotted the old man, generally mumbling and disheveled at the end of a bar, I'd smooth my cowlick, tiptoe over, and tug his arm as gently as I could. "*C'mon, Daddy . . .*" I tried to be inconspicuous. But I was 150 pounds and 5-foot-5 before I was 9. People stared. I'd lean in and whisper in his ear, "*C'mon, Daddy, Mama's ailing.*" But he'd act like he didn't hear me. I wanted to turn around but I never did. I knew what going home without him would mean: Mommy's tears, the crying that turned into coughing fits and blood. Daddy would make a big show of pursing his lips and brushing his coat where I touched him, like some kind of an aristocrat. As if I'd dirtied him.

"I ask you," Daddy would say, talking over my head to the bartender, or whoever else was handy, "does this young rump roast look like he has the blood of William Arbuckle in him? I think not!" Of course I would smile.

The longest exits I ever made were out of those saloons, with Daddy shouting jokes about my "canned hams" and the guys in shirtsleeves doing spit-takes with their beer while I waddled toward the door fighting back tears.

When he was just a little drunk, but not too, Dad would wax rhapsodic about his plans to strike it big in oil and gold. "*Gonna do me some prospectin', and you ain't comin', Tubby!*" I didn't have to ask why. Dad said I wouldn't know how to live rough. He called me a "softy dolly."

Sometimes at night I put on little plays in my head where I'd be standing beside Daddy, in California, panning for gold, and I'd find a nugget big as a cauliflower. I'd hold up my shiny find, and the sun would make it glitter, and Daddy would smile. He would hug me. Maybe muss my hair. Then he'd hold out his hand, palm up, and say, "Give it here, boy. Make your old man rich!" In my little play, I'd just stare at him. I'd play the gag long. Then, finally, I'd say, "*Forget it, you drunken, good-for-nothin' bastard.*" And leave him pawing in the dirt while I went off and lived like a fat pasha.

Years later, whenever I thought about Daddy in those bars,

pretending not to know me, my cheeks still burned. (Not the canned ham ones—the ones on my face.) There's no loneliness in the world like your-own-daddy-don't-want-to-know-you lone-liness. The bartender was always nice, though. He'd slip me a couple of Scotch eggs and whisper. "I got a fatty at home, too. *She's a big ol' sad peach just like you.*"

That winter—our first in Santa Ana, and nothing like the numb-toes months we had to chatter through in Kansas— Daddy got a "business opportunity" in San Jose and left us. The idea was he'd send us money when his ship came in, but either they moved the harbor or it sank outright, 'cause we never heard from him. Once we got word he was pickin' fruit in Barstow. We'd done this as a family a few times on the trip from Smith Center. (I broke a ladder on a farm outside Lovelock, Nebraska, and Daddy brained me with a crab-apple branch when he found he had to pay.) It didn't seem like all that great a business opportunity to me.

Despite everything, I loved Daddy and still believed he would round us all up when the time came. Of course, all us kids were already workin' before Dad left, but with him officially gone— instead of just gone to the bar—we all felt we had to chip in a little more. Mama had been dying for a long time and couldn't do much more than pray.

Happy Is As Happy Does

But happy is as happy does, and—here's a lesson for all you kiddies—opportunity knocks when you quit school in second grade. I was around 8 when the Frank Bacon Stock Company rolled into town for a festive production called *Turned Up*. Their first night a colored boy in the troupe went missing. Mr. Bacon was eating his arms trying to finagle a last-minute replacement. As I happened to be lounging around the theater, in my 8-year-old way, I offered my services. At first Mr. Bacon, an actor *and* impresario, pooh-poohed the idea. Then, reconsidering, he decided having a white chubby-cheeks in the role of a pickaninny might make for good chuckle-bait. I could greasepaint my face, he said. "But you have to go home and get black stockings from your Ma to cover up your gams. You also want to get some shoes. People ain't gonna pay cash money to see those stompers of yours."

Around that time, see, I pretty much went around barefoot, as getting shoes to fit feet as wide as mine was nearly impossible. Even if we had the money to send away, by the time the brogans showed up I'd be a quadruple E instead of a triple.

Well, I couldn't go ask Mom for stockings, I knew that. My mother was a pious woman. For all I knew, she was probably home quoting Revelations 12 that very moment. If I told her I was consorting with actors and needed her lingerie, she might think my Daddy's worst predictions for my future were on the mark. "*I betcha*," he was fond of saying in the grips of rye whiskey and despair, "*you turn out to be some sissy-boy. Betcha you end up peein' with your knees bent . . .*"

Speaking of sissies, nobody wants to see a fat boy cry. So Mr. Bacon pulled me into a closet-sized dressing room full of half-dressed ladies—actresses—who stopped fussing with their own makeup and, at Mr. Bacon's direction, began to slather me in cold greasepaint. (Strange ladies were always undressing around me, even then.) They smeared my face, my arms, all the way from my stovepipe ankles to the tops of my giant, too-tight drawers. (We never had money or new things; I just wore the old ones until they burst.) I felt myself going fluttery. This was more affection in a single moment than I'd known in my entire eight years. I didn't know what to do, so I closed my eyes.

"*Oh, he's a big one!*" cooed an actress named Lil, who had a dime-sized mole painted due north of the cleft between her ample bosoms, like a doorbell. Those amples spilled over her corset inches before my face. It was like a candy dream, where I could have all the chocolate and peppermint snaps I wanted. But instead of candy it was Lil, and Miriam, and Madge O'Scanlon, a.k.a. "Shambina, Mistress of Arabian Dance." Madge, an Irish redhead in an Indian headdress with kohled eyes and a yellow lace brassiere, took me right in her arms and held me. "You're just a big butter pat, that's what you are. You're just a big fat butter pat and I'm gonna squeeze you until you melt and run down my tummy . . ."

Done blackening my flesh, the actresses—half a dozen of 'em, from waif of 18 to boozy matron of 35 or so—began to make carnival with me. They pushed my shirt up to my boy-breasts, a source of embarrassment from my first day in the schoolyard. They started giggling and pinching. They tickled me everywhere, stealing little kissy-bites of belly and paps until I couldn't breathe and laugh-tears burned out of my eyes. I thought I was going to black out or pee from happiness. It was that unfamiliar.

One of the ladies planted a smooch on my mouth and made her own lips black from my greasepaint. Before she got sick, when Mama used to give me a hot bath on Saturday nights and wrap me in old burlap, it felt like this. Floating and loved deep down. I filled my nostrils with gardenia and baby powder and the olive oil the ladies used to keep their elbows smooth. I wanted to stay in that cloud forever.

Right then, I was smitten. I knew before I stepped onstage, this was the place for me. The home you get when you don't have a home you feel at home in. Mr. Bacon showed me where to stand and what to do with my arms. By the time I felt the stagehands' beefy palms on my buttocks, shoving me onto the boards for my debut, I thought that life had gotten as unlikely and wonderful as it was ever possible to get. Then I heard the laughing. A couple of barks from the back row. A few scatter-shot guffaws. . . .

For one, hammering second, I thought: *I did something wrong.* My panic must have shown on my face, for when I turned to Mr. Bacon—now dressed like a buccaneer—he cracked a smile, which brought on still more chortles, along with howls and cackling and full-barrel *Har-Har-Hars.* So many kinds of laughs in the world. You don't know, till you hear them all at once. And then, after *that* happy cacophony, the applause. The clapping like firecrackers going off in your heart.

Mr. Bacon must have seen how I felt, because he leaned in, whispering so only I could hear: "*Like mother's milk, ain't it, Butter Bean?*"

People were standing up and pointing at me and roaring. It was no different than any morning in the schoolyard, but with grown-ups and clapping, instead of bullies and beatings. So that was show business—the place where everything that gets you myrtilized in real life could get you adored.

I came back to the theater every night for three weeks. Mr. Bacon gave me 50 cents after the Saturday matinee and I dropped the coins in Mama's lap as soon as I got home. That was enough for a neck rub and a few minutes of affectionate Bible chat. Mama said she was proud. She thought I was sweeping extra at the grocery store.

This was the life I wanted before I even knew it existed. Everything else in the day was just stuff to get through before coming to the theater, before getting tarred up and tickled by ladies in brassieres. The ladies didn't just tickle me, either. They kept me supplied with sandwiches and other goodies backstage. It got them giggly to see me gobble down a ham-bun or a buttered roll. I always tried to get a little something for Mama too, but I was afraid of getting caught, so I shoved the booty down my pants. One time, Irish Madge, my favorite actress, noticed the bulge and made a crack. "Why, ladies," she tittered, "Roscoe likes me so much I make his pants tight." For some reason this entertained them mightily. Then she reached right down the front of my shorts and pulled out the crumpet that was making the pup-tent. After that they made sure to slip me a little package of snacks to take home, so I didn't have to walk around with crumpet-pants.

A Chance Encounter with Marvo

After my auspicious debut as the Fat Little Moor, I made it my business to be in as many theatrical productions as I could. Though they weren't all in the theater. My next big money job was working for a man named McIvor Tyndall, who went by the stage name of Marvo the Magnificent. Marvo always galloped into town on a speeding carriage with a scarf over his eyes. He said he could tell the horses when to stop with powers of animal telepathy he'd learned in the Orient. It was something, seeing that little fireplug in a purple turban come thundering down the street blindfolded. People would stop what they were doing and rush out to see what the ruckus was.

When he had 'em where he wanted 'em, Tyndall would tug the scarf off his eyes and announce that this was their lucky day. For today, the fates had delivered him, Marvo the Magnificent, to stage a performance in their town, to enlighten them all on the wonders of hypnosis, "the most godly of the psychic sciences."

Marvo stood on his buckboard in flowing robes, arms spread wide, and declared that he needed a volunteer to be hypnotized. "Marvo is looking for one lucky boy to be transported to another world, a world of ether, though in material body he shall remain here with us . . ."

The magician drew more gasps when he revealed that he would pay 10 real dollars—and three free restaurant meals—to his brave subject. My hand shot right up. Of course I wanted the money. But what I wanted more was to be transported to another world. I wouldn't have said this to a soul—Daddy taught all his kids not to snivel—but even the cosmic ether had to be better than Santa Ana, with no father, a sickly Bible-quoting Mama, and the daily sadness and aggravation of kids throwing stones and calling me "The Prince of Whales."

Tyndall's routine was pretty cute. Roll into town, get a store to let him use their display window in return for free goods and publicity, then find a shill, usually a little kid willing to look gaga in public for a ten spot.

I've had a checkered career in entertainment, but no job was ever more suited to my temperament. After Marvo hypnotized me, my instructions were to climb into the window of Mason's Department Store, lie down on the display bed, and pretend to sleep. And I didn't even have to pretend.

Unfortunately, when I missed supper, poor Mama, weak as she was, was driven to throw on her shawl and drag her sickly self around town to find me. Which wasn't hard, as there weren't a lot of other boys who weighed a tenth of a ton snoring away in a department-store window. The crowd of hypnosis fans watching me saw logs drew Mama over. I had never laid down on an actual mattress before, and I promised myself, as

Mother dragged me by the earlobe back to our house, that someday I'd have one of my own to sleep on. Though preferably with a little more privacy. Mother claimed I was touching myself in an unseemly way when she came upon me. (An accusation that strangely presages the one to come.) But, of course, I'd been transported and could not recall.

Will No One Help the Widow's Son?

Less than a year after these first performances—and a dozen more, as everything from oaf to orphan girl, at the Grand Opera House, where I'd first met Mr. Bacon—dear Mother succumbed to her infirmities and left this world for the next. For a time I stayed with my sister Norah and her husband, Walter St. John. But they had an infant of their own, and once baby Al began to crawl around the tiny bungalow, it was feared that his 200-pound uncle, ever graceful on stage and unwieldy off, might accidentally step on the toddler's head or puncture his soft spot. Thus it was decided that I would be shipped off with a box lunch to San Jose, where I would live with my father and my brother Arthur. The pair had apparently purchased a hotel in that romantic and faraway city, and I was to help them maintain it.

The box lunch, donated by the Ladies' League at my mother's church, contained two ham sandwiches, three deviled eggs, some johnnycake, and a hard green apple. The apple was sour, but I ate it anyway. The train ride to San Jose was five hours. I polished off my charity vittles a quarter mile out of the station.

By the time the porter hopped up the aisle shouting *"Next stop, San Jose!"* I felt like I *was* being transported to a different world. Only this one did not promise to be as pleasant as the cloud-soft window-display bed to which Marvo had dispatched me. Now I was staring out another window, only no one was watching me back. The image in my head, as the train pulled into the station, was the exact one I didn't want there. I was unable to stop remembering Daddy, his burning eyes when he shook me awake by the shoulders at five in the morning, his fist waggling in my face like a cobra's head in a snake-charmer act, his whiskey-stench breath singeing my nostrils.

I squeezed my eyes shut, but the memory came anyway. The train's screeching brakes set off sparks inside my head. Buried in the grinding squeal of metal on metal was Daddy's voice, mocking and nasal: *"Betcha yer so fat ya can't see yer weiner, can ya, Señor Lardo? I betcha yer so fat yer weenie's like a toothpick pokin' out of a stoat's bee-hind."* Then his hands on my pants, his fumey grunt when he tugged my skivvies south of my baby hippo knees. *"C'mon, pull down yer pants. Show Daddy whatcher packin' . . ."*

His hacking laugh booming in my head, Daddy marches me outside, naked; and parades me around the street. As neighbors come out of their houses, cackling, he begins to bellow, in his drunken slur: *"Boy's so fat he can't see his weewee. Has to pee sittin' down."* And then, roaring, *"You got a dick under them trousers, son, or you been gelded? Huh?"* Pinching me, hard. *"This castrato fat? Huh, Pansy-boy? Am I squeezin' femme-lard?"*

Recalling all this, on the train, I had to pinch my own thigh through my pocket until tears came, to create an outside pain big enough to blank out the pain inside, the pain in my fat boy's heart.

The funny part—when he wasn't around, I could love Daddy. But when he was, all I could do was fear him. Fear didn't leave any room for love, except in fuzzy retrospect. Stepping off that train in San Jose, the fear froze me. Just to be able to walk, I played make-believe with myself. What if the memories were just a bad dream? Or, better, just scenes from a play whose run had ended. A play that was never going to be revived. Yes! I was going to step off the platform into a new production.

In this version of the Roscoe Revue, debuting in San Jose, the man who played Daddy would be glad to see me. He would not get drunk and show me what belts were for. He would rub my head and call me by my real name, Roscoe, instead of the other. Instead of *Fatty*. The Daddy in this play would muss my hair, take my suitcase out of my hand, and toss it to my big brother Arthur, who used to say that all you need in life is a wink and a nickel. We'd walk off, the three of us—the proud Arbuckles!— almost like a family.

For a while I stood on the platform in the blazing sun, afraid that if I stepped into shade for a second Daddy and Arthur might not see me. It never occurred to me that if they didn't spot me straightaway, they would look. It was like some unwritten rule inside my head. *You have to hurt yourself for other people . . .* Finally I got dizzy and found a shady bench. I watched the people who got off the train with me being greeted by loved ones. I pretended their lives were my life. That *I* was the young soldier being hugged by his gingham-clad Mom and overalled Dad. That *I* was the tall blond boy meeting his sweetheart. But that only worked for a few minutes, then I just got even sadder. So I started staring at people's feet, the way their shoes raised little clouds of dust. I studied the whirling dust and thought: *I am the only person in this whole station who even notices these teeny tornadoes. The only person in the world . . .*

I never minded the dark, but my whole life I had a fear of being alone. This was the most alone I had ever felt. And what I remember about it, along with the fear and the hunger and the urgent need to evacuate my bowels, is the clench-jawed vow I made to my little-boy self: Come hell or Tabasco sauce, as Daddy used to say, I was not ever going to be alone like this again.

Then the last straggler was hugged and led off the platform by someone who loved him. The train was so far out of the station it was only a speck. I studied my hands on my knees, trying to catch my fingers moving when they didn't think I was looking. I whistled. I pretended I was made of butter, like the stage-ladies used to say, and that if I just waited long enough, pretty soon I would melt into a nice warm puddle and—

"Son?"

"DADDY!"

I didn't even know I was crying until I felt his grip on my shoulder. It was like being stabbed by happiness. But it wasn't Daddy. It was a bald man in a clerk's visor with milky eyes. Sniffling badly, I asked the visor-man if he'd seen my Daddy, and he said he didn't reckon, but maybe I should tell him who my Daddy was. . . .

So I told him about the hotel, how Daddy and my brother and I were all going to live there. For a moment the stranger regarded me. Then he sighed and pushed the visor up on his head, revealing a pate dusted with freckles and shiny with perspiration. I memorized every detail of what I saw to block out what I was hearing.

"I know the establishment," the clerk said. "Would your daddy be William Arbuckle?"

"*Yes*, sir!"

Relief flooded through me like sugar-milk. Then I saw how the man was looking at me. Like he wanted to say more, but he didn't want to at the same time. He was plainly trying to hide how aghast he was. At last he wrung his hands together and stared off down the tracks. "Your Daddy sold the hotel three days ago, son. Then he left town. Saw him get on the train myself."

After that I didn't even cry. I was stranded, lost, alone in a strange city with 200 pennies in a rolled-up hanky and a cardboard suitcase. Something like this was too big to cry over. I thought maybe Daddy'd forgotten I was coming. But he hadn't forgotten. This was even worse. He'd *known*. That's why he left. Right then I remember thinking, *What would Marvo do?*

The Lost Boy of San Jose

My pants sweat when I get nervous. Well, not my pants, really, but *me*, inside them. Especially on the posterior. Following the railroad clerk to the hotel, I hoped the San Jose heat would undampify me. I was scared, but I was hungry, and hungry was always stronger. At the hotel, the railroad fella handed me off to a natty, sharp-faced man in spats. He whispered something in the natty man's ear while they both looked at me.

The clerk wished me good luck and left, and the natty man in the suit stepped toward me. "Bill Booker," he said, eyeing me up and down and pumping my hand. "Bought the place from your Pa. Will didn't say anything about a bruiser like you being part of the deal."

"Where's Daddy?" That's all I wanted to know. By now the hotel staff had stepped into the lobby. I raised my eyes from the carpet long enough to see a few girls holding dishtowels and a swarthy fellow in shirtsleeves waxing his mustache and eating a tomato like it was an apple.

"No forwarding address," Bill sighed, looking over my head the same way the clerk at the station did. Like he couldn't stand to see the effect his words would have on me. Later on, I noticed the same phenomenon—how people couldn't look you in the eye when something terrible happened to you, even if it wasn't your fault. *Especially* if it wasn't your fault. They kept their eyes somewhere else. Like maybe your bad luck could crawl off you and sneak into them through their eyeballs. I always figured that's why people liked the movies. They could see terrible things happen to you. But since they were watching at the nickelodeon, they couldn't catch your bad luck. They could enjoy your calamity right in front of you. Of course it would be a while before that little nugget came in handy.

I shifted my gaze from Bill Booker to a portrait of Lincoln looking ill on a white pony hanging behind the lobby bar. *Life gets bad and stays that way,* Abe's big yellow eyes seemed to be saying. Before I could even respond to news of Dad's unknown where-abouts—he didn't just run away this time, he ran away from *me*—a pretty girl with the curliest hair I'd ever seen bounced over and threw her arms around me. "Oh, Daddy, can we keep 'im?" she baby-talked. "I think he's ado-wa-ble!" She must have been 18, and I couldn't take my eyes off her ringlets.

"You ain't my daughter and this ain't a charity ward," Bill replied, but not unkindly.

Then the guy chomping the tomato wiped off his mustache and piped up. "Only vacancy's the dumbwaiter, and I don't think Fat Boy can fit."

"I am *not* going to let you call him that," cried the ringlet girl, squeezing me close. "He's got a name."

They all looked at me, and it was all I could do to stammer out "*Roscoe.*" Adding, for no apparent reason, "Like Roscoe Con-kling. He was a big man in Kansas."

"Well, you're a big man in those trousers," said one of the girls, and it went back and forth like that, all the hotel girls and hotel men saying their assorted pieces—like they were honing their material—until Bill declared "Enough!" Then he clamped his meaty hand on my shoulder and asked if I knew how to sweep and clean. I said I'd done plenty. And he said I'd just bought myself a ticket out of the state orphanage.

Tomato-Mustache brought me out a plate of stuffed cabbage and barrel dill pickles. Then Bill tossed me a blanket and said he'd let me stay in a broom closet for free in return for doing odd jobs. I spilled my cabbage catching the blanket. But instead of yelling, they just watched while I got down on hands and knees and ate the food off the carpet.

"You don't crap on the carpet, too, do you?" Bill wondered drily. I said not unless it's part of the act, which seemed to tickle the hotel's vaudevillians.

Pansy Lessons

The curly-haired girl turned out to be a piano player named Pansy Jones, and she became my guardian angel and de facto talent agent. Pansy'd done some salty entertaining in her day. Lots of nightclub types stayed at the hotel. Pansy's job was to play piano and sing, tell a story or two—anything to keep the guests and visitors entertained and running a bar tab. (*"Fella asked me the other day if my name was really Pansy Jones. I said, 'No, honey, it's really Smith, but I think Pansy Smith sounds too common . . .'"* That kind of stuff.)

A week or so after I went from The Lost Boy of San Jose to humble hotel resident, Pansy heard me singing falsetto as I scrubbed a stew pot. Next thing I know she had me at the piano, learning songs. The plan was for me to show up on amateur night at the Viceroy Theater. If I won five dollars, Pansy said, she'd keep two of them. As agents go, I've had worse.

The night of the show, Pansy dabbed me with rouge so the stage lights would pick up my face. The emcee—a dialect comic named Goody Gunter who said *unt* instead of *and*—recited all the acts on the bill to the audience before the show. Then he waved his long wooden hook over his head, to let everybody know what happened to acts that couldn't cut the mustard. I paced behind the curtain, as wet and nervous as I've ever been. Sometimes, along with wet-seat, I got what Mama used to call "nerve rash," and I'd have to wedge a compress of cold cornstarch between my bum-cheeks. But there was no time for cornstarch now! Blushing, I whispered my problem "downstairs" to Pansy. She took me by the shoulders and looked me right in the eye. "You wanna be a professional, you gotta learn to play with an ass-rash," she said.

And I would! I *did*. This wasn't just a performance, after all. This was for Pansy. (Of course I was sweet on her—which half meant I wanted her to be my Mom.) My slot was between a trained monkey act—the chimp's suit was better tailored than mine—and a German by the name of Eddie Meyers, who billed himself as "Tires Meyers, King of the Unicycle." When the emcee finally introduced me, I felt my heart sink. "*Unt now, ve haf a young blimp, I mean boy, named Fatty, I mean Roscoe R. Butthole, I mean Arbuckle, who vill sing you a very lively tune . . .*"

Why was he so mean? I turned to Pansy, in a sweat. She made kissy-lips and gave me a gentle shove from the wings. Actually, it wasn't that gentle. I stumbled, then caught myself and zombie-walked out in front of the lights. I started singing right away.

When I hit center stage, I clasped my hands in front of my heart, swaying left and right the way Pansy'd said the pros do.

I thought things were going fine, but halfway through "Tell Mother That You Saw Me" I saw Goody, standing just behind the curtain, waggling that long hook at me. I didn't want to stop, so I sidestepped him. He tried to hook me a second time, and I broke into a crazy didder-jig, spinning around with my finger poked into the top of my head like a ballerina. I thought this got some laughs from the front-seaters. But I wasn't sure. The blood was so loud in my head it drowned everything else out. Goody took another swipe with the hook, nearly catching me, and this time I definitely heard some stomping and hollering. Finally, when the emcee ran right out onstage with the hook and had me cornered, I stopped singing altogether and took a tumble into the orchestra pit.

I landed on a pine-top piano bench that ended the evening as firewood, but I didn't feel a thing. Even Goody was laughing, though I could see Meyers stewing on his unicycle, spinning around in tight, angry little circles just offstage.

I won the five dollars. As promised, I gave Pansy two. She gave me a smooch when we got back to the hotel, and my heart felt like a burst pumpkin. It was all I could do to breathe. She waved goodbye with her pinky, the way fast girls did at that time, and scampered off toward the bar while I slunk to my cubbyhole.

Later that night, emboldened by a half-full short dog of rye I found in the Men's latrine, I left the broom closet and went searching for Pansy in the lobby. I saw her in a dark corner, sitting on a man's lap. The man looked distinguished. Even his lap looked distinguished. I was 13, and not distinguished at all. I started back for my closet, hoping she hadn't seen me, but Pansy called me over. When I'd skulked across the lobby to their couch, she introduced the distinguished gent as Mr. Grauman. "Of the Grauman theater chain."

I'd never crossed paths with an important man before, and when Mr. Grauman took my hand, I didn't know whether to shake or just let him hold it. But Mr. Grauman grinned. "Heard about your stunts, son. Pretty fast on your feet for a husky fella. You and I may be doing business someday."

You hear that, Daddy? I thought to myself, then wondered if I'd said it aloud, and looked at Mr. Grauman. But he was still smiling—like any man would with Pansy on his lap. When she pecked his distinguished forehead, Grauman winked at me. "I'm not kidding, son. I'll be watching out for you." Between Grauman's wink and Pansy's pecking, I felt like I was having my heart broken and my hope lifted all at the same time. The combination made me dizzy. Though it may have been the rye I found in the bathroom. The inside of my head felt stuffed with dead little animals.

Spilled Meat and Chihuahua Fear

Events after this take on a speedy and peculiar turn. I'm driving a meat wagon for Bill, picking up prime steaks and cutlets, when a giggly girl with a chihuahua in her purse hops out of a doorway onto the seat. I didn't even see her!

The rule was no riders. Especially female riders. (Pansy told me the last meat-boy had a habit of trading ground round for a round on the ground. I had no idea what this meant, so she explained that he gave girls free meat if they were nice to him. I often felt that she was entertaining me at her expense, but how could I mind?) Only it wasn't the female that got me into trouble. It was her pipsqueak pup.

Right away, the horses got skittish at the smell of dog. Rounding the corner in front of the hotel, they bolted. The cart tipped over and skidded, sending the meat spilling into the gutter. Giggling wildly, the girl jumped out, holding her Mexican hairless to her breast like a baby. She scampered off at the exact moment Bill came tearing out to see what the ruckus was. Plenty of hotel guests saw the accident, and those who didn't heard progressively inflated versions of it. (In one I was riding bareback, throwing chunks of prime rib at a pack of lady bandits.) Those ignorant few who ordered steak at dinner found themselves picking grit out of their T-bones.

I tried to tell Booker that I didn't even know the girl. She was some stranger who jumped me out of nowhere. "Sounds like my first wife," he said, with surprising good humor, considering. As we stooped to scoop up the strewn chops and flank steaks, I thought I was off the hook until my employer added, almost as afterthought, "I'm not accusing you, Roscoe. I'm firing you."

Now I'm no Hindu, but this was the second time I'd been blamed for doing something with a woman that I didn't really do. The first, of course, was when Daddy blamed me for breaking Mom's "vageena." (That's how he pronounced it, if that tells you anything: "*vageena*," like "*Pasadena*.")

If a swami'd walked up and told me that I'd been a tight girdle in a past life, and *that's* why women in this one kept making me miserable, I would not have called him crazy. I would not have said anything but "Thank you, O Mahubba Bubba. Where do I sign up for my monk-suit?" Because that's exactly how it felt—like I'd done something I didn't know I did, and now I was being punished for it.

Still, this being *my* story, bad always leads to good—before it leads to more bad. I walked straight from the hotel to the Empire Theater. The manager, a seedy Brit named Thurwell who affected a monocle, saw the ratty suitcase in my hand and immediately made me an offer. "I'll give you the Friday night slot and a fin, but if you want to kip here, you gotta pluck gum off the seats and scrub floors."

Deal!

Top Billing

The night after I moved my worldly goods to the Empire dressing room, I pulled a Woolsey. I was shining the spittoons when the unicyclist—my old friend Meyers, King of the Unicycle—staggered into the lobby clutching a torn-out newspaper page, tears streaming down his hatchet face. "Calamity Jane died," he wailed, and turned around and staggered out again. The manager ran after him, then ran back in the theater, literally pulling his hair, and started screaming that his opening act was too distraught to perform. "The idiot wrote letters to that cowgirl. He thought Calamity Jane was gonna jump off her Palomino and hop on his uni."

Well, sure I felt bad, but when you're broke you always look for an angle, so I told Thurwell I could fill in. At first the manager said no. "Opening act they want acrobats. Ring-spinners. The unicycle act was the best I could do—and now he's murphied out on me." Then I said I could sing, and Thurwell said he'd think it over. And that's how, much to the consternation of the other acts, "Roscoe Arbuckle, Boy Singer of Illustrated Songs" ended up on the marquee.

I'd waltzed in and pulled a Woolsey—stolen top billing from more established acts. And I'd have to pay.

*   *   *

As an illustrated singer, I offered up popular songs against a screen on which happy scenes and lyrics were projected. My job was to get the audience to sing along. Of course, I didn't mention that I had never actually experienced such happy and romantic scenes myself. Never frolicked with my sweetheart in a wooded glade. Never been the boy in the straw boater on the porch swing beside his special girl. Never snuggled close to Sally Cinnamon on a moonlit hayride. But, thanks to Pansy, I had memorized five songs which could be sung while tableaus depicting a kind of happiness and romance I'd never known flickered behind me.

All I had to do was remember the lyrics. A task made harder, on the occasion of my first marquee appearance, by the stagehands' savage scenery-banging—punctuated by the overloud farts and whinnies of my fellow performers from the wings. Lesson learned.

Soon enough, I learned something else. After I'd been opening for a couple of weeks, ladies began to visit me backstage. Ladies my mother's age. I'd tell them how Mama died and they'd bring me picnic baskets stuffed with poundcake and beef buns. They'd tap the sofa for me to sit beside them and then talk to me about church. They'd get dewy-eyed, pull me close to their fragrant bosoms, and tell me how much they'd like to have me as their own son. Sometimes one would put her tongue in my ear.

Girls from the troupe would come giggling into my tiny room after these ladies left. Irene, the box-jumper in a magic act, told me that if I'd "give 'em a good bomp," these Backstage Betties would give me a lot more than supper and a cuddle. When I mentioned this to Thurwell before a Saturday matinee, he worked his lips up and down and spat tobacco juice into the spittoon I'd just polished. "All actresses are snatch-peddlers, kid. Don't listen to 'em."

I never went any farther than cuddling. Not because I thought that was bad, but because I still didn't know there was any farther to go. The most I received from one of these backstage ladies was a whole meatloaf and a brush-and-comb set monogrammed with the initials LLR. I'd never seen a monogram before. The letters stood for Lucky Little Roscoe, she told me. And I believed her.

A Big Thirteen

I was as close to happy as you can get if you're a homeless prepube the size of a polar bear. Every day I'd learn a little bit more about juggling, or a new dance step, or a line of patter from one of the Hungarian, Italian, or German dialect comics. I even met celebrities.

Cy Young worked the Empire on a swing through the West. He demonstrated the pitches he used to beat the Pirates twice and help win the first World Series for Boston. The second part of his presentation focused on physical hygiene, and at one point I was supposed to come onstage and ask him how I could get to be as strong as him. The gag was, Cy tells me I should get more exercise and cut out sweets, and I pretend to faint.

That same night I nearly fainted for real. I was setting out a chair for my legs before going to sleep—I'd gotten used to catnapping sitting up between shows, and had taken to spending my night that way—when I heard a voice that made my milk curdle. I knew before the door swung open.

"Hey, fat-ass?"

"Daddy?"

"Shut up and pack. I'm taking you away from these people.

It's a good thing I saw your name on that marquee poster, or we might never have found you."

I felt like a runaway slave tracked down and dragged back to the old plantation. Except the plantation was a dirt farm outside Santa Clara, and the massah was a mean drunk who cursed the day I tore his wife's innards coming hiney-first into Kansas. I couldn't meet anyone's eyes as Daddy led me out. The whole troupe ran up to watch my kidnapping, but nobody could muster the courage to say a word about it. Daddy's glare *dared* anybody to step in his path and challenge his authority over his wayward heifer. I kept my eyes on the ground in front of me, a habit I'd acquired as a child in the face of Daddy's rage.

Turns out Daddy had remarried. Once he got me to his ragged farmhouse, he pinched my neck until I raised my eyes from the earth long enough to see his mealy-mouthed new wife and called her "Mother." I was used to quick changes, but not like this. I'd gone from performing and sleeping on theater chairs, surrounded by show folk, to sharing a moldy bed with a gang of rangy "brothers." They were athletic and good-looking and hated me from the gitgo. Or did, until the next week, when I won a county fair pie-eating contest and came home with a blue face and a trophy. The following Saturday I consumed 43 hot dogs in 10 minutes, a local record. After these triumphs my perfect stepbrothers began to brag about me. I had my sport, and I was a champion. The sport just happened to involve shoving a week's worth of food down my throat in five minutes.

Beyond the glory of pie-eating, farmwork was mostly just trudging around in the mud digging up boulders. Miserable as it was, it was still better than going to school. Onstage I could charm an audience of strangers twice my age, but in the classroom I got nothing but scorn. So Daddy and I made a deal— without ever saying that's what it was. In return for me staying home (the name of this play is *Unpaid Day Laborer*) Daddy didn't belt me when I snuck off to San Jose to moonlight as a singing waiter at the Pabst Beer Café. At the Pabst I served all the beer I couldn't drink, and warbled for the clientele till the wee hours.

One night Sid Grauman, whom I'd met with Pansy, ambled into the café for a drink with *his* Daddy, David. Grauman Senior heard me sing and asked if I wanted a job at the Unique Theater in San Jose. "You got connections?" I asked, playing the rube. Like I didn't know who Dave Grauman was! But the old character played it straight. "I don't need connections, Slim. I own the joint."

Just like that I was back where I swore I never wanted to be again—in the Illustrated Song biz—and d–double e–lighted to be there. But this didn't mean I was free from Daddy's business. He let me spend my evenings working in the theater as long as I spent the rest of the night working for him—at his new hash house.

Seeing the cash that floated around the Pabst, the old man decided the real money was in all-night eateries and sold the farm. When he wasn't ranting about how Orville Wright gypped him of his biplane plans, or the time Hank Ford—it was always, for some reason, Hank—drunked him up on rotgut and pinched his idea for the assembly line, Daddy liked to lecture his stepsons about Where the Real Money Was. Not that he ever found it.

Much as I grew to hate the work, slinging hash to hacks and insomniacs in Daddy's dive did not make me nostalgic for agriculture. Sometimes a theatrical company would troop in after their last show and I'd pretend my restaurant job was an act. I learned to flip pancakes behind my back, which always snagged a lot of laughs—and came in handy down the road.

Every night I'd die a little, watching the troupes head to the station while I returned to serving burned biscuits and fatback. I'd learned a bit about meat in my hotel days, and knew enough to tell that whatever Daddy was slapping on his plates and calling T-bone had probably started off life as a pony. From then on, I shaved a year off when people asked how old I was. I didn't count the year I spent breathing grease and serving Man O'War at Daddy's 24-hour ptomaine parlor.

Goodbye, Pig-in-a-Blanket

One night, after I finished my rendition of "Darling, I Adore You (But Mother Does Not Approve")), old Mr. Grauman showed up in my dressing room at the Unique. Owners did not often frequent their own venues, unless they were on fire. So I hoped this meant my pig-in-a-blanket days were over. When Grauman asked if I'd want to sing at the Portola Café, in San Francisco, for $18 a week, I did a jig on the spot. I'd have signed on as a talking dog if it meant getting out of the horse-frying business—and away from my jackass of a Daddy.

I'd been San Francisco's favorite light-on-his-feet-fat-boy singing waiter for a year before I considered writing the old man with my whereabouts. Eighteen bucks was 11 more than the 7 Daddy was supposed to pay me every week and never did. Even better than the greenbacks was the mattress. After sleeping rough for so long—on sod as a kiddie, on chairs in theaters—I still got giddy at climbing into a real hotel bed every night. This was the best sleep I'd had since my stint in the department store window with Marvo the Magnificent.

The Portola attracted all kinds of big names. One evening Jack Johnson stopped by. I pretend-sparred with him and got a laugh when I "knocked myself out" with my own roundhouse. Jack London came in knee-walking drunk at least once a week, and a couple of times we got rubber-legged together, passing a flask of Tokay after hours. Drunk as he was all the time, I don't know how the man could sign his own name, let alone crank out *White Fang*.

Then Mr. Grauman turned up again, with the richest-looking man I'd ever seen. The man's skin was golden—a shade I wouldn't see again until I met old money in Hollywood. Even his eyebrows looked rich. The pair planted themselves at one of my tables, and Mr. Grauman crooked his finger for me to come over.

"Roscoe," Grauman crowed, "shake hands with Alexander Pantages."

Pantages! I was so flummoxed my fingers felt like turkey legs. Pantages had his own vaudeville circuit, as prestigious as the Orpheum, Paramount, or the Hammersteins'. He owned theaters all over the country, plus smart cafés in lots of the same towns.

A job with Pantages was the biggest break you could get—if you could get it. When Mr. Pantages himself complimented me on my singing and asked how I felt about traveling, I told him I took my best naps in train stations. Grauman chuckled like an expensive game hen and said he couldn't pay for my napping, but he'd start me at $25 a week for using my other talents. The next morning I headed north from S.F. to Oregon.

For the next few months I got to play theaters from Eugene up to the top of Washington, then all the way south to Arizona, where I finally scratched out a letter to Daddy. I made sure to tell him I wasn't plucking the gum off theater seats, I was filling them. I did not tell him I'd gotten a raise, to $50 a week. I wanted to impress him—not give him a reason to grift me. Why risk the old man tracking me down to some hall in Bisbee or Speonk and putting the tap on?

Daddy was the one who spent his life scheming about Real Money, and now I was the one making it. I had no doubt that, just as he'd done with Hank and Orville, he'd find a way to convince himself every dime I made was rightfully his. Until I turned 18, he could legally take it, too. I'd seen lots of young performers lose their wages that way. One reason so many folks starting out made up new names to go with their acts—they were runaways. That, or they had warrants out. Or both.

A Frisco Shaker and a Big Decision

Come 1905 my Pantages stint was up, so I got together a little troupe—employing myself as singer, comedian, and manager— and started us swooping up and down the West Coast again. By this time I had to look at a newspaper to know what city I was in. You never notice how many states have towns called "Liberty" until you've played matinees in eight of 'em.

Round about April 1906, my road days nearly came to an end. And not because an irate customer threw a bottle from the balcony, either. (Though that happened, ladies and gentlemen. One Saturday late show in Tucson, a Polish comic named Paps Krakow insulted a cowboy who kept belching during his act. "Gee," Paps snapped after the umpteenth interruption, "I heard you ranch hands sometimes snip your balls off accidental-like—I didn't know it made you *burp!*" Before the crowd even got the joke, Ten Gallon up and brained the Polack with a dead man of rum. I sent Krakow home to convalesce with his mother and filled in with a local Comanche who did rope tricks.)

But back to that April—the 18th to be exact. I'm in my hotel room in San Francisco when I feel the walls wobble. *Now that's a hangover,* I remember thinking. I figured a little peach brandy would steady things. Before I could get hand to flask, the floor started to shimmy. The pitcher tumbled off the nightstand and the most ungodly sounds of mayhem rose up from the street.

I ran down 10 flights in my dressing coat and breached the sidewalk in time to see a three-story building collapse a block away. I can't describe the sound, the wave of choking dust and rubble that sprayed up to the sky and blotted the sun out. The haze was so unnatural, some people had to remember to scream. A frantic girl with twin babies and a table lamp in her hands ran right into me, shouting "Earthquake!" at the top of her little lungs. Before I could see if she was all right, the young mother careened off again, dragging her lamp and babies in the other direction.

Pretty soon you couldn't move for all the terrified citizens scrambling for their lives. I still wonder what that good mother was thinking when she grabbed a table lamp along with her offspring. At the time I imagined she was simply panicked. In my dopey dotage, I realize that she probably looted the thing while passing a lamp store. (Life is bound to do something to your view of human nature.) Either way, a fire had begun to rage in the wreckage of the fallen building, spewing smoke thick enough to make your hair gray. Genius that I am, my first thought was to run back into the hotel. My money clip and my brandy were upstairs. But no sooner did I step inside than I felt a hand grab my shoulder, followed by something hard and round, jammed with no politeness into my back. "Stop right there, suet."

I turned to see an Army fellow with a handlebar mustache spotted white from plaster. Behind him was a colored boy dragging a wagon full of shovels. The soldier grabbed one and shoved it in my hands. "I could shoot you right now for intent to loot," he barked. "Dig or die!"

The soldier pointed his revolver somewhere between my belly and my bellringer. "Happy to help," I heard myself yelp. So, for the next 24 hours, I dug, along with every other man around with matching arms and legs. Including, I am told, the great John Barrymore. It was the first and last occasion in which I'd get to play the same role as a Barrymore. Had I known, at the time, scared stewless and digging up bricks at gunpoint, I could not have found a moment to gloat. Debris seemed to be falling out of the sky. Screaming came from all directions. Worse than the screams were the muffled cries from under the chest-high piles of rubble. The way they died out. . . . By my 20th hour on the job, arms heavy as coffin lids, all I could think, stupidly, was, *San Francisco can be a dangerous town.*

If I had any idea how dangerous, I might have asked Sergeant Shovel to shoot me on the spot.

PART 2

Yuck Huckster

MY MOTHER'S favorite saying was "God can stand on one leg longer than you can." I never did figure out what that meant, but one day, back in Portland at the Star Theater, I was halfway through an illustrated rendition of "Silver Threads Among the Gold" when I noticed an amputee in the front row. One trouser leg had been trimmed to the hip. A stump like a puckered fist poked out of it. I took that as a sign—as if Mama herself was telling me, *"Look, Son, one leg! That could have been you!"* Then and there I made a decision I'd been wrestling with since surviving the San Francisco shaker.

I was done being the Illustrated Singer! This time I meant it.

Illustrateds made a fine career when I was a young sylph. Now they just seemed old-timey. But to be a crackerjack comedian, a high-tone actor . . . that was the new thing. *There* was a future worth pursuing. You could come up with your own acts. You could do some soft shoe, tell a joke in wiener-schnitzel German, or fall off the stage. I'd seen enough of the greats to know how much I had to learn. But I would devote myself.

After the show, I locked myself in the dressing room and pulled out the stocking I'd filched from Mother's bureau after she'd passed. I pressed it to my face. I inhaled her astringent scent—witch hazel, cedar, and vinegar—and made a pledge to her loving memory: *I will work harder than any boy ever worked.*

When the stranger in the checked suspenders opened the door and tumbled in, I barely had time to hide Mom's stockings before he got up and dusted himself off. His look was appraising but not judgmental. A long-faced clown without makeup. "I don't know what you were doing and I don't care," the man said, in what I soon learned was an Australian accent. "I'm Leon Errol, theatrical manager and comedian, and I think you're a natural. Join up with me and I'll show you all the tricks."

I was so stunned I forgot to ask how he'd picked the dressing-room lock. Leon took me out for soup, and after five minutes I was halfway sold. Maybe there was something in my oyster crackers. I followed him from the greasy spoon back to the Orpheum and caught his act. Talk about a hodgepodge! Leon mixed up burlesque comedy, funny ditties, tumbling, black-faced monologues, and, when the spirit moved him, the odd birdcall.

We opened a bottle in his dressing room and by the time we closed it I had agreed to go on tour with him, for barely more than a third of what I was making now. Still. . . . The way I looked at it, the money I wasn't making was paying for my education. Seeing as how I'd dropped out in second grade, it was about time I went back to class.

Funny School

Starting right there in Portland I got lessons in funny dialects, in tumbling (the trick was hitting the ground without cracking your tailbone), in picking the right makeup, keeping the sweat out of your eyes, and making your stage-clothes into cutaways. All the tricks of a world-class burlesque yuck huckster. My graduation was held in Idaho, at the Last Chance Saloon.

The Last Chance featured a diva named Lilly-Bell, a big blond maneater who cake-walked across the stage like she had hot coals in her drawers—which, if her reputation was accurate, more than a few members of the audience had shoveled. The crowd was nothing but tough-as-nails miners. We even got paid in gold dust, in little sacks that tied up tight at the top. But on our second day, the Sweetheart of Boise failed to show, and Errol got as nervous as I'd ever seen him. Lilly-Bell was nowhere to be found.

Out front the natives were stomping their feet, causing a thunderous racket. Errol and I both peeked through the curtain to see what we were up against, and backed off without a word. There was no question one of these woman-hungry gold dusters was going to grab the six-shooter he checked at the door and put holes in our clothes.

Then I had an idea. Without telling Errol, I slipped into Lilly's dressing room, fished around, and managed to slip out again in a tight ruby dress and a blond wig big as a birthday cake. Call me a cat burglar. Errol saw this burly female stroll onstage and gulped. "May I help you, madam?" He had no idea it was Yours Truly. Neither did the wide-eyed miners, who began to clap and stomp all over again when I broke into my first song.

We did four shows that night with me as the opening blonde. But the next night, when I sashayed out in gown and cake wig, the real Lilly swept in and came after me with a steak knife. My wig flew off as I ran through the joint, jumping tables, careening up the aisles, scrambling back onstage, and knocking Errol over when I tumbled into the curtains. The miners thought the chase was staged, and rolled on the floor. Errol was so impressed he said we should keep it in the show till the run was over. Lilly-Bell would have none of it, however, as she felt it impugned her womanly dignity.

Errol's company zigzagged north and south, from the West
Coast halfway to the East and back. One long afternoon on a
train I took out a map and pencil and connected all the dots we'd
visited. The result looked like a run-over porcupine. And after a
couple of months of hard traveling, Errol announced he was
dissolving the act. He had a chance to join with Ziegfeld in New
York City, and he wanted to take it. That's showbiz. I wished
him well—by then I was calling him "Professor"—and knocked
around till I snagged a spot with the Ellwood Tabloid Musical
Company as—never say never, you big ninny—illustrated singer.

I convinced myself it was temporary, and, besides, it was that
or find a brothel that needed a towel boy. The entire run was in
San Francisco—you'd have never known that whole chunks of
the city had burned and crumbled in a quake—and when it was
over Ellwood offered to bring me down to Southern California.
We were to play the Bide-A-Wee Theater in Long Beach, with
Roscoe "Fatty" Arbuckle getting star billing.

The Professional

So here I am, free, fat, and 21. Rolling into Long Beach with a
hotel bed and a slot as headliner in my future. At that moment
about the only thing I was less interested in than romance was a
job in movies.

Working in "flickers," as they were still being called, was out
of the question. Everyone knew that the only people who'd
lower themselves to step in front of a camera were stage actors
who couldn't get work—or couldn't stay sober enough to keep it
if they got it.

As for the romance part, love and marriage were for other

people. Why would anybody who had survived my family want to even *think* about starting another one? How many prisoners of war reenlist?

Well, tickle my knickers! No sooner did I step onto the streetcar from Los Angeles than I spied the tiniest, sweetiest-petitiest creature I'd ever laid eyes on. I soon learned that what she lacked in stature she more than made up for in attitude. When I asked if I might help her stash her suitcase on the overhead rack, the tiny lovely acted positively indignant. "No, *thank* you!" Even as she shunned me, I could not help but notice those beautiful brown eyes. They were dark as chocolate-covered onyx. Though the way she glared they might as well have been matching stop signs.

"My mother warned me never to talk to strange men," she went on, standing on tiptoes to hoist her bag on to the rack.

"How do you know I'm strange?" I heard myself say, helping stash her baggage in spite of her protest. I was more surprised by my retort than she was. I've always been painfully shy around the fair sex. Up to now I'd pretty much just let them feed me. But this girl looked more likely to hit me with a brick than slip me a ham sandwich.

"Well, for one thing," she replied, her face tilted up to mine like a gorgeous pixie's, "your derby's too small for your head."

Without thinking, I whipped off the offending hat, then stood there looking at it with no idea what to say next. I was tongue-tied, and felt myself flushing up, until I raised my eyes and saw that she was aiming a sly half-smile at me. Then we both burst out laughing.

The truth is, I was always self-conscious about my appearance. A lifetime of being stared at like a carnival act will do that to you. But the more abnormal I grew, the more I tried to look normal. Presentable. I never left the house—or hotel room—without making sure my shoes were shined, my suit pressed, my face and fingernails scrubbed clean, and my bowtie just so. Fat men tend to look sloppy even when they're not. So I was always careful to come off neat and dignified—especially when I was a tittle lipsy, as the great mick comic Muggles O'Reilly used to say. Happily, at this particular moment on the Red Line to Long Beach, I was sober as a dead senator.

Donning the offending bowler, I smiled, then lifted it off again, then rolled it down my arm, as Errol had taught me, and bounced it on my knee with a flourish before taking the seat across from her. "I'm going to the Bide-A-Wee Theater," I said. "Do you know it?" At this her kewpie-doll mouth opened in a little O. "Do I? That's where *I'm* going!" For a second she looked suspicious, but when it turned out this pint-sized beauty and I were in the same production, she extended her child's hand and curtsied. "My name's Minta Durfee."

"Minta Durfee," I repeated, the four strange syllables like candies in my mouth. I'd never had a girl curtsy at me before. I was so enchanted I curtsied back, a maneuver that turned more than a few heads. "Pleasure to meet you, Minta Durfee. I'm Roscoe Arbuckle." For the rest of the ride, we chatted away.

As I was already a bit of a stage veteran, I needed less rehearsal. While Minta, an aspiring local who'd been in only one production before this one, was required to spend more time at the theater. Naturally, I found a reason to show up at the Bide-A-Wee every day. But the real reason was little Minta.

Fat Man in Love

I may have been 21, but I had never courted before. My experience with the fair sex was more or less limited to affectionate smooches from those women who brought me backstage snacks. I did not even know what courting *was*. But even if *I* didn't know what I was doing, the other cast members certainly did. Minta herself told me how much the other starlets teased her. We met for walks on the pier every day. By only our third or fourth seaside stroll, I realized, with a shock, that I wanted to marry her. I also realized that I'd blown nearly all my money on whiskey, new clothes, and big meals. I knew, if I was going to ask for Minta's hand, that I had better have some extra cash in mine. Maybe some guys could rely on looks. I needed some solid signs of finance. If I couldn't be dashing, I could at least be dependable.

So, without telling Minta, I held my nose and made an appointment to visit Colonel Selig, a filmmaker whose name I'd gotten from a trick yodeler at the Portola Café. The yodeler, a yellow-eyed son of the West Virginia hollers named Piedmont, told me over a plate of catfish what Selig had told him at his audition. "Boy, the movie business is really just the face business, and the camera ain't been built could make a mug like yours anything but terrifying. If you're lucky, you'll just scare people. Most likely you'll make 'em upchuck." I half-hoped the Colonel would greet me with similar enthusiasm, and I'd be spared the humiliation of aping emotions for cash in front of those white-hot camera lights.

Selig had made a splash after releasing a film about Teddy Roosevelt bagging a lion in Africa. I happened to catch the short when I had some time to kill in Cleveland. All I could think while I was watching was, *If that's Teddy Roosevelt I'm the Czar of Tasmania* . . . You'd have to be really stupid to believe—as Selig insisted—that you were actually watching Roosevelt. I've seen more resemblance between a sofa and a walrus. And Selig was considered one of the good ones!

Moving pictures, as far as I could tell, were made by hacks and peddled to idiots. Only an actor with no regard for the dignity of his own profession would let himself appear on film. Or one who needed the five bucks Selig was shelling out more than he needed professional dignity.

Hot Lights and a Grown Man in a High Chair

Dodging the rabid dogs and dazed pedestrians Los Angeles seemed to breed in equal number, I made my way to Eighth and Hill, where the Colonel and his team worked out of a lot behind a Chinese laundry. With hardly a how-do-you-do, Selig, a man so nondescript you couldn't forget him, asked how much I weighed. When I told him 266 he seemed impressed. I'd expected the same treatment Piedmont the Yodeler received, and was surprised when I didn't get it. "You got a good fat face," Selig said, sounding genuinely glad about it, as if a fat face was something you'd want to grab strangers and brag about. But that was pretty much the extent of our exchange.

Twenty minutes later, my fat face pancaked and rouged, I was led out of the dressing room to the camera like a condemned man to the firing squad. The director was a downy-cheeked, likable baldy by the name of Francis Boggs. Before starting off, Boggs gave me a few brief directions. Chief among them, I'll never forget, was "Don't look at the camera until I tell you to, then don't stop looking at it!" After this sphinxlike edict, I went through my paces with a couple of other actors, moving from scene to ludicrous scene with a woodenness that shamed me deeply.

Mostly, I had to look surprised. An effect I achieved crudely, at the director's behest, by making my eyes go wide and holding my mouth open. I've seen trained seals display greater range of emotion than my fellow actors and I that fateful day. It was like a dumb show with hot lights and a grown man barking orders from his high chair.

That first epic was a one-reeler called *Ben's Kid*. About which the less said the better. For my second Selig effort, a half-reeler called *Mrs. Jones' Birthday*, I got a review in the *New York Dramatic Mirror*. "The Jones of the picture is a fat fellow"—why, thank you!—"a new face in picture pantomime, and the earnestness of his work adds greatly to its value."

I did not show the review to Minta, even though, by the time it ran, we were a lot farther along than walks on the pier. What respectable girl—let alone performer—would let herself be seen with the likes of a movie actor? Why not find somebody more respectable, like a purse snatcher?

Still, the most memorable thing about my virgin moviemaking experience was not what happened during it but what happened after.

Two months after I'd taken my money for playing japes to the camera, the Colonel's gardener, a Japanese fellow, got the heebie-jeebies and shot poor Francis Boggs dead right there on the lot. Selig took a slug in the arm, but shrugged it off and kept producing. As far as I was concerned, the mad Jap's attack on Francis was one more reason to stay away from the movie business. Nobody bothered to explain the shooting, and there wasn't much in the papers about it. All I kept thinking was, theater may be grueling, but at least you didn't have to worry about people getting murdered.

Despite this, I continued to hold my nose and make my sneaky way to Selig Studios, earning my 500 pennies a day cavorting like a monkey in front of the unwieldy camera. I'd done worse for less, but still . . . While I was courting Minta, the last thing I wanted was for her parents to find out their daughter's beau trafficked with film types. They were salt of the earth. Her Dad drove a streetcar. My profession aside, I could tell, when they first met me, it was a shock for Mom and Dad to find their pretty, 98-pound pride and joy involved with an orphan nearly 200 pounds heavier than she was. (You could see it in their eyes: *My God, he'll crush her!*)

Once I was able to make the old couple laugh, they seemed to get over my bulk. Mrs. Durfee even said I was "a charmer." But I knew she wouldn't think I was too charming if she found out I'd been consorting with "film people." Might as well let your daughter run off with a hobo. Though a hobo would have been preferable to a movie actor. At least no one could go to a Nickelodeon and see your hobo son-in-law jumping around on screen with a bunch of other hoboes. Not so with a film actor. Anyone with a nickel and a pair of eyes would be able to see what kind of moral leper the girl you raised left home for.

For a while, I kept mum on the movie work, and had some extra folding money in my pocket to spend on trinkets for the gal of my dreams. (Even though I never really dreamed about girls all that much; mostly I dreamed of my mother.)

Before the season closed, I asked Minta to marry me. Much to my surprise, she didn't laugh. Though she later confided that she believed me when I was said I'd drop her in the Pacific if she turned me down. (Did I mention I was holding her by the shoulders, three feet over the pier railing, when I popped the question? This sounds more sinister than it was. At least I *hope*.)

At the suggestion of the manager, we were wed onstage at the Bide-A-Wee, after the last show.

I can hardly recall the weeks before the ceremony. Let alone the ceremony. I was extra-polluted, but back then I could hide it pretty well. I'll just tell you what happened later. I do recall an awkward moment with the mayor of Long Beach, on hand to recite the vows. "Do you, Fatty Arbuckle," His Honor intoned, "take this woman to be your lawful wedded—" etc . . . etc . . ." And I wasn't having it. The one place I did not want to be Fatty was my own wedding.

"The name is Roscoe," I corrected him, pronouncing "Roscoe" very *slowly*, which got a few tentative cackles, before people knew it was okay and began to laugh outright. There was a hefty crowd, on account of the publicity the manager generated—the highlight of which was a display of wedding gifts at Buffums, the crown jewel of Long Beach department stores.

Each gift had a handwritten card underneath it, describing the benefactor and the franchise they were promoting. "M'Lady's Oven Mitt courtesy of Kelso's Family Restaurant. *'Strap on your feedbag and come to Kelso's!'* "

The Virginia Hotel, where the actors and crew were staying, threw us a wild reception. Or so they say. I was 21, and plastered. Minta was 17 . . . and 17. Before we retired for the night, I overheard a couple of tipsy actresses kidding my new bride that she had better be careful, " 'less you wanna end up like a flat tire, honey—you make sure and ride *him*, not vicey-versey."

The rest of the evening the shame of those words laid me low.

Fatty, Lover

I could not perform at all on my wedding night. I kept thinking that the next day everybody would *know*, and the prospect crippled me. I tried to tell Minta how horrifying this was, to have everybody *know*. But when she asked why, I couldn't really say. Also, I did not tell her how scared I was of showing her my body. Of what the sight of fat might do to her. I'd never been nude in front of anyone but my mother. And she always looked away.

"Honey," I finally confided, "I couldn't stand everybody gaping at us. Making comments." Minta said nothing. She had a very serious expression, as if she'd just discovered something, and she had to decide then and there what to do about it.

After we lay side by side for a while, Minta quietly got up from bed. She was tiny and pale as a porcelain doll in the white lace nighty from Paris that Buffums had bestowed on her. She stepped carefully through the flower-strewn suite of the Long Beach Hotel the City Council had provided us and disappeared into the powder room for what seemed like a long time. I stared at the picture of President Wilson over the bed, wondering if she'd get the wrong impression if I got the bottle out of the suitcase. Maybe a nip would settle my hash, but I wouldn't want her to think I *needed* one.

Minta stepped out of the powder room, saw me on my feet, and mistook my start for the bottle as ardor. She moved dreamily closer and put her arms around me. Or as far around me as they would go.

For a moment, we just stood there. Holding each other. Minta in the terry cloth robe she'd thrown over that lacey nighty, me in purple Chinese silk pajamas, courtesy of His Honor the mayor, still buttoned to the chin. We just stayed that way, in awkward embrace, swaying slightly. Looking into each other's eyes, then looking away. Then looking again and holding each other tighter still. The whole experience, in one way wonderful, was so unnerving in another I began to shake uncontrollably. When Minta offered to pour me a drink herself, I knew that I had taken the right woman for my bride.

Honeymoon in San Berdoo

The next day we were off on our honeymoon, if you can call five shows a day in San Bernardino a honeymoon. We'd signed on to a tour with an Irish comic named Walter Reed. Nine days later, in Arizona, we had still not consummated our union. Painful as it was to go into, I explained to Minta about Mama's little flower, and what Daddy said I did to it. Minta insisted that she understood. But I could tell how bad she felt.

I did not try again to fulfill my manly duty until one night in Bisbee, Arizona. Bisbee was one of those towns so rife with vice, it was decided that Minta would keep to her rooms. Drinking with the fellows after the show, I was overwhelmed by the number of sporting girls in the street. A bunch of them let on that they liked husky boyos, and I even kind of accidentally let one lick me behind the ear, if you can imagine that. Somehow, visions of these ladies' painted faces played in my head like scenes in a one-reeler and spurred me to fulfill our union as God intended. Or almost. Unfortunately, as soon as my car pulled into the garage, I flooded the engine.

I was—I know I've said it already—very self-conscious about my body. And I could not stop thinking how wide Minta's eyes went when she saw my drawers. I was so afraid she would laugh, my mouth dried up. Not knowing what else to do, I laid her down on the bed, kissed her forehead, then licked it a little, which made her giggle, and waited for something to happen. Neither of us spoke, but I could see Minta's bosom rising and falling with an urgency she seemed both shy and proud of. I closed my eyes, touching my new wife where her hand guided me. But then I froze. I don't know why.

Finally, when the sound of the clock ticking had begun to feel like pounding, I leaped out of bed. I told Minta I was going out for a nightcap. I scrambled down to the hotel bar and tipped back a few—fast. Maybe more than a few. Next thing I know the room was swirling and my eyes burned from watching the sporting girls hike their slips up to scratch their thighs. It was around this time I returned to our nuptial chamber, determined.

Entering the suite, I aimed myself directly for the bed, found my pint-sized bride, and pulled her towards me, careful not to paw. I held Minta as close as I could without hurting her. Then, as mentioned, I made my entrance. And a little bit of a mess.

Later, the almost-official husband and wife spooned in the dark. I held Minta to me, telling her all over again about *the little flower*, trying to explain, but always ending up repeating *"I'm sorry I'm sorry I'm sorry I'm sorry I'm sorry I'm sorry I'm sorry I'm sorry"* until the words sounded like a jungle chant.

Most of the above, I confess, I know only from Minta's accounting. I'd drunk so much, so fast, what remains in my memory is a perfumed blur, punctuated by one strange thought that lingers to this day: *This*, it occurred to me at the height of the act, *is how they make jelly doughnuts . . .*

Each night from then on was spent in honest cuddling. Occasionally we made the effort, but when we got close my pipe burst. If I could even find it. Although, as Minta pointed out some time later—under much more savage circumstances—those may have only been the nights I remembered. There were, she hinted, many other nights. And many things she was not going to tell me, if I was going to insist that I didn't remember. Which may be true. When you pass out, your body and mind go down together. But when you black out, your mind says good night and your body heads off without it.

When kidders in the company made jokes about our life as man and wife, when they hinted about my manly capacities—"Fatty's just a big *softy!*"—little Minta could always be counted on to take my hand and say, "That's all right. There are other ways to be affectionate . . ." This actually made me feel more embarrassed, though I never could find a way to tell her, since she meant so well.

Still, for the rest of that tour, when I watched my wife descend on a cardboard crescent to sing her nightly showstopper, "By the Light of the Silvery Moon," I'd feel hot tears in my eyes. That's when I needed a drink the most. But mostly I just tried to keep chuckling. A good chuckle will always see you through. Although, in El Paso, a chuckle nearly got me killed.

The Mexican Revolution Pie-Fight

A free afternoon in El Paso is a mixed blessing. On this scalding April day, I was dragging the troupe around town, trying to find a keno game. When that plan fizzled, we ended up having a picnic on the banks of the Rio Grande. We were all amazed how, at that point, the mighty river was no wider than a good-sized trickle. When we looked up from the water, they were standing there. Soldiers. On the other side. A dozen of them, half-starved and filthy-looking, like they'd been in the jungle for so long they didn't know they were out of it. A couple of the soldiers saw us gawking and pulled their guns on us. I yelled, "Hold your fire!"

Then I grabbed a ham sandwich and tossed it across the river. (If somebody's gonna shoot you 'cause they're hungry, why not feed 'em?) The soldiers didn't know whether to smile or fire. The boy who picked up the sandwich examined it seriously, then began to delicately peel off layers of ham, cheese, tomato, and bread and pass them out to his cohorts.

One by one, after the boy dismantled the sandwich, the whole troupe started throwing whatever they could grab: apples, muffins, hard-boiled eggs. We were whooping it up good when a short, wild-haired pistolero with a giant mustache and twin cartridge belts criss-crossed over his chest rode his horse right into the middle of the soldiers, who instantly dropped our theatrical offerings and looked solemn. The power accorded this surly figure was apparent without a word being uttered.

El Jefe turned his eyes from his soldiers to us and we all fell silent. Then he announced, in a commanding voice, "*I am Pancho Villa!*" There was a long, tense hush, until I bellowed back, "Have a pie, Pancho!" and threw a blueberry pie I happened to be holding across the river. An audible gasp rose from soldiers and actors alike as the pie sailed over the water. And then, an ever bigger gasp—this time of delight—as the Mexican leader turned on his horse, almost casually, and caught the pie one-handed with flawless timing. An amazing feat!

Pancho tossed the pie back to me. I bobbled it but managed to hang on. His men and my own ragtag troops cheered wildly. I wasn't sure if I should throw it back again, then figured the Mexicans had probably gone a lot longer without pie than I had, and flung the thing back over. This time Pancho smiled and fired two shots that winged the pie plate before snatching it out of the air.

Now this was a showman! I shouted, "Viva La Revolución!" Then "Bravo!" Pancho acknowledged my kudos. He smiled big, took a bite out of the pie, and fired his pistol straight in the sky as he galloped off with his freshly fed soldiers in the same direction he'd galloped in.

"My God, that was Pancho Villa!" Reed kept saying. "There's a thousand-dollar reward on his head!"

"Well," I said, "if he ever gets out of that jam, he's got a future in vaudeville."

Something, I'd be lying if I didn't admit, I was no longer sure I wanted for myself.

The Grind

After the El Paso run was over, we were out of bookings, so Minta and I worked our way back to Los Angeles doing pass-throughs. We'd announce to whatever theater we could find that we were passing through, then I'd snag us a slot on the bill, pop onstage for some songs and patter, and finish with a surprise duet with Minta. Of course the regular acts weren't too happy about a "name" showing up. And half the time I had to practically sit on the manager to get us our money.

The two of us got back to Los Angeles ragged and crabby—with little more cash in our money-sock than when we'd started out. This meant we had to live with Minta's parents. I actually liked the Durfees. I liked their little house on Coronado Street in Echo Park. But I felt more squeamish than ever taking to bed with Minta knowing her Mom and Dad were two inches of plaster away. Lounging around one morning—"Pick up your feet, Roscoe, I'm dusting!"—I read a story in *Variety* about James O'Neill, who made 50 grand free and clear touring as the Count of Monte Cristo. For one role—*50 grand!*

That was the thing to be: a real actor, making real money. Like I told Minta later, I must have forgotten about the money part when I prayed to the theater gods for a long-running role. (I also forgot to pray for the *right* long-running role, but never mind.) When, out of nowhere, impresario Ferris Hartman offered me a part in *The Mikado*, my first thought was *Why me?* But what was even stranger than the idea of Roscoe Arbuckle in *The Mikado* was the idea of where we were performing it—in the Far East. What could the audience possibly think?

Still, after lounging around imitating furniture for all those weeks at the Durfees', I'd have played Queen Victoria in Pago Pago just to get out of the house.

The Mysterious Orient

The closer we came to departing, the more the whole notion made me nervous. How would *we* like a bunch of coolies coming to our shores, playing white men and making carnival of us? As I kept saying to Minta, it's like taking a minstrel show on a tour of plantations.

But hunger, like I told you when I was stranded in San Jose at 10, always trumps nerves, so off we went. First to Honolulu and a command performance for Queen Liliuokalani, at the Royal Hawaiian Opera House. During the reception afterwards, I misjudged the potency of the native cane liquor. According to Minta, I made an appearance in a hula skirt, attempted to dance cheek to cheek with the queen—who looked 96 if she looked a week—then took ill and spewed poi on a royal show pony. My poor wife had to apologize the next day. (Not, sadly, for the last time.) I was ushered unceremoniously out of the palace, and advised not to try and return to Hawaii without armed guards.

All the way to the boat in Honolulu, I was convinced I was going to be hijacked, skewered with an apple in my mouth, and left for pineapple fertilizer. Sadly, my boorish behavior, and poor Minta's inevitable apology, set the tone for the expedition.

Round-Eyed Demon

When the 43 of us arrived in China, it was obvious at once this was 43 more white people than any of the natives had seen before. Men and boys followed me everywhere—including to the public latrine—where, to my amazement, I'd find them brazenly ogling my privates.

Our host, a Chinaman who spoke English like a landed duke, explained that your average Chinee believed "round-eyes" were endowed with jumbo equipment, and could not resist the chance to catch a glimpse of the big fat white man's package. I felt like a zoo animal, and became too self-conscious to urinate. I held it in till my scalp felt damp. I was afraid of what would happen if they weren't impressed. I was a big man, but I wasn't a big man.

To keep the locals out of pee-peek range, my host told the throngs of curious that I was a wrestler, and it would be dangerous to stand too close in case I got riled. After less than a week in the East, I found myself cupping my wiener when I passed water, blocking the eyes of the curious, like a man trying to light a smoke in a strong wind.

We spent a year and a half in the Far East, and halfway through I stopped drinking after the show. Instead I started drinking before it. Thank you. It was all just too much. In Tokyo we saw prostitutes kept in swinging cages. They looked about 9, with eyes so dead you wanted to rip your heart out and feed it to them to make them alive again. In Shanghai, to get to our restaurant we had to step over children in the street, old-looking babies grown big-headed from starvation. My wife wanted to adopt every one, and I had to pull her away with more force than either of us cared for.

Minta was even more livid the first time I paid for a rickshaw. How could I be so insensitive? It took four dainty yellow men to move this big fat white one an inch and a half. The Chinese on hand to catch the spectacle seemed to find it highly amusing. Especially the other rickshaw drivers.

What the Chinks enjoyed more than anything was watching their friends get hurt. The perfect Mack Sennett audience. Stick four Keystones in coolie hats, let 'em lose control of the rickshaw on a steep hill with me in it, and you've got yourself a two-reeler. Culling a chuckle from the suffering of others appeared to be a universal plot.

When Minta ranted about the rickshaw ride, I told her that, harsh as the work might seem to her, if she had never been broke, *really* broke, then she could never understand how much our little slant-eyed chums would appreciate having it—not to mention how gaga they'd go over my sizable four-way tip for a job well done.

But Minta didn't see things that way. We fought constantly, not just about the beggars—she couldn't pass an outstretched hand—but about whatever impropriety I'd perpetrated on our gracious host or fellow cast members the night before. The worse my behavior, the more uncomfortable my wife's next-morning apology was to the other actors and local society swells whose carpets I'd waltzed on with poop on my shoes the night before. Poor Minta had sacrificed a promising career to become a professional apologizer. But to give the angel her due—she was good at it.

I loved my wife, but I hated myself when I was around her. Does any drunk like to be called an ogre by his glass widow before he knows how big a hangover he has to sweat through that morning, or what manner of shame he brought on himself and his loved ones the previous evening? I suppose I could blame the ground rhino horn they put in sake—I've downed tastier paint thinner—but it was my own fault that in Asia I became a belligerent dipso. Somewhere in Nanking Province, the entire troupe began to regard me with that worse-than-hateful, worse-than-angry look that every lush on the planet has had aimed in his or her direction. The look that says, *"Before, your behavior was just disgusting—now it's making our lives a living hell."* The words may as well be plastered on their foreheads: *"You're an asshole and we wish you would just go away."*

Still, when Fatty was buying, Roscoe always had friends. Anything was better than the tension of being cooped up with Minta. My wife's mounting disappointment in me made it hard to breathe. I couldn't wait to head out with the boys at night and get roaring. Since women weren't allowed in drinking joints, Minta remained behind. Some nights I'd crash back into our room at some ungodly hour, screaming so loudly the entire company would get an earful. *"I'm tired of having to carry the whole damn show on my back! What am I—a white sumo?"*

"Two sumoes!" someone shouted from down the hall. Or so Minta told me. I, of course, have no memory of Nanking Province whatsoever.

Somehow, in my hooch-addled brain, it was Minta's fault that we were slaving away in Riceland instead of doing respectable theater and getting rich like that O'Neill fellow. *The Count of Monte Cristo*, every day of your life. And wouldn't *that* be heaven?

If I really concentrate, I can squeeze out a cracked memory or two of the *Mikado* tour. The worst image is Minta cowering on a tatami mat—the fear in her eyes so damning it made me want to hurl somebody out the window. Probably myself. *Did she really think I'd hit her?* She must have, or she would not have looked so scared.

I could tell the company was turning on me, so I picked up every tab. Bought everyone presents of shantung silk. Organized tea parties that started out pleasant and ended up with me sweaty-faced, doing the Black Bottom with nervous women I'd yank out of their chairs—often as not the wives of respectable businessmen too polite to kill me.

The cast knew how much cash had gone to keeping me out of scrapes. They also knew how much it cut into the net profits. My assaholic behavior was taking money out of everybody's pockets.

By the time we hit the Philippines, the strain and firewater caught up to me. My voice went. I got a fever of 104. For three weeks I soaked the sheets in Manila, stinking up a hotel room and shutting down the show—leaving the rest of the company unpaid and justifiably hateful.

Living with In-Laws
Is Its Own Kind of Death

All I wanted to do was crawl back to Los Angeles. Once we actually returned, though, it was back to Minta's parents' house, back to scraping around for work. It didn't take too many botched auditions before I had to admit I was never going to be a high-paid serious stage actor. With my body, I was not likely to be a serious anything. Who was I kidding? They were paying to see a dancing elephant, not a dramatic one.

Minta grabbed some chorus work through a man her Dad met in his capacity as streetcar conductor. This gave me more time to hunker in the Durfees' easy chair and stew. Some days my big activity was lifting my ankles when Minta's Mom vacuumed around me.

For hours, I sat in that chair, sneaking sips from a flask and pawing my tattered scrapbook to see what a big-time headliner I was in vaudeville. But sooner or later I'd have to raise my eyes and admit what I was in life: a dead broke, bone-tired 22-year-old who'd been hustling nonstop for 12 years, a young man who'd known top billing and now lived off the charity of his wife's parents.

That night, waiting at the streetcar stop to meet Minta and walk her home after her night on the chorus line, I ran into a hoofer named Davey Woods. Woodsy and I had worked a tour or two together and crossed paths on the circuit for years. The last time I'd seen him he was fanny-out-of-his-pants broke in Idaho, stranded after a promoter stiffed him. Now here he was, back in Los Angeles, in a spanking new suit and boater. When I told Woods how well he looked, he smiled sheepishly and looked down at his shiny new shoes. "Movies, Roscoe."

"Movies!" I launched into my usual diatribe: "*Only people so poor they couldn't afford a vaudeville ticket go to the nickelodeon. . . . Any actor who would demean himself by blah blah blabbity blah . . .*"

Then I heard myself and laughed. What was more demeaning than living off your wife's parents? Even if I could go star in a vaudeville show, right now I couldn't afford a ticket to one. Years after this, Buster Keaton told me how, in 1914, William

Randolph Hearst offered his father big money to put the Three Keatons, the family vaudeville act, in a feature movie version of the comic strip *Bringing Up Father*. Pops Keaton turned Hearst down flat. "The dough's great, but the work's beneath us." He'd sure change his tune down the road, but then who wouldn't?

Like Errol the Aussie used to say, sometimes the truth sneaks up on you and whispers. Sometimes it smacks you in the face with a catfish. This was definitely a catfish moment. For once, instead of boring myself and everybody else with my antimovie spiel, when Woodsy mentioned that the Selig-Polyscope Company was casting for some fluffball called *Alas! Poor Yorick!* I just thanked him for the info and shut up. When he told me the part was for an actress, I thanked him again and told him I didn't care. I couldn't afford a streetcar ride, let alone something as upscale as dignity.

The very next day, I showed up at Selig's studio dressed like a respectable woman. It hadn't been that long ago I was sashaying across the stage for the gold-dust thugs in Boise. And I hadn't lost my feminine touch. I got the part, and appeared on screen—not for the last time—dressed as a female with an exceptionally large torso and lovely hair.

Hands off, Cowboy!

To keep from scratching under my wig during filming—the brute light got the studio temperature up to 110—I focused on the details of this peculiar process. How the camera had to be cranked to keep it whirring. How an actor had to exaggerate every gesture—like doing pantomime for the nearsighted. How you learned to stick out your lower lip so you could aim your breath upward, cooling your face, staving off that dread moment when the pancake starts running down your face.

Filmmaking was an uncomfortable, impractical, and highly irritating endeavor. On the other hand, it paid well and you got to sleep in your own bed at night.

PART 3

Comedy Has a Special Stench

T HE FIRST thing you noticed about Mack Sennett was his breath. Mack crunched raw green onions, lettuce, and radishes for breakfast, washed down with straight whiskey. The rest of the day he skipped the rabbit food and stuck with the whiskey. The stink of those booze-and-onion fumes was legendary—a fact in which Mack, if this tells you anything, took great pride. His belches could singe your eyebrows, and he liked to aim them.

I did not particularly want to meet Mack Sennett, and only went because Fred Mace happened to sit down next to me on the streetcar—another Red Line moment—and told me I had to. I didn't know Fred from Adam. But he was as hefty as I was, and when he saw me he told me he'd been working as an actor with this Mack Sennett character and he was getting ready to pull up stakes. It might be the perfect opportunity for a fellow fat man.

Gumming a silver toothpick, Fred filled me in. "Mack used to work with D. W. Griffith. He's the only moviemaker who writes his own stories. Comedies only. No dialogue. How it works is, the director tells you where to stand, yells 'Action,' and then you either wing it or do whatever the hell else he tells you to do."

"Like what?"

"Fall off a roof. Drive over a cliff. Squirt yourself in the face with a firehose."

"Sounds crappy."

"It *is* crappy," Fred said wearily, staring out the window as we clattered past a cowfield. "But what it really is is five clams a day and lunch."

If I had had any work coming up, or even the prospect, I would not have bothered. But I didn't, so I did. Next day I rode the streetcar to Effie and Edendale, the end of the line. Which was exactly how I felt, trudging through the dusty weeds, clutching Mace's back-of-a-matchbook map to the unmarked gate of Keystone Studios.

Once you were inside, things weren't much better. To get to Mack's office, you had to pick your way through an obstacle course of muddy scenery, camera parts, bits of tattered-looking clothes, and the odd, unexplained mannequin with breasts and pubic hair painted on. Those mannequins gave me pause, but I pushed on.

The Keystone grounds, if you could call them that, looked like a theatrical trash heap—a symbol I did not want to dwell on. Mace had told me to just go upstairs and introduce myself. On the top step, I checked the collars of my suit and shirt, wiped the dust off my shoes, then straightened up and knocked on the door. Nobody answered. Then I heard what sounded like splashing, and the voice of someone clearly used to barking out orders. *"Get in here or get out!"*

After a minute's jittery consideration, I chose the former option. Inside, Mack Sennett reclined in a full bathtub in the middle of a private office, flanked by a giant Turk in a turban and a tired-looking accountant type. The Turk had a towel over one arm and carried a whiskey bottle in a bucket. The accountant slumped on a folding chair tapping a notepad with his pencil. The bathtub was set on a raised wooden platform, like a fruit bowl on a dinner table. It faced a window so Mack could soak away and still have a bird's-eye view of whatever went on in his domain.

"Too neat to be funny!" Mack bellowed as soon as he saw me. Before I could protest, he raised his head and delivered a stream of tobacco juice into a spittoon 20 feet away. With a little shoe polish, his spittoon trick could have made a first-class carny act. It was impossible not to stare.

"Still here, fat boy?" Mack stood up in full manhood and raised his freckled arms while the Turk toweled him off. "What makes *you* think you're chuckle-bait?" By now I was so nervous, all I could do was throw my arms up in the air and do a backflip. I bounced out of that into a forward tumble—like I was going to join Mack in the bath—and landed square on my two flat feet.

Sennett just nodded, like fat guys were flying around his bathtub all day long. Then he kind of whistled through his teeth and jiggled his testicles. It didn't take long around Mack for the rankest behavior to seem ho-hum. That was part of his charm, if you could call it that.

Thrusting his empty glass towards the Turk, Mack asked him with great sincerity, "What do *you* think, Abdul?" The swarthy character poured more whiskey and grunted. Mack then turned to the harried man with the pad and pencil. "How about you, Glassmeyer?" The fellow fiddled with his glasses and gave a weak nod of approval. I later learned that Glassmeyer was a writer, and that while Mack kept a restaurant stocked with food for actors and hands, he never let the writers eat. Mack believed if he kept writers hungry, they'd think more. That's why all the Keystone writers looked so miserable. On the other hand, they were all pretty damn trim.

Mack was always cheap with talent—especially actors—which is why he lost them. Ford Sterling, Harold Lloyd, Chaplin . . . They all asked for more money, and they all got the ax. When Paramount made me the first actor in Hollywood to make a million a year, Sennett said it would be the end of me. So how'd *he* know?

Anyway, Mack's standing up in the tub in front of me, naked as an imbecile, lifting one gam so the Turk can dab the underside of his thigh, then lifting the other. After that Abdul wrapped him in a towel, like a big hairy-legged baby in swaddling. Then Mack stepped out of the water and grabbed a Panama hat off a rack. When he put it on, his dyed black hair poked out of the top, where he'd cut the lid out.

"Nothing beats sunlight for a healthy scalp," he declared, as if daring Glassmeyer or myself to try and tell him otherwise. Then, bare feet puddling the floor, Mack stepped out of the towel Abdul'd just wrapped him in. He padded up to me twirling his penis like a dandy with a little cane. Later he said Charlie stole his routine. I suppose he wanted to shock me. But I grew up around farm animals.

Mack put his face close to mine and rattled off his stellar offer. "Players make five dollars a day, extras a box lunch and a buck. Be here tomorrow at eight, fat boy."

I managed to breathe without inhaling onion gas, and smiled big.

"Sure thing, Mr. Sennett. And nice hat."

Keystoned

Imagine. I'd known Mack Sennett 10 minutes and already felt a physical revulsion to the man. Even after his bath, he reeked. The poor Turk who dried him must have mastered some Muslim rite of nostril blockage.

The whole scene distracted me so, on the way down the stairs after our "meeting" I collided with some Dapper Dan in a monocle. The man I bumped protested, in a stage-French accent, as though I'd shown him some grave offense: "I beg your pardon, sir!" Then he made a show of looking me up and down, before sniffling at me and wrinkling his nose. By now I was too frazzled for false propriety. Mack Sennett had just showed me his one-eyed milkman. Was I supposed to mind my manners?

"Frenchy," I snapped at him, "if you don't like how *I* smell, the guy upstairs is going to *kill* you."

Henry Lehrman—the kind-of-but-not Frenchman I'd bumped—did not think this was funny. Like he did not think most of what I did was funny in years to come, when he started directing me. Sennett held Lehrman in such contempt that he called him "Pathé"— in mocking homage to the cinematic pedigree this Belgian ex–theater usher liked to claim—but he let him direct because he was adequate. And he worked cheap.

From the second he gave me the okey-doke on the stairs, Pathé always made me uneasy. My world would explode nine ways to Sunday—in good ways and bad—before I found out why. In the meantime, I just wanted to grab the streetcar and run back to Minta, just to tell her I could pay for groceries. That I had a job. This was a night we were going to celebrate. Of course, after all the embarrassment in the Orient, I'd promised I wouldn't drink. But I easily convinced the little missus that champagne was okay, and we went dancing.

This was the last good night for a while. My first day at Keystone Studios, Sennett stuck me in some bit of nonsense called *The Gangsters*, which as far as I could tell involved a bunch of misshapen miscreants running up a hill, bumping into each other, and falling down the hill. The script left a lot of room for what Sennett called "improvisilization."

In the dressing room—the men's was side by side with the women's, leaving less privacy than Union Station at rush hour—I had to squeeze into a Keystone Kop uniform so tight it felt like an ankle-length corset. Sennett saw it and said it was perfect.

Worse, after that fake Frog Lehrman yelled "Action!" on my virgin outing, he didn't *stop* yelling. "Fatty, go right! . . . Fatty, look scared! . . . Fatty, stub your toe!" *You forgot to say "Simon says"!* Every time Lehrman opened his mouth during shooting, I'd look over at him. And every time I did, he yelled at me not to look at him during shooting. On top of that, people in the neighborhood were hanging out their windows, waving white hankies, trying to get our attention.

It was all so chaotic, I had to ask Edgar Kennedy, one of the other actors, what the heck was going on. *Why are all those housewives surrendering?* Edgar explained they weren't surrendering, they were trying to get the company to film over at their place. Everybody in the neighborhood knew Sennett paid $10 for front yards, $15 if the actors were going to run around the sides of the house. If it was hard to concentrate with the director yelling at me, the cheers and waves of the Edendale locals made it all but impossible. These people never needed to pay to go to the movies. They saw them in the raw on their front lawns. And they wanted to cash in.

To homeowners insane enough to open their doors to the Keystone Kops, Mack would pay $25—with no responsibility for damage. But that's not the craziest. Right before quitting time my second day, a firetruck clanged by and Mack yelled for us all to follow it. A house was burning down on the corner, so we ran around like idiots while the firemen were trying to do their job. Chester Conklin grabbed a hose and tramped on it.

When I picked up the nozzle to pretend to see what the problem was, Chester lifted his foot and blasted me in the face. After that I climbed on the roof to save a baby—which turned out to be a doll—and promptly fell off. The fire was actually in a barrel of rags somebody had torched in their backyard. But Mack worked with whatever came his way. If he didn't need the footage for the film we were shooting, he'd use it in another one.

After a week, Mack said he needed to talk to me upstairs. Walking behind him up the stairs, all I hoped was that he wasn't going to run a bath. What happened was worse. Sennett told me he didn't think I had anything on-screen. My hair was too light for the camera. My eyes looked watery. But the biggest problem of all, I was stiff.

"The gag's gotta come right after the plant. Slam-bang!" he yelled. Sennett only spoke in yells. "I don't got a yuck every 100 feet of film—*every 90 seconds*—I don't got a film." A week of smashed cars, dismantled kitchens, tree jumps—and all I got was I'm too *stiff*? My *hair's* too light? My anger must have shown through—or else he was afraid I was going to cry. Whatever the impulse, Sennett decided to try and let me down easy. "Look," he said, "I liked the way you fell off that roof. I'll call you as soon as more roof stuff comes up."

Saved by the Mabel

As luck would have it, Mabel Normand was walking into Mack's ramshackle office just as I was walking out. Mabel Normand, of course, was the big reason Keystone made nearly a million in its first eight months of existence. She was the only actor who got a private dressing room. Mabel was more than pretty. She'd been an artist's model in New York, and had these big soft eyes that made men she'd never met want to throw their lives away for the chance to take care of her. When she wanted, Mabel could look sophisticated enough to write operas in heels. But her favorite mode of attire, shockingly, was overalls and an old shirt with a straw hat on top.

You didn't expect a woman with Mabel's class to be madcap. But prior to signing on with Keystone, she'd worked for D. W. Griffith's Biograph in New York. She made a name for herself when she spent 10 minutes on top of a box-kite plane, in mid-flight, for a daring aerial sequence. Mabel was more fearless than any man. When Mack made his parody of Griffith's last-minute-rescue films, hiring Barney Oldfield for *Barney Old-field's Race for Life*, Mabel agreed to an amazingly dangerous high dive. It took so long for her to hit the water Sennett had to use two cameras, which had never been done before. But she was just as comfortable in a suds fight.

Mabel was also Sennett's girl. Why a woman like her would go near an onion-breathed, womanizing, testicle-juggling crack-pot like Mack was a subject of much speculation. One wag on the lot claimed that Mabel'd sniffed so much cocaine, she was the only starlet who couldn't smell him. It was as good an explanation as any. Though the goofer dust didn't really become a problem—or at least a noticeable problem—until later, when Mabel's whole life began to unravel.

That afternoon—which looked like my last on the lot—Mabel smiled and said, "See you tomorrow, Big Otto." I told her probably not and she stopped dead, as though completely shocked. Mabel'd been nice to me from that first day I showed up at Keystone. She dubbed me "Big Otto" because of how German I looked. We weren't close exactly, but we were friendly.

Now here was Mabel Normand, ready to stand up to the boss to make sure I stayed at the studio. Without so much as a blink, she stomped over to Sennett and poked her finger in his chest, while I dawdled self-consciously behind her. "Keep the big kid around, Mack. He's funny even if you don't know it yet."

Sennett, who hated conceding to any opinion but his own, stalled for time. He made a show of wiping some crumbs off his foul suit, then spat a chaw like Annie Oakley shooting a bull's eye into the corner spittoon. "You wanna keep Fat Boy, then *you* work with him," he finally told her. It was probably the most lucrative decision Mack Sennett ever made, even if he did it out of spite.

All the way back to the Durfees' on the streetcar, I thought about the day's strange turn. I'd never wanted to work in the movies, but the prospect of working with the actor friends I'd already made—and the ones I knew who would end up being more than friends, like Mabel—was hard to turn away from. I even got excited at the idea of learning a little more about working for the camera. The possibilities were there—it's just that the movies were so new, there was no way to say what those possibilities were.

Even if Minta and I didn't need the paycheck, I would have been sad to leave Keystone. Still, underneath my relief and gratitude, what stuck in my craw was the way Mack called me Fatty. I was more than used to teasing. For better or worse, Fred Mace, Charlie Murray, Edgar Kennedy, Slim Summerville, and the other Kops already had nicknames for me: My Child the Fat; Matching Saddlebags; Sir Hefty Dumpling, Esquire. Somehow those were okay. But the one that stuck—the one that always stuck— was the one that hurt the most. The one Daddy called me. Fatty.

Fatty! What made this one different was the way Mack spat it out, just like my father. Like it was something disgusting. Thanks to Sennett, I was listed on title cards as Roscoe "Fatty" Arbuckle. And pretty soon most people forgot the Roscoe and just remembered Fatty. From that moment on, the joy of my accomplishments would be forever tainted by mortification over the name I accomplished them under.

And I had not been consulted.

The Happy Factory

That first year at Keystone, there were 50 title cards with my name on them. *Fifty.* Some weeks we'd grind out three or four one-reelers. To say my life changed is like saying Vesuvius got a little hot and burped. The pace made vaudeville seem stately. On the other hand, no more sleeping in train stations and skipping meals for 50 weeks. I took a streetcar to work in the morning. Sennett supplied decent grub. (Unless, like I said, you were a writer.) And the money was good and steady.

Let me wade into it, though. Because everything seemed to happen fast and slow at the same time. True to his word, Sennett paired me with Mabel for my second movie, *Passions, He Had Three.* Mack's idea was that the whole film should play out on a beach full of "bathing beauties." Mack was big on bathing beauties. That was the joke around the Happy Factory: "*If she wants to be a Sennett bathing beauty, a beauty has to bathe with Sennett.*"

Anyway, what happens in *Passions,* Harry Langdon plays the wolf and starts giving my gal Mabel looks. Naturally, I get jealous. Harry and I end up rivals for Mabel's affections. We compete like schoolboys. Not that I know too much about being a schoolboy. The school I attended, your final exam was getting hymied after a nine-show-a-day run in Bakersfield, helping the juggler pawn his Indian clubs so you can cadge a train ticket.

Arbuckle, you're rambling . . . I know that.

"Hey, Mishter, your whiskey's showing!" Mack used to shout this at himself whenever he passed a mirror. Or, on occasion, when he passed Yours Truly. The conditions under which I'm trying to rein in these memories is less than stellar. Whiskey helps. So does Aunt Hazel. The doctor said it would kill me—but he was always the optimistic type.

So where was I? Keystone. Mabel. *Passions, He Had Three.* There we are. *Passions* was Mack's version of light romance. In the course of the seaside shenanigans, Harry pops me one in the beak and Mabel takes off in Harry's balloon. Which makes me so mad I call in the cavalry. The Keystone Kops wobble in to end things with suitable chaos and injury.

Macking

Sennett came up at Biograph under D. W. Griffith, whom he idolized. According to Mack his mentor had a blind spot: Griffith didn't see the point of filming "guys chasing other guys." Especially if the guys doing the chasing were policemen. That was the difference between them. Wark—I love saying Griffith's middle name; he was David *Wark* Griffith—wanted to make people good. Sennett wanted to make them happy—which to him meant making the cops look like morons.

This creative difference gave Sennett his brainstorm: a studio that only made comedies. He raised the money for Keystone with a couple of bookie pals and kicked off in New York with

Mabel, Ford Sterling, and Henry "Pathé" Lehrman, the fake Frenchman who hated my guts. They shot a one-reel stinker in Fort Lee, New Jersey—*Cohen at Coney Island*—then Mack got the California bug after his god D. W. hightailed it from East 14th Street to sunnier climes.

In New York everything was shot indoors. In the winter, it got dark at four. If it rained or snowed the light was gone altogether. To people who started as pups filming in freezing New York studios, just the *idea* that you could shoot outside in December was enough to send them running. The lush scenery meant you didn't have to spend time and money building sets. The cheap labor and material were just gravy.

After Tom Ince got rich in five minutes making his California westerns, movie people started flocking to Los Angeles like the proverbial lemmings. Some went straight over the cliff; some took a while.

Keystone had been in business eight months by the time I rolled in. Mack and the gang worked off a simple formula: create mayhem and film it. When I first got there, I though the plots were ridiculous. Worse, actors had to improvise much of the action. And the stories made no sense. But Sennett had a different take. He loved to tick off the ingredients of a Keystone Comedy on his fingers: pace, gags, motion, and the expression on the actor's face when, just when he thinks things are going his way, they go all to hell.

"It ain't a comedy till the wheels fall off" was another Mackism, which may as well have referred to the crates the Kops used to bang around in. Mack never minded seeing an employee get hurt. He was fine with it. As long as the camera was on and you didn't bleed in his whiskey. One time, after making me do five takes of tumbling out of a palm tree into a mud puddle, he strolled over to watch me putting ice on my jaw. "Hurts, huh, Fat Boy?" I just looked at him: this big Irish lug in a soiled suit, his face smeared with dust and that open-top Panama askew on his head.

"What do you think?" I asked him back.

"What I think," Mack cackled, "comedy is *you* fall in a ditch and die. Tragedy is I get a hangnail. It all comes down to human nature, Arbuckle. People just naturally love watching bad go to worse."

"Worse," in the case of the Kops themselves, meant more than just a laugh. At any given time half the guys nursed broken bones. And Sennett didn't pay for their time off, either. In his mind, there were two kinds of comedians: fast or f—ed. I never liked that kind of cursing in my presence, but Mack didn't care, any more than he cared about calling me Fatty. That explained another Fun Factory fact: Keystone spent more on bandages than on makeup. We were usually shooting on some hill on Manzanita, Hyperion, or Effie, or down in Echo Park, so whoever got gandied that day would recline in the sun back at the studio, which would turn into a Red Cross center. Somebody was always hobbling around the Keystone lot on crutches or nursing a fresh bloody nose. The injured would try to lure a bathing beauty over to clean their wounds. This was as much as Mack was willing to provide in the way of balm for the wounded.

Did I describe the Keystone stage already? The whole thing was nothing but three exterior walls with muslin slung over the top, for filtering. The worst job in the studio was moving that muslin sheet on the roof. After a rain, it stayed mildewed for weeks, and the pigeons who called the lot home liked to relieve themselves on it. Why am I telling you this? Because, if for some reason Mack wanted to shoot inside and needed to alter the light, he'd assign whoever he hated that week to Sheet Duty. My first months at Keystone, I got used to coming home with pigeon poop on my kneecaps.

Pain Lessons

What Sennett said over and over was that comedy was not about being funny. It was about being desperate. What, besides desperation, could make a person walk on telephone wires 30 feet off the ground, then smash through a skylight and bang off a busted-out mattress 20 feet below? They weren't doing it to be funny. They were doing it because, in the movie, they *had* to! You can watch that wire-to-mattress sequence in *Fatty's Tintype Tangle* and say "That's one brave fat man!" But maybe the fat man doesn't think it's particularly brave. Maybe he thinks that's what he has to do to keep his job.

No matter. After 20 years of struggling, *Movie World* magazine called me an overnight sensation. They declared my face "more familiar than the president's!" President Who?

Back then, Minta would always tell me that I worked like a man being chased. Sometimes she'd ask me what was chasing me. All I could think to answer was, "I won't know until it catches me. That's what scares me . . ."

She told me to read Freud.

Mabel-and-Fatty Magic

Here's the funny thing. After the first three Mabel-and-Fatty pictures—*Passions, For the Love of Mabel,* and *The Waiters' Picnic*—audiences went berserk. They could not get enough of us. But even after I knew Mabel and I were making hits, I didn't know what it meant. Not really. I knew I had steady work. I knew that after six years of marriage, I was finally able to buy my wife flowers. That every morning, Minta, who'd gotten a job at Keystone thanks to Mabel, would wake up, make me a breakfast of eggs and bacon and a tureen of coffee and ride the streetcar by my side to the lot. I had a future, even if it wasn't the future I'd imagined. What did I know? I'm a fat kid from Kansas. My own good luck scared me. Life seemed unbelievably livable.

Then the fan letters started. Every day, a limping Irish girl who called herself Harvey would bring me a stack of fan letters and I'd go around the back of the stage, sit on a barre, and try to read them. "Dear Fatty, Me and my sister think you're Tops. She's got the goiter . . ." "DEAR FATTY, I DON'T HAVE A DAD, BUT YOU WOULD BE SWELL . . ."

One time I made the mistake of showing a note to Minta, from a Greek boy with tuberculosis. Naturally, the next day we took the train to the hospital, and when I walked in the room he had my photo in his pale little hand. I said, "How are you, scooter?" The kid just smiled. Pink lips in a little gray face. Then his mother, a nervous woman who kept wringing her apron, whispered something to the father, a big bald moussaka with arms like pylons. Dad looked at the floor and asked if I would mind touching his boy on the head. I was embarrassed.

It was awful. Knowing this kid put so much faith in me. An *actor*.

I patted his head, surprised that his hair was so damp. "Fever sweats," the doctor said. The youngster—his name, I'll never forget, was Paris Tsangaris—raised his sunken brown eyes to mine. I don't remember what I said to him. What was I supposed to say? The poor nipper was so scared he shook. I looked into his eyes and knew everything that was going on in there. That's when it hit me: this kid was scared before he got the TB. You could tell by the way his brothers and sisters cowered. The way he kept sneaking looks past me, at his silent father, as if expecting a backhand any second.

That shook me up good. Made me remember Daddy. Waking up with his belt buckle across my face. Once I made my way out of my own childhood, the last thing in the world I wanted to do was remember it. When magazines asked, Sennett's office passed out an official press release about my happy boyhood. Much to my surprise, "*I was born in an average, middle-class family of five . . . A graduate of Santa Clara College . . . A football star and glee club feature . . .*"

Sometimes I almost believed this hogswaddle. I preferred it to the truth, which the terrified look in Paris Tsangaris's eyes made me recall all over again. I remembered what it felt like to be scared. To be Daddy's punching bag. To be told you're a piece of dogmeat so many times you're embarrassed to even look anybody in the eye, 'cause after a while you just believe it's true. I looked in that little TB boy's eyes and saw the 200-pound 12-year-old me, crying on my suitcase in the San Jose train station. What could I tell him but "*Run! Gawdamighty, run, you little lunger!*"?

The second we got home from the hospital I picked up a bottle and didn't put it down till it was empty. Minta tried to comfort me and I pushed her into the wall. I shouted at her. "*I'm just a comedian! I'm too fat to be Jesus!*" Minta didn't understand. "But honey, don't you feel for that child?" How could I tell her where I'd been at that boy's age? I used to *wish* I'd come down with the croup, or something else that killed you. Even coughing myself to death seemed like a better deal than lying awake, keeping my eyes open, never knowing when Dad was going to bang in with a belt in his hand and rotgut on his breath.

I didn't say any of this, of course. Minta came from a real family. Her Mom and Dad loved her. They loved each other. How could I begin to tell her about life in the Arbuckle asylum? The last thing I remember about that night, after the Greek TB boy visit, I picked up a vase that had been in the Durfee family in the Old Country and hurled it across the room. And the only reason I know I said that bit about Jesus is because Minta told me the morning after, when she was cleaning up the crockery.

The next day, at Keystone, I must have still been in the mood for throwing things. We were looking for a slammer—something to break up a sequence—during *A Noise from the Deep*. We were shooting on the stage that day and I couldn't get anything right. I was still out of sorts. Mack asked what the problem was, and when I told him I'd skipped breakfast, he sent Harvey to the bakery. She came back with a tray full of cupcakes, turnovers, and a fresh blueberry pie—just like the one Pancho Villa and I tossed across the Rio Grande. That's when it came to me. I yelled for Mack to run camera. I whispered to Mabel what I wanted to do. As film rolled, we concocted some squabble. I was waiting to give the cue—*"when I pull my ear, that means I'm going to throw the pie!"*—when, Lord in a latrine, she scooped the thing up before me and threw it right in my kisser.

I thought Mack was gonna wet his drawers! Which happened to be all he was wearing, it being bath day. He sent Harvey for more pies and by the end of the day I'd mastered the two-handed hurl, the side-arm, and the over-the-shoulder. From then on pie-throwing was de rigueur. The lucky duck who ran the bakery down the street, a Hebe named Greenberg, even developed a blueberry-and-paste pie that didn't fall apart midair. For long-distance throwing.

Greenberg retired at 35, bought a mansion near Santa

Barbara, and hung a sign over the front door that said THE HOUSE THAT PIES BUILT. All thanks to a poor little chest case who made me feel so bad I wanted to fling something at my wife. That daddy-scared boy with Greek TB.

But look at me, I'm tearing up!

Zipper Money

Mabel used to toodle over to the Durfees' and visit after a day shooting in Echo Park. Then Mack gave me a raise. From $5 to $18 a week, and from there to $25. Eventually it would hit $150. Even before I got that much, I was able to buy a car. An Alco. We arrived in Echo Park homeless vagabonds and moved out in a spanking-new coupe to a beach house in Santa Monica. Praise Jesus, Hollywood be thy name.

No more living with the in-laws, uplifting as that can be. I even suggested we get a butler. At first we had a Brit, named Mackens, but he spoke better English than I did, and I always felt like he thought I should be picking up *his* socks. So we found a Japanese. His name was something like Oka Lima Beana. So we called him Okie. I don't think he knew five words of English, which was fine. We communicated in pantomime. Minta bought me a pair of pants with a zipper—the new rage in men's fashion—and that's when I knew I was making money.

I taught Minta to drive, but after two weeks there was a permanent indentation in the driver's seat—*from* the driver's seat—and when poor Minta sat behind the wheel, she said it was like sitting in a pothole. So I had to get her one of her own. Which I swore not to sit in and ruin.

*   *   *

Across the globe, world war was breaking out. Nobody got too fussed about it in California. Mabel thought Archduke Ferdinand's wife had peculiar taste in hats, but otherwise we were a merry band—or at least a busy one—working 12 hours a day, sometimes seven days a week. The biggest problem for the writers was finding new ways to keep Mabel and me in hot water in front of the camera. But it didn't seem to matter. We could make a two-reeler about doing laundry—*Mabel and Fatty's Wash Day*—and it would turn into gold. The trick was to keep coming up with new places for Mabel and me to mix it up. Airplanes, autos, motorcycles; opera house, outhouse, a mother-in-law's house flooded with water and floating down the street. Et cetera. And that's when I wasn't dressing up like some tarty woman and showing my knickers.

When ideas ran low, Mack was always ready to throw us in some public event and film whatever happened. "*Okay, kiddies,*" he'd say, with that greasy-radish grin of his, "*let's go drop the piranha in the goldfish bowl.*"

One time we all went down to the San Diego Exposition. Sennett pretended to set up a demonstration of how movies were made. But our cameras were empty. What Mack was really doing was filming us cut up in front of the crowds. Same thing at the World's Fair in San Francisco. The films we made from crashing parades or gallivanting through collapsed water mains were no different than the ones we shot normally. They just had different extras. At public functions—or calamities, as we used to call them—half the action was made up. More than once, we had firemen stop to wave at the camera, much to the consternation of families waiting for them to rush in and save Grandma's knitting basket. Basically you could get killed any minute.

What started to amaze me on these outings was how many people felt the urge to approach us. How excited they were. It never stopped being a surprise, having total strangers skittle over and talk to you like you were old friends. Course, I still hated it when folks called me Fatty. If it was a little tyke, I'd grin and tell 'em my real friends call me Roscoe. If it was an adult, and I'd had a couple of nips in me, I'd say something really classy, like "How'd you like it if I called you No Neck?"

One time we ran across a sideshow setting up in Echo Park and met the Fat Lady. She must have had 200 pounds on me, all packed in a bathing suit. Mabel said she looked like a pile of albino tires. The funny part, she kind of shimmied up behind us and yelled, "Hey, Skinny!" Me, Mabel, and Mack turned around and nearly fell over.

That was the one time Mack was caught flat-footed. A jalopy had backed over his camera when he was taking a leak, so me, Mack, Mabel, Minta, and Lehrman were standing around waiting for somebody to show up with another one. Mack nearly died at missing a shot of me and Jumbelina. He bit through his knuckle-skin when he saw the Fat Lady wobble off. First time in my life I ever felt normal. Minta said the woman was actually quite sweet. Just a little slow. "She'd been manhandled as a child," she told us. "All that fat's just a wall between her and any man who might get ideas."

"She'd be safe if Fatty got an idea," Lehrman cracked. "Those two couldn't mate without a crane and tweezers."

Right away my face got red. The way it did when Daddy browbeat me. Pathé stood there, waiting to see what I'd do. When I didn't do anything, he said, "I rest my case." I can still see that self-satisfied smirk. Until Mabel opened her mouth and the smirk disappeared. "Oh, Henry," she said, in that slit-your-throat-but-make-it-sound-chipper way she had, "everybody knows the only time you get laid is when you meet a girl dumb enough to think your accent is real. Just 'cause you *smell* French, honey, doesn't mean you are."

Escaping Lehrman wasn't the only reason I decided to direct. But, like I told Minta, he was the bite in the ankle that made me run the 50-yard dash. My first two one-reelers were *Barnyard Flirtations* and *Chicken Chaser*. I got out of animal husbandry with *A Bath House Beauty*, my third, and hit my stride teaming up with Mabel in *Where Hazel Met the Villain*, which has a burglar scene in it. Nothing opens more doors for comedy than burgling. We'd write 'em, we'd shoot 'em, and then we'd write another one. Those were great days: jumping out of our chairs with comedy Eurekas, then pullin' the stunts under the sun with the camera runnin'—if that ain't heaven on earth, it sure beat shining shoes.

Pretty soon Minta got in the act. She costarred in *A Suspended Ordeal*, also known as *Hung by a Hook*. Both titles, Minta claimed, pretty much summed up our marriage when I was on a bender. Which wasn't all the time, just almost. When I wasn't drinking to get drunk I was drinking to kill the hangover. Unfortunately, I was the only one who could tell the difference.

Liquid Refreshment

You could say it was the pressure that made me guzzle the hard stuff. But pressure was having no work, not working too hard. And drinking didn't make pressure go away. It only made you have to work harder walking across the room. Trying not to tip over took your mind off of whether you were breaking the gag-a-minute rule.

Minta used to tiptoe out of bed at three a.m. and find me slumped in my easy chair, pencil in one hand, bottle in the other, and a pad on my lap. That's how I got my ideas. Stinking drunk in my easy chair. But try telling that to a sweetie who thinks a sip of gin on the Fourth of July is plenty, thanks for asking. Sadly but truly, as they used to say in the minstrel shows, I felt more pressure hunkered in our house some nights than I did at work. I just couldn't turn off the action-gland. So we started going out. Minta and me. The Sunset Inn on Ocean Boulevard was our big haunt. Later on, Buster Keaton and I hosted a party there every Saturday. We even booked the bands . . . But where was I?

Minta hated going to the Sunset 'cause of the time I ran out of the bar, down to the beach, and into the Pacific fully clothed. I would have swum a few laps but I banged my knee up on a rock. Later that knee got revenge on me, but that's up the road, and the road ain't built.

Sennett lived at the Alexandria, on Fifth and Spring, so sometimes we'd slide by for a pop at the hotel bar after work. Lots of show people stayed there. My favorite bar was Goodfellow's Grotto, on South Main Street. Goodfellow's installed a special reinforced booth in the back, extra-wide, so I didn't have to worry about getting stuck going in and out. It would have been easier sitting in a chair, but I hated eating with my back to the dining room. I could feel all those eyes on me, like spiders. Made the back of my neck rash up red as an orangutang's ascot.

By then the world was calling Mack the King of Comedy. And Mack was calling me his right-hand man. I still remember his stellar quote from the *New York Times*: "Roscoe may act foolish before the camera, but he is one of the most sensible young men in pictures." Why, *garsh* . . .

All the old onion-gobbler had to do was plunk a poster of me or Lady Mabel in front of a theater and the crowds poured in. It's a weird feeling to be lying on your back at three in the morning thinking, *People I'll never meet pay money to laugh at me.* When I was little they did it for free. I guess that's success— getting paid for the same thing that used to make you wish you were dead. I should have asked the Fat Lady if she ever thought she'd grow up and be fat for a living. Not that that's what I was doing. Why, not at all! I was fast on my feet. I could cook up a scene. And I was pretty when I was fed and watered.

Put it this way. I didn't like what it was people liked about me. I was grateful, but I wasn't happy about it. At 26, what the newspapers called my "cherubic" and "innocent" face, my "infantile charm"—this was before they switched to "porcine," "imbecilic," and "evil"—made me popular with people who couldn't agree on anything else. Little kids and crotchety uncles. Tee-totaling blueblood spinsters and drunken micks. They all loved me. Or was it something else? Was it, maybe, that no matter how poorly any of 'em felt, they could all wake up glad they weren't me?

I spent a lot of time whispering inside my head, *I am so tired of being the Fat Guy.* But of course, a diet would have ruined me.

Trampled

When Chaplin showed up in 1914, Lehrman was as nasty to him as he'd been to me. During their first film, *Making a Living,* Lehrman's veins bulged out at how long it took Charlie to work out a simple gag. Charlie was a serial rehearser. Pathé went whining to Mack, as was his wont. Even though Sennett's the one who discovered Charlie—at the Orpheum, doing a falling-down act—and even though Mack knew all about Charlie's compulsive rehearsal habits, he acted shocked when Lehrman came to him and complained.

Charlie *was* the slowest-working man in show business. He had to be great—because everybody else on the set hated him in five minutes. Mabel worked with him a grand total of one hour and called it quits. Though later she confessed it was due to their "animal attraction," she sure didn't say that to Mack, who put my Minta in the role and was busily contriving a way to squeak out of his contract with Charlie when he called me in.

Shortsighted as a sewer rat, Mack just cared about getting the films shipped on time. When he came to me and said, "Big Butt, I don't think the Brit's for us," I said keep him. "The guy's a little queer," I said to Mack, "but he's funny. *I'll* get the GD films out on time."

So Lehrman quit, I started directing, and Charlie stayed. For a while. Chaplin wasn't much happier than Mack was. In fact, right before we stumbled onto his Little Tramp getup, Charlie was the one ready to pack it in. I can hear him now, snotty as an earl: "*Really, Roscow*"—that's how he used to say my name— "*the cinema's just a fad anyway. No real actor should get caught doing this.*"

In case it ain't obvious, Charlie spilled that whine about an hour before me and the boys made him the gift of a lifetime. What happened is, Mack heard there was a soapbox derby going on in Venice, so naturally he wanted to jump in and film it. The caper called for Charlie to play an inept shutterbug, a real "schlemiel" (Mack's favorite word). It was a classic film-on-the-fly: get the footage and we'll find out what we need it for later. Mabel used to say, if Jesus Christ came back to save mankind, Mack would show up with the Keystone Kops and toss him in a jalopy.

The problem this particular day was a fiscal one. Mack had given Charlie $25 to go out and buy shutterbug duds. And Charlie, justly famous for being so tight his keister squeaked, pocketed the money instead. Five minutes before we were supposed to leave for the ride to Venice—which, of course, Mack would also film—Charlie tore into the dressing room, where Chester Conklin, Mack Swain, and I were sharing a bit of liquid conviviality. "I'm in a bit of a spot," he said—his Yorkshire-pudding way of telling us he needed to mooch a wardrobe.

So that's how it happened. I slipped him one of my too-tight derbies and a pair of pants that ballooned on him. Chester supplied a cutaway. Mack Swain lent him that toothbrush mustache. He still didn't have shoes, so I gave him an old pair of mine. While I watched, he put the shoes on, walked around in a circle, then took 'em off and—scratching his head for a second—put them back on *the wrong feet*. That's when I knew he really was a genius.

By the end of the year, the Little Tramp was as popular as I was. The big diff: highbrows loved Charlie. I, on the other hand, was lowbrow as a beer-hall crapper. Charlie was Maine lobster to my sardines in a can. The other difference, natch, a Little Tramp stops being a tramp when the camera stops rolling. But a Fatty stays fat. Not something you probably ever thought about, but glug-glug-glug. Chaplin was always a better businessman than me. So when he announced to Mack—Charlie never asked, he announced—that he wanted $200 a week, Mack gave him the heave-ho. The Little Tramp—who would have made a world-class accountant—ambled over to the Essanay Company, who scooped him up for $1,500 a week. Not long after that he funny-walked to Mutual, where they hooked him for a mere $670,000 a year.

But I'll tell you something about Charlie—or really, about

Charlie and me—that I've never told anyone. See, everybody at the studio was always impressed how nice I was to the upstart limey. From the beginning, I made sure he didn't get fired. I gave him the "Buck up, it happens to everybody" speech when a critic called him "Chapman" in a review of *His New Profession*, one of his first Keystones. And not to harp, but I already told you about helping cook up the whole tramp thing. He never paid me for the pants, but never mind. Noble Roscoe never acted anything but proud when CC wiggle-waggled from mangy vaudevillian to biggest comic in the world. But here's the truth:

I was nice to Charlie Chaplin 'cause of all the times I tried to kill him.

Okay, I'm exaggerating. But I hurt him a little, and I can't say I lost any beauty sleep over it. Once Charlie and I were being filmed in a rowboat in Echo Park. I think it was during *Pastime*, but with enough tom-tom juice all those two-reelers blend into one big fall-down-and-bite-my-mother-in-the-neck car chase. I already knew Charlie hated the water. And not just 'cause he never met a bathtub he couldn't avoid. "Gamy," I do believe, is the technical term—though Mabel said that was being cruel to game. No, I knew because Chaplin didn't know how to swim. Not really. He'd been out to Casa Arbuckle, on the beach, and he wouldn't get in the ocean on a bet.

Water-wise, I was the opposite. The happiest times of my life were in the water. Out in Santa Monica, I'd swim every day. It got so the local dolphins knew I was coming and would swim along. I learned how to jump straight out of the water, like they do, and even used it in a picture. Just don't ask me which one. I don't have wet brain, I'm just a little damp under the ear flaps. Mack was convinced the dolphins thought I was their homely pink cousin.

Anyhooch, there we were, halfway to the middle of the Echo Park lake, when I kicked out the stopper of the rowboat with my shoe. When he saw the water gushing in, I thought Charlie's eyeballs were going to crack like eggs. He started chewing his lips. He even peed himself before the Echo Park lake made the rest of him wet. But, I gotta give it to Charlie, he never stopped acting. Even when the boat was nearly under, with us in it, all he did was make sure his derby didn't float away. He kept vamping till we were up to our necks.

And this wasn't a one-off event. Me nearly killing him, I mean. From doing odd jobs around the Durfees', I'd gotten handy with electric wiring. So, when the opportunity arose—as it did, oddly, the very week I heard Mack was going to be paying Charlie the same as I was getting—I wired the toilet so whoever who sat on it would get a jolt. This time, I told some of the guys, and we crouched in the dressing room trying not to giggle when Charlie went in. Five seconds later—"*Yeeoww!*" Out flies Chaplin, skivvies at half-mast, clutching his nuggins doing that herky-jerk shuffle that turned into his trademark.

Again, part of me feels bad, another part figures, "C'mon, Roscoe, he got that funny walk out of it, so why feel guilty?" After he left Keystone, I couldn't look at a Charlie Chaplin movie and not think: *What would the public do if they knew that famous walk was the product of electrified testicles?* File under things the world will never know.

Life's a pie-fight, and then you die.

A Thought on Comedy, from a Tragic Perspective

In slapstick, the hero can never relax. As soon as he thinks he's got things licked, a safe falls out the window he's strolling under and that's that. I guess you could say Mabel Normand walked under a lot of safes. And I'm not talking about in the movies.

Even in life, Mabel was always a script that needed work. More than anyone I ever met, she had a unique way of doing things. Like, one time, tired of the Keystone Kops flirting with her, she waited till they broke for lunch, then, looking springy in her flowered dress, did cartwheels all the way across Echo Park and back right in front of them. "There," she said when she finished, "now go home and kiss your wives and think of me." Coincidentally, she'd left her panties in the dressing room. So they had plenty to think about.

Mabel liked being known as the wildest woman in Hollywood. On another occasion, when Mack got on her about disappearing from the set in the middle of the day, she rolled her eyes at all of us, then let out a big put-upon sigh. "For gosh sakes, Mackie, even a movie star sometimes has to relieve herself. But if you don't want me to take the time to walk to the little girl's room, fine!" With that, in front of everybody, she pulled up her dress and sat on his lap. And wet all over him.

Still, for all the cocaine and hijinks—did I mention she had a bit of an inhalation problem?—Mabel was an old-fashioned gal. All she really wanted was some lunkhead to pop the question.

Old Onion-Breath finally proposed in 1915—they'd only been engaged seven years—and Mabel went out driving with Minta and another actress named Anne Luther to celebrate. That's when Anne decided to let Mabel know Mack might not be the man of her dreams. At that moment, according to Minta, Anne felt compelled to tell her good friend that her future hubby was having his manly way with one Mae Busch. "Mae!" Mabel shrieked. "But she's my *friend!* She didn't know a soul when she came out, so I let her use my apartment."

Poor Mabel wasn't naïve about anything—except her own

life. But after her chat with Anne and Minta, she dumped those gals out and drove like Barney Oldfield back to her own place. Big surprise, Mabel found Mack in her bed, clad in nothing more than a milk mustache, alongside the New York stray she'd taken in. Her good friend Mae.

Mack insisted, and you almost have to respect him for this, that he and the actress were discussing tomorrow's script. "We're working out a gag." Before Mabel could think of a comeback for that, Mae Busch panicked and cracked a vase over Mabel's head, leaving her bloody and stunned. "I'll tell you the scary part," Mabel told me later, in one of her own more scary moments. "The movie they were about to shoot was *One Night Stand!* Maybe they *were* rehearsing." Her cackle was hellish.

Ten days later, Mabel tied rocks to her waist and jumped off the pier in Santa Monica. If she couldn't find a safe to fall on her, she'd improvise. Fortunately, more or less, she was quickly rescued by a clammer and hospitalized for a month.

Understandably, even after her release, Mabel stayed away from the set for a while. And Mack being Mack, when the press wanted to know why there were no Fatty-and-Mabels slated, he blamed me. Not that *I* knew about it. No, I knew nothing of my own heinous behavior until I opened a *Photoplay*, and there it was in black and white. The article was called "Why Aren't We Killed?" Mack—who wouldn't stop filming if an actor's spleen plopped onto the sidewalk—was lamenting how dangerous, how *careless* those doggone actors could be. Case in point, Roscoe "Fatty" Arbuckle. Apparently, I was always throwing myself around and breaking things. I had, in fact, "recently nearly crushed poor Mabel in a good stunt gone bad." That's how Mack Sennett made me the heavy. The public believed that *I* was the cause of their favorite actress's head injury. Do I need to tell you how good this looked later? "*Why, ladies and gentlemen of the jury, Mister Arbuckle's irresponsibility has already been well documented.*"

Funny how I'm always the last to know. About anything. I didn't even know how big I was. I'm not talking about weight, either. The studio loved to tell movie magazines I topped off at 286, when I wasn't a nosehair over 260. What I'm talking about is how much clout I really had. How much I was worth. Folks knew me most places I went. But even that doesn't give you the global perspective.

What did give me an inkling was Luke the Dog. Willie Lucas, a Brit director, dumped this crazy pup in Minta's lap after they made *Love, Speed, and Thrills*. For one shot, Willie asked Minta to dangle from a tree root by a piano wire—over a 100-foot drop down the Arroyo Seco. Minta looked a little skeptical, so Willie promised her a bonus. Back then, directors were always promising bonuses if you'd stick your face in a fan or dive off a flagpole into a bucket of coleslaw. In this case, the big bonus turned out to be Luke the Dog. Who, if I do say so myself, ended up one of the most dependable stars in the Keystone kennel.

Now back to how it started sinking in I was really a star. As a joke I asked Sennett to put the canine on the payroll. And damned if that mutt didn't start pulling down $150 a week! This was a lot more than most two-legged dogs were making. In fact, my wife's canine was making a lot more than *I* did for the majority of my professional life. I would have been jealous if I didn't know that she made him eat out of a bowl.

Even more than making a bull terrier wealthy, what showed me how far things had come was New York City. In 1916, figuring to make some movies with different backdrops, Sennett dragged us back East with a full crew. We stayed six months, shooting out in Fort Lee, New Jersey—where Mack made the execrable *Cohen* way back when. And every day, even in sleet, you could hardly get to the set for the mob that showed up to see Fatso Me-o. The half that were press you might expect—I was their bread and butter. But the rest were regular people. Which was even stranger. "What's going on?" I asked the coffee boy, the first time I saw the throng of folks on hand at the start of *He Did and He Didn't*. "They givin' away hams, or is President Wilson in the neighborhood?" He thought I was kidding.

I guess the best way to find out you're a real celebrity is when people *you* think are celebrities want to meet you. When Enrico Caruso showed up on the set, I nearly fell off my high chair. We had an Italo dinner together, and after we both dumped a bucket of vino down our gullets, Caruso asked me to sing. I declined, like any sane man. But after another bucket of paint peeler, I got up the nerve. I did my old vaudeville tune "Find Me a Girl Like Mother (and I'll Meet a Girl Like You)."

When I was done, the whole restaurant applauded—Caruso the loudest. Then, taking my hand in his—if I didn't know he was a ladies' man I would have blushed—he leaned over the table, very serious, and asked me why I wanted to "put on ze clownfeet" when I could be a serious singer.

I still couldn't tell you if this was the biggest compliment I ever got—or the worst insult. Maybe both. But it did get me thinking. Knowing the money Chaplin was making, and knowing that what Mack paid me was cashews compared to that—though we were equally popular—I started listening to offers. They'd been pouring in for a while. But the one I went for was Max Hart, the big-time agent. Hart not only guaranteed me 200 grand a year, he promised that wherever I went, Minta would be hired, too. Then came the real head spinner. Max told me Sennett was making $200,000 off of each movie I made for him. And that's just in the States. "You're so big in Europe, there's fistfights from Germany to England every time Mack sends over another picture, 'cause everybody wants a ticket. You're an international star, Arbuckle."

All this was news to me. And $200,000 sounded pretty sweet after being treated like the House Negro by my good friend Sennett. Imagine not telling me I was internationally adored! So I signed. Big mistake. Or actually, it wasn't a mistake. *Thinking* it was a mistake was a mistake. Or—never mind. You'll see. Let's just say, before the ink was dry another show-bizzer, a guy with sweaty palms named Lou Anger, invited me to Atlantic City to meet the legendary Joe Schenck. Schenck called himself "the second most powerful man in the movie business." Joe would be there on behalf of Adolph Zukor, then head of Paramount. He didn't have to tell me that Zukor was Numero Uno to his Dos.

We all got a little tipsy on the boardwalk, and I heard myself tell Schenck, a little slurrily, "It isn't just the money, I'm sick of making pictures I don't want to make. I wanna call the shots." Schenck excused himself to make a phone call. I stared at the Atlantic and peed. The ocean was calm. It was beautiful. But for some reason I kept thinking, *That just makes it easier for the monsters.*

When he came back Schenck announced, with no fanfare, "I can get you artistic control, 1,000 bucks a day, and 25 percent of the profits." While I was trying to filter this through the alcohol in my brain, sweaty Lou Anger felt compelled to chime in. "That comes to more than a million per, Roscoe." "Izzat so?" I said. I wanted to ask if I'd heard him right, but I didn't want to look like a simp. A lot of people assume all fat people are stupid. Which we all ain't.

"Here's Zukor's idea," Schenck continued, tossing his fat cigar into the sea. Insanely, I remember thinking, *What if it lands on a clam?* "You can create your own film company, call it Comique. All you gotta do is make—you should pardon the expression—Fatty pictures. Adolph says Paramount will keep its mitts off. Famous Players–Lasky distributes. Lou here runs your studios. Deal runs for 10 years, with annual sit-downs to figure out bonuses."

By now the stars were whirling in the sky. I had to sit down myself before I introduced the clams I'd had for dinner to Joe's suit. But that wasn't the only thing bothering me. I knew there was something, I just couldn't find it in my juice haze . . . Then it came to me, and I did feel sick. "What about Max Hart? I just signed with him."

Schenck and Anger exchanged looks, then Schenck nodded and Lou signaled to somebody I couldn't see. Next thing I knew, this Rolls-Royce the size of Canarsie comes rolling right up the boardwalk. "I like Max," Schenck said, "but could he give you anything like this?"

By then I was too drunk to drive. In my looming stupor, I just gazed at that beautiful machine and hoped I didn't pass out in it.

The morning after my boardwalk kibbitz with Schenck and Anger, my head felt like I'd used it to crack walnuts. But I managed to have breakfast with Hart and lay things out. I figured he'd be upset. Maybe throw his eggs at me. Max wasn't mad, though. He was sad. "You're making a mistake," he said, so quiet it gave me the willies to think about it later, when I realized he was right—and it was too late to matter.

Max just smiled sadly and put his hand on my cheek, the way you'd touch a child. "God help you, Roscoe. These guys are gonna chew you up and spit you out."

With that my agent for five minutes picked himself up, shook my hand somberly, and told me to give my regards to Minta.

Minta! In all the excitement about the Rolls and the millions, I forgot to ask Joe and Lou about putting her in the contract. I called Lou and he acted put out. We made a deal and that wasn't part of it. When I wouldn't let it go, he said he'd see what he could do and hung up. His tone was a lot chillier than it had been the night before.

When I told all this to Minta, over Waldorf salad at the Waldorf, she threw down her napkin, as mad as I've ever seen her. "First you walk over Max Hart, then you walk over your own wife. After all the years I've looked after you . . ."

Maybe it was the hangover. Maybe it was some part of me, deep down, that didn't want to admit she was right, but I pounded my fist on the table so hard the plates rattled. "Nobody ever took care of me but me," I yelled at her, in front of the entire restaurant. "I've been doing it since I learned to waddle."

I regretted this as soon as I said it. But Minta, who never failed to surprise me, just took my hand in both of hers and started to cry. "Oh, Roscoe," she kept repeating, over and over. It was as if I'd tugged her heart out, jammed a nail in it, and put it back. "Oh, Roscoe, you don't even know what you've done . . ."

PART 4

Everything I Want I Get

Celebrated comedian to begin work on production of two-reelers in March. "Fatty" Arbuckle, the funniest man on the screen, who has long abandoned his first name of Roscoe, has entered into a contract with Paramount Pictures Corporation . . .

The secret of Arbuckle's great popularity is the fact that he makes his audience laugh at him as well as with him, never fearing to be made the victim of a joke.

—*Moving Picture World*, 1915

THERE'S ONE for the tombstone, huh? *He never feared being the victim.*

I look at these scrapbooks now and I still don't get it. The Russkies were running Czar Nicholas II out on his can. The Anti-Saloon League was passing dry laws in 24 states. The Marines were landing in Santo Domingo and clouds of mustard gas were burning boys' lungs to bloody mush over there at Verdun and the Somme. But for some reason the international newshounds could not get enough Arbuckle-alia.

Predictably, Sennett cursed me up and down. Like Ford Sterling, like Chaplin, like his own Mabel before me, I was an ingrate abandoning the saint who'd turned him from vaudeville hack to movie star. Oddly, Mack's words echoed Max Hart's. And there could not have been two less similar characters. "Fat boy," Sennett spat at me, "you sign on with those bastards, they'll work you like a packhorse, then sell you for glue. Zukor would stab *himself* in the back if he could make a shekel out of it." Then Mack did something I'd never seen him do before. He actually choked up. "Keystone may be a nest of freaks, but we look after our own. That's how it is in the sideshow, sonny. You walk in the center ring, your life ain't even gonna be yours anymore."

Then he gave me a stinky hug, and I went home to shower.

Très Comique

A few months later, Keystone was history, and I was being sent scripts by my new studio. Only they weren't movie scripts. Months before I even set foot in front of a camera, Anger, Schenck, and Zukor had me doing more interviews than Woodrow Wilson. But they weren't really interviews, either. They were performances. For *Photoplay*, for *Movie World*, for—who cares? Listen: "*My pictures are turned out with clean hands and a clear conscience, which, like virtue, is its own reward. Nothing would grieve me more than to have mothers say, 'Let's not go to the movies today, Arbuckle is playing and he isn't fit for the children to see . . .'*"

No need going into how *that* came back to bite me on the bowser. I never liked slinging this kind of guff in the first place. But that was Paramount. They had me saying a lot of things, things I didn't know I'd said until I picked up a movie mag. I may have thought I'd signed on to make silent pictures, but the brass had a whole wing devoted to making an ass out of me. "*'Let me handle the Huns,' boasts jokester Arbuckle. 'I'll find the Kaiser and sit on his family!'*"

Anger was always there to make sure I mouthed my lines for the press. If I didn't like what I was mouthing—like I never liked fat jokes—he'd smile, snip the tip of a cigar, and say what a shame it would be if the public found another fat man to love.

Talk about your command performance! "*Whatever success I've had, I credit to my mother's love and my father's guidance.*" That's from "Fatty Talks to Young People," a phony article Paramount planted in the papers. Even stranger than stumbling on these bromides in print was having to deliver them, in person, at whatever women's club or boys' home or studio-staged affair they made me attend. Half the time I was smashed to my dewlaps on heroin when urging an earnest crowd to "join me in thanking Mr. Zukor for making Paramount a studio for the whole family." Though I didn't mention that to any bug-eyed reporters.

Oh, wait—I'm *sorry* . . . Did I forget to tell you about the fairy dust? Boy, is my face red!

Bayer, the Heroin That's Good for You

What happened is, at the end of August, anticipating my Paramount millions, I snapped up Theda Bara's old house on West Adams. Theda didn't say why she was selling it, but my first night, I got a hint. No sooner had I unpacked my easy chair and collapsed in it than I felt a sharp pinch on my left knee. I yelped, then forgot about it. When you're born on a dirt floor in Kansas, you grow up thinking insects are *pets*. Not to mention, I may have had a sip or two of liqueur at lunch and been incapable of feeling the pain in real time. But Minta, who'd decided to stay though our marriage had a toe-tag on it, swears she saw a spider hop behind the couch. I told her spiders don't hop. "Except," Minta said, "when they bite something as big as you!"

Whether it hopped or took a cab home, the eight-legger must have hated me, because a few days later my knee blew up to the size of a medicine ball. The whole leg was so inflamed I screamed every time my pants touched the skin. My luck, though, it was Labor Day, when the whole town was off work and off duty. Minta wanted to drive me to the hospital, but the last thing I wanted was publicity. Even if you're there for a hangnail, the papers get a hold of it and pretty soon nobody can laugh at you anymore cause they think you're sick. Who'd laugh at a sick comedian? Of course, sick was five flights up from where I was headed. Sick would have been good news—but don't rush me.

Finally we tracked down a sawbones who looked no older than a paperboy. Dr. Cub Scout took one look at my limb, announced that I had a poison boil, and explained that if he didn't drain it that minute the toxins might seep into my bloodstream, leak into my heart, and leave me stricken.

I wasn't sure what "stricken" meant, but it sounded bleak. So bleak that, right there in the living room, I let the baby-faced M.D. take my pants off. I lay on the Persian rug with my leg up on the ottoman while he fished in his black bag. He swabbed the unsightly growth with alcohol and asked Minta to bring a washrag. This he rolled up and stuck in my mouth, telling me to bite down when it hurt. "*When what hurts?*" My words came out muffled around the rag. By way of reply, the doctor pulled a gleaming scalpel out of his bag and stabbed me in the leg.

I thought I knew what pain was, but I was wrong. When Junior started rooting around with the blade I bit through the gag and saw red and yellow stars. I screamed so loud the Dohenys, our snooty neighbors, sent a colored servant over to say they were calling the police. The Dohenys were old money and resented the influx of actor types creeping into their sanctum. "Boy, listen!" I yelped, delirious, spitting the rag out and spewing at the startled visitor. "Tell Mr. Dodo I have photos of Mrs. Dodo doing the funny can-can. That'll shut 'em up!"

Minta and the servant went wide-eyed. No surprise, considering I was ranting through a bloody mouth, with what looked like a rabid wolf bite on my knee.

"What photos?" Minta wanted to know.

"The ones of her and the pack mule," I cackled, winking at the colored fella, who didn't know if he was allowed to laugh, but when he started he couldn't stop until I sent Minta to the pantry for a glass of brandy and made sure she got it down him.

"Consorting with the help," Minta tut-tutted, in that way she had, where you didn't know if she was joking or not.

"It's that or scream," I said, and meant it. The pain made it hard to breathe. Then the pink-cheeked doctor, who'd remained mum through my little performance, stuck a drain in my leg and I started yowling all over again.

"Roscoe, please!" Minta shushed me. "The *Dohenys!*"

Before he fled, I made sure their loyal servant—dressed in a red jacket some organ-grinder might have stuck his monkey in—received a second brandy to fortify himself. It was a long slog through our back garden into theirs. I'd done it myself once, having mistaken their front door for mine after a long night imbibing furniture polish with Chaplin. At least I *think* it was Chaplin. After the first hour I went blind for a while. They don't make hooch like that anymore!

To shut me up—Minta claims I was howling—the medicine man pulled out a hypo and asked for my arm. With the pain I was in, I'd have given him both arms and an ankle. Doctor wrapped my bicep with a rubber tube, squeezed tight enough to find a vein floating in the fat, then stuck in the needle. Next thing I know I'm Floaty M'loaty. Falling down never felt so good. I wanted to thank the doctor, but my tongue seemed to have moved, with no forwarding address.

"That should settle you," the young sawbones smiled, almost like he knew a secret. Boy, did he, the peach-fuzzed little fraud! Then he snapped his bag shut and shook my hand like a grown-up. "That leg is too dangerous to play with. I'm putting you on a daily dose of heroin. Stay off your feet a few weeks and you should heal up just fine."

I was more concerned about the staying-off-my-feet part than I was about taking the heroin. Though, now that I'd had a bang, I wasn't too concerned about anything, except maybe how soft the armchair felt when I ran my fingers over it. Funny, I never noticed before . . . Back then Bayer advertised heroin to mothers who wanted to calm their toddlers' cough. It was that bene-volent. Oddly enough, it was their newest product, aspirin, that had solid citizens of the day concerned.

Heaven in a Tube

My new friend the doctor left enough medicine for a month. For the first two weeks while Minta went off to work—she was still at Keystone—I stayed at home, in that easy chair, happily staring off. Sometimes I'd move my toes. By the end of the third week, I was still staring off, but the pain had gotten worse. And the swelling doubled. When the doctor came for a follow-up he looked grim, said he'd heard of cases where this happened, and doubled my daily dose. Yum!

I'd had a screening room put in at the house, so every day I'd arrange my audience-of-one narcotic film festival. The studios were wild about drug movies—especially if there was a pretty girl who turned into a prostitute somewhere in the story. So I'd take my feel-no-pain shot, sit back, and nod in and out of *White Slave Traffic, The Devil's Needle, The Girl Who Didn't Care,* or this really strange one, *Half-blood,* directed by some pervert Kraut named Fritz Lang, about a party gal who lures a regular Joe to Hades with an opium pipe.

By early November, it was obvious that not only wasn't I healing, but the infection had spread. Now my entire thigh had swollen like a drowned man's. I had to measure every breath. The slightest movement was excruciating, like someone plunging a fork in my flesh and twirling the nerve ends like spaghetti. When the doctor made his next house call, he looked very grave. After administering a healthy injection (enough to set me off in a drooly smile, even though I knew, underneath, the pain was screaming) he announced, from very far away—possibly Ohio— that "the leg will have to go."

"Go where?" I asked, feeling positively blithe after the injection. "On vacation?"

Minta knew what he meant, and she was aghast. Paramount had paid for a whole comedian. They were funny that way. If they shelled out a million, they wanted the whole star. Panicked, Minta called everyone she knew—up till now, my condition'd been top secret—asking them if they could recommend a doctor. It was Max Hart, of all people, who provided one. The new medico was a serious old gent who informed us that, first of all, the so-called doctor who'd been treating me was actually an intern, and had no business not telling us. And second, the infection in my leg could be treated in the hospital, but once that was done, there was the other problem.

"What other problem?" Minta and I both wondered aloud.

"Heroin addiction," said the doctor, looking so doctorly he could have been acting. "It usually affects housewives." Here he paused, raised his eyes to the ceiling, as if appealing for divine guidance, and lowered them to me and Minta again. "I know what kind of pain you've gone through, son. But that's nothing compared to what you're going to go through coming off this stuff."

I Get a Kick out of Life!

Minta wasn't surprised that I was scared. Being the reasonable type, she assumed that what I was scared of was the pain of withdrawal. Which was true, as far as it went. How could I tell her I was even more scared of living without heroin?

From that first shot, when the turned-out-to-be-an-intern pushed in the needle, it was like I was home. Returned, in swaddling, to a blessed baby-state I never knew existed. The pain relieved was not the pain the drug was prescribed for. Or not just. It killed everything—the agony in my leg and the anxious, restless Daddy's-Right-I'm-A-Freak-And-Everything-Good-Is-For-Other-People heebie-jeebies. It's as if the fingers wrapped around my throat since childhood began to loosen. I'd gotten so used to them, I didn't know I was being choked until they were gone. Even when I closed my eyes and relived Daddy's drunken punches, heroin made them fluffy pillows.

I had two choices, the new doctor told me: six months of slow, careful withdrawal—uncomfortable, but not *that*—or three weeks, over and out, of utter hell. I wanted to go for careful. (I never said I was brave.) But my career required over and out.

The hell route. Paramount had set up a nationwide tour to promote its hearty new star. And when I asked Anger for more time to get well, he turned me down flat. "Zukor," he said, "doesn't give more time."

The doc arranged for a private hospital, so nobody would know I was in there, plus a padded cell, so I couldn't bang my head off the wall trying to knock myself out. Talk about a dream vacation!

At the last minute, naturally, I chickened out. But not all the way. If I was going to bite my feet and claw the walls in a padded cell, I'd rather it was *my* padded cell. So we set up a room in West Adams. The place was so big, even the closets had closets.

My home kick-bin had all the amenities: rubber sheets and foam rubber walls. I don't know what the workmen thought when they installed the stuff. I was too busy shaking and sweating to inquire. For two weeks Minta listened to me scream and beg and upchuck like a gut-shot buffalo. The people we trusted, like my friends Barney Oldfield and Charlie C., came over to empty my barf buckets. Friends like that you can't buy more than once.

I wasn't even allowed alcohol, so on top of the pain-shakes and puking I got DTs. God knows what my poor wife thought when she heard me thundering around in there, trying to dodge the tiny red-eyed rhinos. I would have killed for a good old-fashioned pink elephant, but they never showed up. She said I cried so much she had to put cotton in her ears or go crazy herself. But all I remember is those rhinos. The scut they left all over the room. And the rat-sized fleas that hopped out of them, then burrowed under my skin, until I had to rip the skin off my flesh to dig them out.

By the day the doctor came and let me out, I'd lost nearly 100 pounds. From 285 to 190. My pants fit about as well as the ones

I lent Chaplin way back whenski, as Mabel used to say, doing her Polish-maid routine. Anger stopped by, but he was all business. All he said when he saw me was, "The studio better send some tailors."

Minta, brazen as ever, told Anger I couldn't go on the tour—now only weeks away—and you'd have thought she said I planned to rape his grandmother. His rage was instant, but he kept a lid on it.

"Roscoe's going on that tour," Anger said. Then he looked my way, adding icily, "He can't disappoint his public."

When the film business started, the Myrons who ran the companies tried to keep actors and actresses no-names—so other studios couldn't steal 'em. Now the big boys played it just the opposite. They did everything to make us famous. When you signed on the dotted line, you didn't just pledge your talent, you forked over your life. The real acting job was trying to make the public think you were what the studio said you were. Which, in my case, meant being the perpetual happy-go-lucky fatso funster. Not a half-dead junkie, a fraction of his normal size, who shuffled like a piped-up Chinaman and burst into tears 'cause his hair hurt. The slightest breeze raked my skin like a cheese grater. And I hadn't had a bowel movement since Lincoln died. I felt like one of those sideshow boas with a gopher in it. At the other end, whatever I tried to eat had a round-trip ticket. But I'm lying about shuffling like a Chinaman. I could barely crawl.

Needless to say, the studio put out a story I'd injured my knee doing a tricky stunt.

Party Problems

Zukor insisted on an elaborate bash, a "kickoff dinner" at the Hotel Alexandria, to publicize the nationwide tour. I spent the weeks beforehand practicing walking in my living room. By the morning of the event, I could make it from the Victrola to the couch without a pair of canes. While Anger, pragmatic right down to the soul he didn't possess, had arranged to have three suits of clothes made for the journey: one for the svelte new me, one a bit bigger, and one, optimistically, for my old nearly 300-pound self. My Svengali made it clear I needed to get back up to Fatty status pronto. In case I didn't, however, he laid in a fat suit of foam-rubber padding, to slip over my skin and bones so the public would never know I was secretly wizened. Already clammy, as a by-product of my narcotic problems, beneath that foam suit my sweat turned to horse lather. It was like wearing a portable steam room. Even Minta, most tolerant of women, remarked on my pungent new stench.

The night of the big do, Paramount prez Zukor sat on the dais with Jesse Lasky and Marcus Loew, alongside Doug Fairbanks, my pal Barney Oldfield (who walked around with a steering wheel in his hand), the lovely Mary Pickford, and Charlie Chaplin. For the occasion, Thomas Woolwine, L.A. district attorney, served as master of ceremonies. Woolwine showing up gave the soiree a kind of legitimacy most movie events couldn't claim. Zukor, whose past was said to be slightly less than legit, was always big on legitimacy. In fact, Woolwine was in Zukor's pocket. When William Desmond Taylor was killed, and Mabel Normand was involved up to her coke-addled eyeballs, it was an open secret big Adolph had his boy Wooly quash the whole thing. When it was my turn in the barrel, I had no such gestures made on my behalf. But why barrel into that maw before we have to?

Anger made me promise I'd walk up to the dais. *On my own.* The sight of me crawling might have scared exhibitors. So we waited in a hall backstage for my entrance cue. Drumroll, please, and a big bleat from the band. Off I go, and—uh-oh!—here comes the floor rushing up to my face. S-*LAM!* Before I even made it out of the wings, I fell flat on my kisser.

Thinking fast, Minta and Lou wrapped their arms around me from either side. They propped me up that way, linked like ice skaters, till I made it to the podium.

Not to go misty-eyed, folks, but I gotta say, the standing O I got from the crowd helped keep my pins steady. I was able to stand upright and say the few words I'd prepared with Anger. Cornpone stuff. "Well, friends, as some of you know, I almost didn't make it up here tonight. No, not cause of the knee injury—I couldn't fit through the ballroom door . . . Who'd they design this dump for, anyway—some little tramp?"

That got a hoot or two, even though I kept waiting for a hunk of foam rubber to pop out of my collar and give me away. My fat suit must have soaked up 40 pounds of perspiration. And it chafed where it dug into my privates. It took a little maneuvering on the part of Lou and Minta to make it look like I was walking under my own steam to my seat on the dais, but we pulled it off. By the time the waiters—all smiling Negroes, who'd seen me flop in the wings—delivered our filet mignons, I was so happy I was able to eat three bites of meat without throwing up. It was the first solid food I'd had since my detoxification in the family rubber room.

I have a dim memory of thinking, at the writhing height of withdrawal, that this whole thing could be a funny two-reeler. Really! I'm a kick-crazy patient. Mack Sennett's the male attendant. Mabel's the cutie-pie nurse he flirts with—forgetting that he's left me tied to the bed with my head over the bucket! I scream, but Mack just pooh-poohs my pleas. Until Nurse Mabel, concerned, pushes past him and finds me flopping like a hooked cod. "*It's the H*," Mack says. "Poor baby," coos Nurse Mabel, kneeling to stroke my sweaty brow while Mack looks on, aggrieved. In a fit of jealous pique, he straps me to the bed and covers me with a sheet so just my big toe's sticking out. A fly lands on my toe. Hijinks ensue. Later, when Minta told me how much I screamed my first week in the room, I told her, "Darling, I just wanted a pencil. I had an idea."

After my debut, so to speak, it was off on the grand tour. For the trip, we were packed into a private railway car. Zukor, pulling strings as usual, got it on loan from Evalyn Walsh McLean, a Washington, D.C. society lady and newspaper publisher. She was also owner of the Hope Diamond. According to Anger, who knew this kind of stuff, she'd loaned it to President Roosevelt's daughter for her honeymoon trip.

I understand that some couples find long train rides romantic. Mabel said train wheels had "sex rhythm." But that kind of thing was not exactly a big part of my marriage to Minta. Every city we went to the routine was the same. I would hop off the sleeper, show up and make some snappy patter to a Women's Club or a cadre of local theater owners. Then I'd repeat the performance until there was no place left to sing the praises of Paramount's family fare, and we'd hop back on the train for the next whistle stop.

Travel Contracts as It Broadens, and Vicey-Versey

Twenty miles out of Kansas, the pain in my legs grew so bad I sat down on the floor of the sleeper and cried. Minta heard me, and swore she was going to make Anger stop the tour, whatever it took. I tried to grab her ankles, but she was too fast for me. Five minutes later, Anger stormed into the room, railing. "These people pay your salary, and you're going to earn it!" Five minutes after that bit of kindness, a doctor showed up. Before you could say "Drop your pants and lick your kneecaps," I had a needle in my buttocks. Five seconds later, my pain was gone. The world took on a fuzzy glow. Anger led me out on the platform, where I waved gaily to the crowds, feeling love in my heart for every one of them. By then my eyes were so crossed the people looked more like seaplants. A happy gaggle of seaplants, gently waving underwater.

At first I thought it was the goofer dust, but no! There really *was* an ocean of humanity out there. Zukor had worked out the Local Boy Makes Good angle, and—be still, my heart—about a quarter-million proud Kansans waggled their hankies and screamed for a glimpse of Y-O-Me. When it came time for me to say a few words, my tongue felt coated in wet concrete. But somehow I managed. "I'm not gonna lie, folks, I had to come halfway across the country for some decent barbecue . . ."

They loved me up. I hobbled back to the pain chamber. Then I collapsed and cried in Minta's lap till I passed out.

And that, my friends, was how it went. By the time we hit Massachusetts, I was back to taking my medicine in the morning like a good boy. My butt cheeks, by this point, resembled elephant hide from the constant poking. Zukor kept an elephant-leg umbrella stand in his foyers. But I tried not to think about my own gam with parasols sticking out of it.

Every night Minta and I would fight about my "dependence"—on Lou Anger, on Paramount, on the painkiller. Maybe even on her, though I was too dense to see it then. I'd stalk off, as best as a fat man could stalk with two canes, and go drink with whoever was up. Let her hole up by herself!

The worst fight we had was just outside Boston, near the end of the line. After saying a lot of things she'd already said a million times, she got quiet and said something she'd never let slip before. *"You didn't even care enough to get me written into your deal with Zukor!"*

I was flabbergasted. How dare she accuse me of not caring. *Me!* I informed her, with as much dignity as I could muster while drooling, that a lot of gals would be pretty damn happy if their hubbies handed them the kind of career I'd handed her. I'd given her a pretty fine run, all things considered. I don't know if her horrified silence was the result of my words or my by-now-nightly practice of lying in bed and wetting myself. It's not the kind of thing you really want to know, anyway.

Boston

My wife and I were not quite speaking when, per usual, I made my way off the train leaning heavily on her shoulder. Paramount was footing the bill for a banquet for the New England Theatre Association at the Copley Plaza, a stuffy old Back Bay hotel. This was a big one: about 10 dozen Paramount exhibitors, along with Zukor, Walt Green, and Hi Abrams, the three owners of the studio. Plus—just to round things out—Marcus Loew, who happened to run the most massive theater chain in the country. And don't let me forget Jesse Lasky, Paramount's resident genius VP. Blow the place up, and you'd wipe out a quarter of the big brass in the movie business. Why didn't I think of that then?

Shrewd Zukor was always big on dragging locals into the act. So along with the showbiz bigwigs, the attorney general of Massachusetts was on hand, accompanied by a gaggle of staffers from the governor's and mayor's offices. All in all, the kind of affair you'd have to be either drunk or ambitious to attend. I'd rather have kissed a stoat than show up, but I did, and performed my public duties with dispatch. Then I collapsed, more or less.

Having tooled all the way from Los Angeles to Beantown, I was so tired I was seeing triple. But the Paramounters announced they were going for a "private party" after the Copley dinner, at Mishawum Manor in nearby Woburn. The "manor" was run by a sporting lady who called herself Brownie Kennedy. Not exactly my cup of fun.

Pleading honest exhaustion, I bowed out of the festivities and went to bed. Though you wouldn't know that from the publicity later, after the press got wind of the nonstop debauchery these rich, respectable giants of commerce and government indulged in—and the whole affair became known as "Fatty's Orgy."

Anger said it was going to be a "chicken and champagne" party, code for whores-and-hooch. I'd never heard of Brownie's but I'd heard of Woburn. Everybody had, since four years earlier the Woburn town council passed a resolution banning movie theaters. They didn't want citizens of their fine burg to sample any of that "celluloid degeneracy" and end up a pack of raving sinners.

From the sound of that party, the Woburners may have had the right idea. Madame Brownie—who also went by the name of Helen Morse and Lily Dale—apparently enlisted some underage "entertainment" for the evening. And some of the entertainers returned home so ravaged that their loved ones, demanding to know what happened to the poor girls, got wind of the affair. Even more damning, the piano player, one Theresa Sears, claimed that Hiram Adams, head of the New England Baseball League, paid cash for the party. She also laid out the one detail that made me wish I *had* been there. I mean, if I was going to be blamed anyway.

According to Miss Sears, a giant tray was wheeled out with a clamshell cover on top made of sterling silver. "Gentlemen," Hiram is alleged to have said to the guests, "I bring you tonight's specialty—Pleasant Under Glass." And there, when the straight-faced servant lifted the lid, was a naked girl on hands and knees, an apple in her mouth and a few sprigs of parsley scattered over her body. "Pleasant," that old cutup Hiram continued, "say hi to the boys. Boys, meet Pleasant."

The singing pianist's account spared no detail. As she recounts it, after Pleasant plucked out her apple and said hi, the rest of the entrées sashayed in. A dozen nubile beauties—including three of the Negro persuasion—none of them even wearing parsley.

Not all of the girls were underage, as it turned out. Some were married.

My Once Good Name Tarnished

When the whole affair blew up in the papers, nationwide, writers insisted on referring to it as "Arbuckle's party." Something Adolph didn't seem to mind. I'd go so far as to say he encouraged it. Why? Because my friend Zukor took care of his own rear end first, that's why. The Federal Trade Commission already had Famous Players–Lasky in its sights. They were just waiting for an excuse to pull the trigger. A scandal would do nicely. Thank you. And Zukor would do anything to keep his name out of the papers, including implicate the one high-profile Paramount employee who wasn't there. Namely me.

To know how spooked Zukor was, you have to know how dicey the whole film business was looking, investment-wise. Wall Street money was getting antsy. A big stink linking the top dogs at Famous Players–Lasky to prostitution and political payoffs would have sunk the studio—and Adolph—like a Kraut torpedo.

Long story short, Zukor presented a cool 100,000 simoleons to the Middlesex County DA, an unctuous three-piece suit named Nathan Tufts. One minute Nate was railing about those "amoral Jews at Paramount," condemning "that elephantine debaucher Fatty Arbuckle." The next he was quietly quashing the entire investigation. Funny what a little moola can do.

Zukor and the gang dodged the bullets while I took one for the team. That's how I, Fatty, ended up looking like the host of the depraved ceremonies. A fact that played no small part in the prosecution's case after another party that got out of control, on the other side of the map, in San Francisco.

The Truth, As If It Matters

The truth is, that night, while young Pleasant was appearing under glass, not only did Minta and I stay in, we—*Oh, why lie, Arbuckle?*—I mean *I*, tried to accomplish my manly duties. And was, I do not say proudly, unable. Had Minta gone to the press and made public what everybody at Keystone used to tease her about, she could have easily cleared my name. "*Your Honor, the only thing my husband would be good for at an orgy is serving canapes or getting plastered. He can't even—well, I don't like to be vulgar . . ."*

Sadly, this proved to be but the first occasion when Minta's testifying to my *nether problems* might have spared me a world of trouble. The truth is—and I know this must sound loathsome—I preferred the penalty for committing sin to the shame of admitting that I *couldn't* commit it. There, I said it!

"Honey," Minta explained, as delicately as possible, "if I don't tell them about your condition, they'll think you're guilty. We could bring in the doctor you visited."

"The one who recommended bloodmeats? Never!"

My pained reaction moved her to unusual candor.

"Roscoe, if we don't speak up, your name is going to be associated with sex orgies . . ."

No man should have to make a choice like this even once in a lifetime. Little did I realize, I was a man who'd have to make it twice.

I guess I've just always been lucky.

A Dodged Bullet in My Chest

Happily, the Mishawum Mess blew over fast. At least it seemed to. Until a judge in Boston found Tufts guilty of taking bribes and tossed him out of office. Zukor and Lasky both saw what was coming. Whole chunks of the public were already boycotting the movies, and being tied to "an orgy of drink and lust" did not help with the League of Decent Christian Mothers. That's when Zukor got the idea of finding somebody so respectable they glowed to set up a Hollywood Morality Code.

The idea was to make the rest of the country see how sincere the industry was about "clean living." Zukor's first choice for Morality Czar was Herbert Hoover. Hoover said no, but recommended Postmaster General Will Hays, a Bible-thumping Indiana Republican with close ties to President Harding.

I did not anticipate that Hays's first target would end up being my own wide behind. If you were the suspicious type, you might almost think I was the red meat Zukor cooked up to throw to Hays and his morals squad. I'll give you the details and let you judge for yourselves. See, Zukor had a director with gambling debts named Fred Fischbach. Fred and I were friendly, but not close. All of this will mean something later. I mention it here to show the tiny seeds that grew into a jungle that swallowed me up.

In the wake of Mishawum only one thing was clear. As the old joke around the lot went: *If you pushed Adolph Zukor off the Paramount water tower, someone else would take the fall . . .*

New Yorking

After the tour, it was Schenck's idea to head back to New York, to stay there and work on *The Butcher Boy* at Norma Talmadge Studios. Norma being his wife and all, Joe no doubt had his own reasons for the deal. What he told *us* was that it was convenient—a short hike from the suite Minta and I took at the Cumberland Arms, at 54th and Broadway, to the studio, at 48th.

"Bubby, how many guys get to stroll to work?" Joe said. Whenever he marched out that "Bubby," you knew you were in trouble. The truth was, unless it was three in the morning, we both knew I couldn't do much strolling without attracting oglers the way a sheepdog draws fleas. Plus which, my legs weren't exactly overdependable. But the good news was I could walk, thanks to the top-drawer New York doctors the studios corraled. So how could I complain?

By now, Minta and I were fighting so much, I couldn't step through the door without first arming myself with a fifth. I'd start gulping on the elevator and by the time I stepped out at our floor either the walls were weaving or I was. It got so I didn't want to come home. All day I'd be hashing out ideas with the writers on *Butcher Boy*. And it was so—I don't know any other word—*stimulating!* just to be able to decide what I wanted to film, and how I wanted to film it, without anyone meddling . . . Heaven! I never wanted to stop. But the other guys all had lives they liked, so eventually I'd have to walk back through the door of the Cumberland, and the Battle Royale would resume.

One night I smashed a wing chair off the wall. Another I put my head through a pantry door. It got so bad, people in apartments on either side of us moved, and the building manager threatened to sue if we didn't keep it down. As it happened, Minta'd gotten me a membership in the Friars Club for my birthday. A few nights later, after Minta broke a sugar bowl on my chin when she found a flask in the hamper—breaking the no-booze-in-the-house rule—it just occurred to me: I could *live* at the Friars Club. Women weren't allowed. Heh-heh-heh. If the missus wanted to carp at me for being an overly ambitious, self-centered, selfish, and gluttonous son of a beanbag—all true, by the way—she could do it over the phone to the Friars. We'd save a lot of crockery that way.

Over the next three days I relocated my clothes to the Friars. Lou Anger and Joe Schenck encouraged the move. Both offered cagey advice on how to separate without getting in the papers. Can't ruin that wholesome image! Minta kept trying to tell me I was being manipulated, that Joe and Lou just wanted to get rid of her to have more control over me. (Don't say it, folks, I know.)

Joe suggested giving Minta $500 a week. I felt so guilty, I settled on three G's a month instead. Anger insisted on the proviso that Minta and I continue to live separately "as man and wife" (as opposed to cow and cow catcher, I guess) and that Minta not get involved in any way with the running of Comique. *Butcher Boy*, my first film at my own company, was days away from shooting, and I felt like I needed every ounce of oomph to put into that. The constant squabbling had a way of de-oomphing me.

Later, Minta would always blame Anger and Schenck for the divorce.

Enter the Human Mop

The first day of shooting on *Butcher Boy*, a young vaudevillian named Keaton ambled into the studio with Nice Guy Anger. Buster Keaton—alias "the Human Mop"—had no intention whatsoever of working in movies. He'd been performing onstage since he was three months old and had the same attitude I did before stumbling in front of a camera. Theater GOOD; film BAD. Plus which, Buster was pulling $250 a week onstage. But when I saw him, I waved him over anyway. I just had a feeling.

In the scene we were doing, I was an incompetent butcher boy, minding the shop, when a customer comes in to buy some molasses. By way of cheating me, the customer drops a quarter into the bucket, then asks me to fill it up. To outsmart him, I pour the stuff in his hat. Naturally the hat sticks to his noggin, and—well, you get the gist. Highbrow all the way.

From the second we slapped Buster in that porkpie chapeau and let him loose, I knew he had something magic. Strange, but magic. In a few minutes molasses was everywhere, pies were flying, and the whole crew lined up to watch Buster and me go at it. I got this crazy idea in the middle to hit him in the face with a sack of flour. Buster didn't even flinch. Later he told me that when he was a boy, his father used to throw him into the audience when he got mad. So Buster either had to learn how to take a fall or end up a gimp. A sack of flour in the face was nothing compared to being tossed headfirst off the stage.

I told Buster, the only difference between my dad and his was that mine didn't get paid for throwing me around. And he didn't need an audience. He did it for free. For his own amusement.

The Man of My Dreams

Buster and I did the whole destroy-the-store scene in one take, molasses to flour sack. By the time I yelled cut, the two of us were laughing so hard we had to be helped out to keep from drowning in the muck.

In the second reel I'm back in pretty dress and spitcurls— always a crowd pleaser. But for me it was meeting Keaton that made the whole thing spectacular. See, what I really wanted was to find a way to make comedies that weren't just glorified Keystoners. I wanted laughs without car chases. Without bonehead violence. I liked to think of what we did as more of a ballet, though I wouldn't have spread it around. I wanted to make my plots as funny as my physical hijinks, and to play all kinds of characters. If Chaplin wanted to be a tramp in every movie, God bless him. I needed to stretch my hams a little. With Buster on board, I felt like I had an hombre who wanted all the same things I did. And had his own peculiar way of getting them.

Butcher Boy made a few hollow legs full of cash and the reviews made me blush. Here's the *New York Dramatic Mirror*: *"The spectacle of Fatty as a kittenish young thing in his ruffled pinafore and short socks and his efforts to behave as a young lady boarder will undoubtedly delight the Arbuckle fan. As for Arbuckle himself, he is the best known proof that everybody loves a fat comedian."*

Ouch, and thank you!

Life Gets Good, Then I Listen to Lou

Theater owners hounded us for more *Butcher Boy* prints right out of the gate. Schenck's cut was 25 percent of the net, so he was "Bubbying" all over the place. Me and Lou Anger had a slightly smaller chunk. But by the end of the first year, between one dream-come-true and another, I was rubbing noses with a million smackers. That's when Lou had the bright idea I should only declare $250,000, by way of saving on taxes. When the IRS popped out of the bushes with masks and duffel bags five years later—"Give us all your money, hambone!"—they didn't really care that my manager had prompted the maneuver. By then I was already tainted meat, and it didn't help to see my mug on the front page under TAX CHEAT.

Lou was always full of helpful advice. One time, I wanted to buy a gravel pit in Los Angeles. I'd seen horses pulling wagonloads of the stuff all day long. I figured we could resell the gravel to construction companies, who always needed it, and make a tidy profit. Lucky for me, my fiscal wizard vetoed the idea. A month later they struck oil in the pit I'd wanted to buy. It would have made me a billionaire. God knows what *that* would have done to my career!

But what am I doing here? Huh? Here I am trying to recount the happiest period of my life—back in Hollywood with Buster—and I'm cutting away to the taxecutioner. (That's tax-e-cutioner—no Q, honeybunch.)

When Schenck dragged us all back to the West Coast, I dragged Keaton with me. By then Buster was a full-fledged member of Comique. From hating the idea, he'd become a movie nut. That first day, after we cleaned up the flour and sorghum, he wanted me to show him everything. How scenes got spliced together in editing, how story gets laid out, how what goes in the camera comes out onscreen at the other end. I didn't even know how much I knew until I started filling Buster in. He took a pretty big pay cut to jump from the stage. Schenck offered $40 a week and Keaton took it. A few months later, his Dad, Joe, who'd stayed away from movies as a point of pride, came hat in hand to the set. He wanted his boy to find a part for him and Buster's Mom.

As a favor, I stuck Pops Keaton in a couple of scenes. But after listening to him bloviate about "stagecraft" and "the lure of the boards," I devoutly wished he'd pack his bags and head back to the Herkimer Circuit.

I'm almost ashamed to say how footloose and fancy-free I felt, back in Hollywood, with no Minta to feel bad about. I'd gotten kind of smoochy with Alice Lake, one of the girls who appeared in a couple of our movies. But that wasn't why I was feeling good. Buster was what made being back in California so much fun. Because some funny things had happened to Los Angeles while I was away. The place was twice as full of people as it was when I left. And actors were treated like royalty. I still remember when rooming houses put signs out front: NO DOGS, NO COLORED, NO ACTORS. Not anymore, brother! We were like puddly-faced gods. (Things were still pretty rough for Negroes and mutts.)

During *Out West*, my second movie since coming back to Los Angeles, I was doing deep knee bends in my dressing room when I groaned out of a squat and found myself face to face with a tall blond girl. She was an extra in a barroom brawl. But for our little scene she sported a different wardrobe. Beneath her smile, she wore nothing but a holster, a pair of six-shooters, and sparkly boots. "Kiss me and I won't shoot, Roscoe!"

I can't say if it was her ambition or my puckish charms that inspired the stunt. I didn't ask. Instead I excused myself—and asked Anger to replace her. This kind of thing had become a real problem. Douglas Fairbanks took to carrying around a flyswatter, to keep the sweethearts away. But poor Wally Reid couldn't take it. Handsome Wallace, "*America's Number One Screen Heart-throb*," as the magazines called him. So many girls used to camp out in his garage, the poor cuss had to fight his way to his car every morning. One budding starlet, daughter of a certain titan of industry, bribed Reid's valet to let her hide in a trunk in his boss's dressing room. The valet was fired, but it would have taken him a while to save up the 10 grand Miss Starlet slipped him. The girl jumped out of the steamer in time to see Wallace injecting his wake-up—the morning bang of morphine he needed to get up and shave—so of course she needed to be paid all over again to keep her mouth shut. Which she didn't. Until rumors got so thick the studio had to cook up a story about his "baseball-related" rheumatism. Too late. Handsome Wally's image was ruined, and so was he.

I thought about Wally a lot whenever the pain came back, when I got tempted to go back on God's Own Medicine myself. Of course, Wally's pain was in his brain. Or maybe his heart, and points south. Once, when we were both pretty splashed at the Vernon Country Club, he grabbed my lapels, stuck that pretty puss of his right up to mine, and admitted, eyes tearing up, *"I can't take it, Roscoe. I never know when one of 'em's gonna jump out of a closet. Or from under the bed. It's givin' me plumbing problems, y'know what I mean?"* I told him I knew what he meant.

Everywhere else folks were scraping by, lucky to have 10 bucks a week. Out here . . . Well, let's just say I wasn't the only raised-poor young timebomb with a million in his pocket and an itch to empty it. One minute little Rodolfo Alfonzo Rafaelo di Valentina d'Antonguolla was a gardener. The next he's Rudolph Valentino, the Sheik of Araby. Magazines couldn't get enough of our shenanigans. And studios wanted to give 'em plenty to write about.

The bigwigs would never come out and say it, but they wanted you to spend the dough as much as they hated giving it to you to spend. The studio hacks needed to keep the public panting over your every purchase. A sure crowd pleaser was the Hollywood Home. To show you were a "big" star, as opposed to a little twinkler, you had to snag a giant house. But after a while it wasn't enough to just own an outsized domicile. You had to have the right lawn, too. You had to have sod.

Buster thought this lawn stuff was as D-U-M-B ridiculous as I did. So when we weren't cheating at pinochle, banging a base-ball around, or trying to reel in something off the Santa Monica pier besides truck bumpers, we both loved to take the piss out of the town's fake-grass fixation. Our first victim was Pauline Frederick, an actress who did everything but rent a billboard to brag about her fresh-laid blades.

Like Mary Pickford, Miss Pauline had her green imported from Olde England. So Buster and I swiped a couple of uniforms from Wardrobe, rented a water-company truck, and knocked on the door to say we were "investigating a leak." After the butler gave us the okay, we rolled the front yard up like an old carpet and hauled it off. When the lovely Pauline awoke to see a dirt patch outside her window, you could hear the scream all the way down to Al Levy's Café.

One guy who took advantage of the whole Jumbo House Craze was Al Helmen. All us rich rubes got our hair cut down at Helmen's Barber Shop. Me, Charlie, Rudy, Wally Reid—when he still knew he had hair—and Douglas Fairbanks. Helmen could make a porcupine suave. But knowing the stars were ripe to be plucked, he quit snipping their follicles and started shaving their bank accounts, selling real estate. While the rest of the country was chewing its legs off, us rich boys were busy doing the Black Bottom and the Turkey Trot at the Sunset Inn. Making sharpies like Helmen rich.

But I digress. By the end of *Out West*, Buster was starting to get a little hinky from having Daddy Joe around. He wouldn't come out and say it, but I could see the way he dug his nails in his palms every time the old man started spouting off. I told Keaton Senior we needed to reshuffle the deck, and he should sit out a few films. Daddy Joe's reaction was classic Daddy Joe. "I'm stealing the scenes, is that it? I knew it! You movie actors are all alike. Scared of a little competition. Not like your trained professionals of the stage. Why, in my day . . ."

Buster and I both had our earplugs in before he got out another trained professional syllable.

Daddy Sticks His Hand Out

I have always been an easy touch. A few years before this, when
the war first started, it was almost like folks figured, "I might be
dead in a week, may as well tap Fatty for a C-note!" The tappage
pretty much cooled off after the Armistice. That is, until my
father showed up, with a homely wife and one shaky hand
sticking out, palm up. Daddy said in a tinny voice that he was
proud of me. I wanted to say, *"Thanks, that makes up for
leaving me stranded in San Jose. For making me work in your
lousy hash joint . . ."* But he looked so down-at-the-mouth and
threadbare, stooped in my doorway, I couldn't even lay into
him. For years I'd put myself to sleep planning what I'd say to
the heartless so-and-so if I ever laid eyes on him. But that's not
really my nature. I just make nice, then go out and eat a
poundcake.

What I did, when Daddy showed up, was invite Daddy to visit
the set. There I introduced him to Lou. That was that. Anger
took one look at the ragged old mendicant and dragged me into
the editing room. "Pay 'im, Roscoe. Whatever the old bastard
wants, pay 'im."

Turns out, Lou had heard from his contact at the *Times* that
Daddy was trying to peddle his "Selfish Rich Boy Shuns Poor
Old Pop" line to the papers.

"'Shuns'? Ask him how he ditched me when I was 10!" I
could feel the old hot tears welling up. But Anger got a hard look
and pinched me on the belly.

"He's going to squeeze you, Roscoe."

"Squeeze me?"

"Paint you like a monster in the press, guilt you into payin' up
big."

That was Lou. Always thinkin' the best of people. I would

have paid Daddy anyway. He sounded like he had a mouthful of broken marbles when he talked. The morning I brought him down to the set of A *Country Hero*, poor Buster had to watch *his* Daddy doing high kicks. It was actually funny, seeing an old man do the can-can. I asked Buster why he looked so miserable, and he told me Daddy Joe's high-kick routine cost him his front teeth when he was 12.

That's when my stepmother—I couldn't call her "Mom" with a rake to my throat—inched up to me on tiptoe and whispered in my ear. "Son, your daddy has the cancer in his tongue. He's got to have some medical."

Big surprise. Lou went into his I-told-you-so. I told him to can it and write the check like he'd suggested in the first place. Why not pay for the hospital? Keep the old man comfy.

The first time I visited Daddy at County Hospital he was crying in pain. I walked in as the night nurse was giving him his morphine. Daddy looked a little too happy. It was startling. *Is that what I looked like?* He wore this drooly little smile. When he saw me, he flapped his hand. I thought he was imitating a chicken for a second—sometimes, on one of his 1-out-of-53 happy drunks, Daddy did a drunken-chicken imitation. Kind of a flappy dance where he waved his arms and clucked.

I opened my mouth. But nothing came out. That's when I realized I was staring at the needle. Probably lickin' my chops. *Any left for me, Daddy-mine? Or did you take everything for yourself, as usual?*

I scooped up the old man and hauled him downstairs. Dumped him in the backseat of my Pierce-Arrow. I had to *move*.

"Look, Dad, I use imported civet oil to keep the leather soft."

For a while he acted happy; then the drugs wore off. I could see his happy turn to ragged. After that he acted like every good thing I had was a sign of my treachery. Like I enjoyed myself to spite him. Got successful to rub his nose in it. When he saw the shrub sculptures at my house—I had one done like Luke the Dog, and one like Zukor—all Daddy said was, "Nice, I guess, if you go for that kind of thing."

I could not have impressed my father if I hired President Wilson to pee in the swimming pool. Still, I tried. I took him out to Vernon, to see the ball club I owned, the Vernon Tigers. Dad used to mock me for not being athletic when I was a child. Now I had the deed on a team that won the Pacific Coast League three seasons running. So how did Daddy react to that? He had a hot dog and said it tasted gamy. I did not tell him that half the reason I bought the Big Cats was because the Vernon stadium was next to Doyle's Saloon, which stocked the best under-the-counter cripple-juice green money could buy. Does that make me a bad son?

I left the car at the stadium so we could ride home on the Red Line. I thought he'd get a kick out of the trolley. But he didn't care much for trolleys, either. His only reaction was to ask why all the paddy wagons were lined up at Sixth and Main. "Lot of folks get a little excited when my fellas win," I told him.

Buster was grateful for how I'd helped him deal with his own father, so he offered to come along for part of my outing with mine. Of course Buster had to do it his own way. He showed up at the Red Line stop behind the wheel of my car, dressed like a 17th-century footman. "I, sir, am your son's chauffeur," he announced. "I worship him!" With this he kneeled and kissed my brogans, which alarmed my father to no end. Then, after helping him into the car, Buster offered to shine Daddy's shoes with his forehead. "Secret buffing technique," he said, with that straight face of his. Daddy would not let himself react, which drove Buster to further heights.

*   *   *

But that reminds me. I have to say something here. (Should I stick my hand out when I make a left?) See, Buster could have been a leading man. He was that kind of handsome—whenever he smiled. In *Fatty at Coney Island*, we had a gag where Buster was supposed to swing the mallet at a strong-man gong. He was trying to show what a brute he was and smack the rubber ball up to the ringer. Originally, the gag was that the ball barely moves when he whacks it. But, during the first take, he reared back and accidentally beaned me with the hammer. Buster was so startled he turned around and laughed. Dead into the camera. He made me shoot another take. I stuck with the first one in the movie. Just to show him what kind of face he had on celluloid. But Buster insisted he didn't want to admit what a looker he was. The handsome bastard.

"I can make love to a leading lady anytime," he explained when I nagged him about it. "But if I take her clothes and hit her with a pie, she's going to report me." From that day forward, you never saw Buster Keaton onscreen when he didn't look like his dog ate the baby and died.

Okay, okay, so I'm not supposed to talk so much about Buster. Well, what was I talking about? Daddy? Fine. We were talking about Daddy. The Scotch is starting to affect me. Not like the old days, when a couple gulps flipped the off switch on my worry gland. Those switches don't work anymore. They got switched.

Anyway . . . After we took Daddy to eat at Musso and Frank's, introducing him to Mary Pickford and Valentino— "Never did like greaseballs," was all he had to say about Rudy— we drove him back to the hospital. The whole ride, Daddy acted like he'd finished some much-dreaded and unsavory chore. When I said goodbye at the door to his ward, he even hesitated before shaking my hand. Like either he was afraid he'd catch something, or he just couldn't bear to touch me. I was staggered, which Buster seemed to sense. Walking out the front gate of the hospital, Buster pulled out his flask and stuck it in my hand. "You sure showed your Dad a good time."

"That's not how it felt to me," I confided. "I tried too hard to impress him."

Buster adjusted his cap, ready to resume chauffeur duty like it was the most normal thing in the world. That's what I loved about him. He had to keep that serious look plastered on his face because all he ever did was play. He scooped some ice from the chest behind the passenger seat, dropped it into a tumbler, then grabbed a bottle from the Pierce-Arrow bar and, holding the ice-filled glass behind his back, poured a perfect two fingers of Scotch right into it.

"Well, did you?" he asked, taking a sip of his drink.

"Did I what?" I was still marveling at his over-the-shoulder pouring move, but it would have been unprofessional to make too much of it. "Did I what, Buster?"

"Impress him," he said.

I almost had to pull over. We were driving to Echo Park, where Sunset Boulevard ends, to Buster's apartment. All the New York theater types lived around there. Buster occupied the bottom half of a rooming house on Alvarado. A trio of budding comediennes shared the rooms above him.

"Do you believe what that bastard said," I blurted, "every time a fan came up to ask for an autograph?"

"Didn't notice," Buster replied, and waited for me to explain. He was the greatest waiter in the world. That was the secret to everything he did.

"Well, let me tell you," I continued, my voice cracking a little. "This Mexican fella comes up and says he's a fan, could I sign something for his little boy. That's a nice thing, but before the guy even gets my John Q and turns away, Daddy shakes his head and says, 'Don't his kind have jobs?' 'His kind'! *Right in front of the guy!*" Buster thought that was funny.

Oh, oh, but wait. *Wait.* This will really get you! Did I mention taking Daddy to a test screening of *Reckless Romeo*? People thought I was nuts for showing my movies in public before they came out. But I figured, the freshest eyes you're gonna get are total strangers. So why not corral a few, loiter in the back, and see where everything goes dead? Daddy knew how much this meant to me. But did he so much as chortle, perk up, or at least stop talking when the guffaws rocked the rafters? No sir. No. Not a-tall.

Dad was too busy telling me about the magazine article he read that said I spent half a million dollars on clothes a year. Before I could tell him a lot of that stuff was studio hooey, he stuck his elbow in his homely wife's ribs and chuckled, in his mouthful-of-broken-marbles way. "For all the money those fools make off you, you'd think they could afford to buy you a girdle!"

Buster nearly dropped the flask when he heard that one. He *did* drop it the day he found out he was drafted. Not only was future Private Keaton shy one trigger finger, his feet were flat enough to heat up and iron shirts. Am I jumping around? Well, you'd be jumpy, too.

I kept Buster in front of the camera till five minutes before he shipped off with the 40th Infantry. He was heading to Camp Kearney, outside San Diego, to make $30 a week and learn how to make his bed. That last film, *The Cook*, was our 17th. We shot down on Sixth and Alamitos in Long Beach, at the old Balboa Studios. Schenck said we could make more money working like hermit crabs, moving from studio to studio, than we could if we actually built our own place.

*　　*　　*

Maybe it's because none of us knew what was going to happen next, because Buster didn't know if he was going to live or die, or because the whole world was skidding off the tracks. But that last afternoon, Keaton inspired me to come up with a comic sequence that gave us both goose bumps. I started slicing salami with an electric fan, then stuck a fork in a couple of breakfast rolls and did a bun dance. Eight years later, Chaplin lifted the whole routine for *The Gold Rush*. But by then petty theft was the last thing I had on my mind.

I tried to enlist, myself—don't laugh—but not even the Courtesy Corps would take a hunk of suet 100 pounds over-weight with a leg that looked like it had already taken shrapnel. I'd done a couple of advertisements, lending my name to the glories of Murad cigarettes, for which I received a bargeful of that very product. So one Saturday I rented a truck and went down with a load of smokes to pass out to the Marines on Mare Island. The last bit of America those boys would see before being shipped out.

While I visited the base, I played tug of war, and single-handedly held off 20 jarheads. They couldn't budge me. I did a couple of cartwheels in the mess hall, which got some choice spit takes. Nothing a private likes more than seeing his sergeant spray beans in his lap. Then I marched everybody into the gymnasium to demonstrate reverse somersaults and the art of falling on my keister. "I've got a lot of keister to fall on, fellas, so I understand if you're jealous." Big laugh for El Fattopotamus.

There were a lot more lads than I'd anticipated, so I ordered a gross of Bull Durhams—more to the fighting man's taste than Murads—and had the brass pass them out before I headed back to Hollywood. All anonymous, of course. Don't want to show-boat. So maybe I was trying to impress the unimpressible Daddy in my fat head. The fighting men would get their extra tobacco ration. That's what mattered.

Does that sound right?

Crazy Money

The more you read the papers about what was going on everywhere else, the more you realized Hollywood was like a crazy island, where the natives were off on a spree while the rest of the world crawled through war, inflation, influenza, and food shortages. By now I had to have a brand-new garage built to hold my cars. All five of them. There was a pearl-white Caddy, the Renault (a Frog ride I got as a gift), the Rolls (so lush I used to sleep in it), a Stevens-Duryea I kept for the gardener to drive, and on the way from the manufacturer a 25-grand custom-made Pierce-Arrow.

But just indulge me here. One more Daddy thing and I'll shut up, okay? When Daddy walked up the flagstone path to my house, I said, "Guess how much this front door cost?" He said, "I don't know . . . 50 bucks?" To him 50 was extravagant. When I told him 15,000, I thought he was going to be sick. The Japanese bridge in my garden probably cost more than Daddy made in his life. But I couldn't stop myself.

I dragged the old man, sick as he was, out to Venice, where I'd snapped up another little mansion, 1621 East Ocean. We did so much shooting in Long Beach, it made sense to be closer, save on drive time . . . All right, that's not the only reason. Venice was also a "wet" town. Which, for all you lucky lappers who weren't around for Prohibition, means a city where a man could still get his lips around a whiskey bottle without a fuss. *Round white man buy 'em firewater easy.* You could drink, and get drunk, and the cops were okay with it if you patted their palms a little. And the Sunset Inn was a hop-step-and-tumble down the road. Buster and I spent so much time there we were on the menu. *I'll have the Mammoth Olives à la Roscoe Arbuckle and the Shrimp Cocktail à la Buster Keaton. Thank you. And bring me some breath mints, honey.*

The Sunset Inn was the scene of many an epic bender. Something about that beach air. Whenever we wandered the sand with drinks in our hands, and I started feeling tipsy enough to need a lie-down—generally flat on my face—I'd look at Buster, stroke my chin, and declare, "That darn ocean breeze. It *does* something to me." That was everybody's signal to catch me when my knees buckled. There was no better place to pass out than on the beach. As long as the tide was out.

But what I really loved about my Venice place, aside from the fresh air and fresh hooch, was the tunnel. My private tunnel. Who else had one of those? The President? Underneath our property, somebody'd built a tunnel all the way down through the cliff right out to the surf. Rumor had it this was a bootlegger's drop. Or maybe a smuggler's. The last occupant of the house died under mysterious circumstances. Who knew?

Goodbye, Daddy, Goodbye

My father's last night before going back into the hospital I threw a party for him out at the Venice house. When I led him through the tunnel Daddy kept eyeballing the ceiling, like it was gonna collapse any second. I plopped him on a horse on the beach, between Mary Pickford and Bebe Daniels. I think the old child abandoner got flirty with 'em, because his wife stalked back to the house more stone-faced than usual.

I guess Daddy's visit made me think about things. Before he left, 10-grand check from Yours Truly in his hand, he made that jiggered-up face he always made when he wanted to let me know what he thought of me. "Funny," he said, in his cracked-glass cancer voice, "you used to hate when anybody called you fat. Looks like you're making a pretty decent livin' at it."

No "*Thank you.*" No "*I'm proud o' you, son.*" Nothing. Which may be what inspired me to do *Out West*. See, when I was clowning around for the soldiers, I could tell how impressed they were. Not just impressed, but surprised. Like, they pretty much had the same view of me that Daddy did. I was some glorified carny act. The male equivalent of the Fat Lady. Nobody seemed to understand how strong you had to be to do what I do. How physically sound and coordinated. *Twenty marines* I held off in a tug of war. Could you do that? I rest my crankcase.

Seriously, in my secret heart, I knew I could be Douglas Fairbanks. And after getting that last, disgusted goodbye look from Daddy, I decided to demonstrate that fact on celluloid—to put my strength and agility front and center. If not for Fairbanks's—or my father's—benefit, then for mine.

Understand, Doug-Doug was a friend of mine. We'd shared more than a few "Is it eight in the morning or eight at night?"'s together. He was the Action Hero—the man women wanted and other men wanted to be. But look at what he did in every movie: the roof jumping, the balcony hopping, the swan dives into choppy waters. It was the same stuff *I* did. Except he looked better in tights. So, since Buster was gone, and I figured I'd have to carry things on my own, I got the bright idea of doing a parody of a Fairbanks film.

The gag in Hollywood was that D.F. wouldn't even read a

script if the plot did not involve a couple of balconies to bounce off of. So, in *Out West*. I squeezed in as many leap scenes as I could think up. I didn't play them for yuks, either. I just performed 'em, almost like a demonstration. Did I scramble up church steeples? Did I make bad guys cower? Did I shimmy onto the porches of beauties who got all goose-pimply at the sight of me? Yes. Why? Same reason a dog laps his genitals. *Because I could.* (Not lap my genitals, though later on Mr. Hearst would accuse me of worse. I meant, I shimmied onto porches.) Sure, the audience was laughing, but they also realized something: just cause he's called Fatty doesn't mean he's not an athlete. I was doing this for fat men everywhere!

Out West wasn't the first movie where I was required to show off my physique. (Now be quiet, ladies!) After Jack Dempsey creamed Jess Willard, I asked the new champ if he wanted to do a movie together. What gave me the idea was an item I read in the paper. The Dempsey fight was the first one Willard's wife ever attended. She didn't even show up when Jess beat Jack Johnson to become heavyweight champion in the first place.

Imagine! At the one fight Mrs. Willard sees fit to attend, her hubby gets his hind end handed to him in three rounds. My idea was to play Willard, trying to explain to his wife that this wasn't how things usually went. "Honestly, hon, this never happened before!" Show me the man who denies ever serving up *that* bit of palaver, and I'll show you a liar. But Dempsey's manager thought movies would lower his boy's real estate and took a Pasadena.

Of course, when it came to spire climbing, I got the laughs, but Fairbanks got the sighs. Still, once people in Front Porchville saw me doing all the stunts Douglas did, I earned a new kind of respect. Minta, who'd become somewhat of a Freud nut since we split up, told me Herr Shrinker would say I was trying to get kudos from my father by getting it from the audience. I might have bought this, but she also said Freud thought throwing a cream pie was a "symbol for ejaculation." Don't think I didn't mull on that the next time I caught Mabel in the face with a custard. *Duck!*

What with the war and all, it was incumbent—that's a Joe Schenck word, "incumbent" (he was a college man)—it was incumbent on all of us to do what we could for our country. (The only thing my country ever did for me was dun me till my eyes bled for back income tax, but I don't want to sound like some kind of Red.) Uncle Sam may not have wanted want me in uniform, but, by gum, he wanted me on celluloid. Naturally, I was happy to donate my humble talent.

Alongside Mabel, George M. Cohan, Mary Pickford, Elsie Ferguson, my liquid-lunch buddy Fairbanks, plus Pauline Frederick, William S. Hart, and a smack-happy Wally Reid, I showed up in a morale booster and money raiser with the catchy title *The United States Fourth Liberty Loan Drive*. Not much story, but plenty of stars.

The stars, of course, worked for free. We made a million dollars for the US of A. It was a Famous Players–Lasky setup, and I couldn't help but wonder how much old Jesse was skimming off the ammo money. Then the Armistice was signed, and 10 minutes after Buster got off the train I picked him up and brought him back to Alessandro Street to play a theater rat in *Backstage*. That was the first time we tried for color-tinting the film. Buster said we both looked like we'd been force-fed peaches. We didn't bother with the color gimmick after that.

By now I was pulling down $7,000 a week, and not a day went by without some company or other sniffing round, waving cash in my face, to see if they could "extract" me from my current contract. Loew's, through Joe Schenck's brother Nicky, wagged one-and-a-quarter-million per, plus a cut. Even that hotbed of melodrama, Universal, came at me. Didn't matter to them if I did comedy, they just wanted the name. Oddly enough, one of Universal's biggest stars was Earl Schenck, baby brother of Joe and Nick. I tell you, those people bred like *minks*.

The money I made at Comique never ceased to amaze me. And getting creative control! The whole deal was positively unprecedented. But between you, me and that six-foot sidewinder I've been hallucinating on and off since my padded-cell vacation, I was just happy not to be robbed outright . . . When I was five years old, Daddy gave me a teddy bear for Christmas. I remember, 'cause it was the first and last one I ever got. Right away, I loved that bear. Then I hugged it to my chest, and I noticed a little tear in its tummy. Some stuffing was coming out. So I stuck in my finger and *SNAP*—just like that, something bit it. I screamed so loud Mama woke up from her morphine nap. Then I pulled out my hand and—I could faint thinking about it—there was this baby snake swinging from my forefinger. It had its fangs stuck right under the nail, and what I recall even now is how calm it looked. If snakes had eyebrows it would have probably waggled them. With its shiny little eyes, the snake seemed to be saying, "*Well what did you expect from your Daddy?*"

That's how I felt about all these companies coming up with their fantastic offers. And that's how I felt about the deal I had. Sooner or later, the teddy bear would turn out to have a snake in it. Until you got bit, all you could do was keep an eye on your fingers.

Zukor and I had formed Comique on a handshake in New York. But now Adolph wanted something solid. So he offered the one thing none of the other studios even thought of. I'm not talking about money. He promised more than three million in three years, but I was already making a mil a year. So what does Zukor offer, that conniving son-of-a-gunstein? Features. That's what. The one dish nobody else slapped on the table.

Feature Me

The idea, if I signed, was that my two-reeler days would be over. Zukor wanted seven features a year—with no one but me saying what we do and how we do it. I had to let that sink in. Starting in October 1920, I'd be making 22 features in three years. Chaplin didn't crank out a feature until *The Kid*, in 1922. I might have felt the snake wriggling in the teddy bear when Adolph said Famous Players–Lasky would be producing all of them. But I've always been a simp at negotiations. I started out in vaudeville because I was hungry. I hate this business stuff. Mack always used to say, "You can't trust anybody in Hollywood, so relax."

Balanced on a couple of bar stools on Zukor's boat, nursing a fistful of martini, I tried to let the proposition sink in. We'd spent the weekend at Catalina, and he'd insisted on bringing me back to Los Angeles himself, so we could talk. I didn't know if I should I be jumping up and down screaming "whoopee!" or covering my tender orifice and diving for shore. I should have known something was up when he insisted on feeding me a tureen of drink before taking advantage of me. What was I, a starlet?

Adolph, plainly, thought I was playing "confused" to grind him, biting my lip and scratching my head full of cornsilk hair like a rube in a melodrama. I *was* confused, but if you're an actor, producers just assume you're acting. From where Zukor stood, I had all the power, I just didn't know it. So when it looked like I was having second thoughts—or worse, trying to make him cough up more money—he swung into double-hand action.

But allow me to interrupt myself. Until Buster pointed it out to me later, I did not even realize what Zukor was really going for. Namely, getting me to do more work for the same amount of money. The feature bait was a way of getting my eyes off salary details. *Misdirection.* Keaton's godfather was Harry Houdini, so he knew these things. Buster was a great man in a poker game, unless you liked your money.

Zukor, smart as he was, was a terrible poker player. He had an expressive face, and he was fidgety. When you got to know him, you got to know which twitches meant what. As Buster said, Adolph had more ways of telegraphing his next move than Western Union. But his hands were the biggest tell. Whenever he was trying to sell you on something, Adolph would hold your hand. He didn't squeeze it or anything. Just held it. Looked you dead in the eye. The message was: Adolph Zukor was so tough he could hold your hand like a prom date. Who else could do that?

It's hard to march out a bunch of niggling doubts about a man's veracity when he's fondling your palm. Especially if the man is the most powerful studio head in Hollywood.

"Roscoe, one little thing . . ." Palm squeeze. He's selling me something. "You do understand that Comique will have to fold. Go the way of the Mohicans."

"You said that, but—"

What's he doing with his other hand? No! He's going to *sandwich* me. Now he's got my one hand in two of his.

"All your pictures will be produced under Famous Players–Lasky."

So, I'm still wondering, *Is this good? Is this bad?* Generally,

I'd hire a guy to tell me what a contract meant, then I'd have to hire another guy to tell me what the first one said. But I'm out here on the Zukor yacht. Mano a mano. A captive on the high seas.

Zukor gave me a day to "roll the offer around in my brainpan and see how it feels." While I was deciding whether to hop on the Famous Players train or not, Mabel told me that Zukor, the sneaky Semite, had signed up another jumbo comedian. A human tuba named Walter Hiers. In other words, Zukor already had a Plan B.

So I guess you could say half of me finally went with Famous Players 'cause the idea of features was thrilling. Half because the idea of being unemployed still scared the rind off my bologna. And another half cause the idea of having to go through the nightmare of contracting with another company was too much. That's three halves, but I'm a big man.

I figured hiring Hiers was Adolph's way of saying "Everyone's expendable." It was an open secret that all producers thought actors were idiots. The only bigger idiots, of course, were the public, who were stupid enough to believe we were what the mags and studios said we were. If it weren't for the public wanting to see a few particular idiots in their movies, the studio heads would have probably used each actor once, then shot him, ground him up, and fed him to the next expendable thespian. *Thespy Chow.* Come and get it!

Going Continental

My living room at West Adams sat 24, but more than that squeezed in for my bon-voyage party. Lou Anger had the bright idea we should do a little continental touring at the end of 1919. So, before heading for New York, from where we would sail to London, I invited over a few of my closest reprobates. (Another Schenck word, the man was a dictionary of 25-cent jaw-breakers.) All I really wanted was a chance to rest. But somehow it didn't work out that way. In Manhattan, I kipped at Minta's for a few days. Funny how much I missed her, until we were under one roof again, and then I missed myself. The boat wasn't much more relaxing. Every 20 feet some pipsqueak with a rich Mommy and Daddy would ask me to do a somersault. So of course I'd have to.

Once we hit London, though, I thought I'd expired and gone to heaven. If heaven was a place where hordes of fish-and-chips eaters followed you around like Moses' flock. In Piccadilly Circus, when word spread I was waddling around playing tourist, a spontaneous cheer went up on the street. *Hip hip hooray!* It startled me so badly I dropped the Guinness I'd hid under my coat. *Ker-splat!* My nerves still felt stripped raw from the heroin withdrawal. That gave the alcohol a much bigger job to do.

How popular was I? Claridges had to hire extra doormen and a gaggle of press agents. Ever try to nosh with a mob of strangers smashing their faces to the window, itching for a glimpse of you chewing your dinner roll? After a couple of days I began to feel lonely when a few hundred people weren't shouting my name.

France was even louder. A pack of wined-up Pierres decided to sneak up behind me on the Champs-Elysées and swoop me into the air. I guess that's a thing they do there. Probably started with Napoleon. But a couple of kids could've tossed Pee-Wee Bonaparte up and down. The merry monsieurs who tried to hike my thighs skyward made it about five feet, then buckled. I cracked the sidewalk and my shoulder at the same time.

Ever since the leg thing, my pain tolerance was pretty low. So the rest of the trip, along with icing the bruise, Anger kept me supplied with morphine. The bad part was, the French don't believe the mouth is the place to administer medicine. They weren't big on needles, either. They have their own peculiar notions. A key one, I soon learned, involved something called a suppository. Bottoms up!

The rest of the Paris trip, I am embarrassed to say, was spent keeping my cakes clenched, trying to stop those little butt-bullets of painkiller from leaking out. On what should have been one of the greatest days of my life, when I was bending to place a wreath on the Tomb of the Unknown Soldier, all I could think was, *Please, God, don't let that morphine shoot out of my caboose.* For the occasion I was wearing white ducks.

Still, nobody had ever shown me that kind of respect before. I was honored. Some general shook my hand and they played their national anthem. "The Mayonnaise." Then every man in the crowd saluted me. What do you think about that? This was a situation of the gravest dignity, and I was truly touched. I didn't pretend to fall down until five minutes after the ceremony, when I had the driver step on the gas right before I got in the car. We did that three or four times. I'd open the Renault door, take a step, then the coupe would lurch forward and I'd fall on my face. It sent the frogs into a frenzy. As a race, when they laughed they snorted.

It's one thing to know people like your films, but when they treat you like the King of Hollywood, you come back home thinking, *Yeah, maybe I am royalty!* Until, say, you have lunch with Schenck and he calls you "Bubby" and stiffs you for the check. But, even though I wasn't away long, something else had changed while I was gone. Something I couldn't quite put my finger on—until it laid a finger on me.

PART 5

Cleaning Up the Business

I'D NEVER heard a word about "reformers" before I went abroad. I hadn't heard the word "normalcy" at all. But by the time I came home from Europe it's all anybody was talking about. President Harding—a fellow fat man—peppered every speech with calls for a "return to normalcy." Whatever *that* was. But everywhere you looked things kept getting *less* normal.

A lot of it kicked off with the Black Sox Scandal. The World Series—*fixed?* Kiddies' baseball heroes really a bunch of grifters? You can't imagine what that did to this country.

You could not pick up a paper or ride an elevator without some pasty-face yammering about moral decline. Then, thanks to Billy Sunday, a screaming evangelist, and the schoolmarms in the Women's Temperance Society, Congress voted in the 18th Amendment. Prohibition. And don't think half of them weren't snockered at the time! An Irish bootlegger friend of mine, Joe Kennedy, told me the Senate was full of lushes—all sipping bourbon and branch water. He knew 'cause he's the guy what sol'em the bourbon. I can hear Billy Sunday yowling now, *"Once the demon Alcohol is banished, all men will walk upright. Hell will be forever to rent . . ."*

But banning alcohol wasn't enough. Once they got a taste for outlawing bad behavior, the reformers themselves were like drunks on a bender. They couldn't find enough things to object to. Once, when Luke the Dog crapped on the dining-room rug,

I caught the headline on the paper I was crumpling to whack him with: AMERICAN SOCIETY OF DANCE TEACHERS DECRIES BALLROOM DANCING. There was a picture of a woman who might have been my twin sister. She was that kind of plump, with troubled puppy eyes and pursed pink lips. Underneath her beauteous mug ran the story of her crusade: "Organization President Dot LeMay Says 'Jazz Music Impels Degenerate, Degrading Movement . . .'" I laughed so hard Luke got away without a well-deserved snout swat for soiling another Persian.

What wasn't funny was, every newspaper or magazine article, every crackpot pamphlet, ended the same way. With a call for government censors to oversee moving pictures. Filthy things that they were.

Paramount's very own Rudolph Valentino was held responsible for much of this moral turpitude. Ads for *The Sheik* were so racy some citizens' groups threatened boycotts. "*See the auction of beautiful girls to the lords of Algerian harems . . . See the heroine, disguised, invade the Bedouin's secret slave rites . . . See Sheik Ahmed raid her caravan and carry her off to his tent . . .*"

Arbuckle asks you, what happened to decency?

Well, Arbuckle's had a lot of time to think about this. And Arbuckle will tell you.

You see, the War To End All Wars gave a lot of gals jobs, and when it was over a lot of 'em didn't want to go back to darning socks for Daddy. In my world I was used to independent women. Actresses worked to eat, just like actors. But out there in Hamhock City and Back Porchville, the "authorities" wanted the fair sex to forget they ever went to work in factories, to toddle on home and back to sock darning.

Too late, Gramps. Modern girls didn't want to be like Mother. They wanted to be like movie stars. Like Colleen Moore, the original flapper, who clipped her hair, shortened her dresses, and tossed her corset in the trash. But that's not all. Colleen was so shameful she sucked cigarettes in public, dabbed on makeup, and—get the kids out of the room—rolled her stockings up.

This is when the police, at the behest of said reformers, started arresting bathing beauties. Some towns equipped the officers with rulers, to check on the offending temptress's hem. If her dress was too short, it was off to the slammer. Other cities were more inclined to jail lady smokers. Mind you, if the cops had done that in the Keystone days, there wouldn't have been a female left on the lot. The clams Mack hired showed a lot of thigh and smoked like steam trains. Otherwise they wouldn't get the job.

Before the Reform Movement, managers like Anger or Joe Schenck would encourage successful actors and actresses to buy as much crap as they could: fancy cars, grander mansions, more of everything, as long as it was expensive and wild. Now the talk was about "toning things down." Six million people were unemployed. Striking coal miners were being shot. The Red Scare was on. The folks in charge needed somebody to blame. Why not some movie-star type with a snifter of cocaine and a 40-grand solid-gold bathtub? As long as they could point the finger at us Hollywood types, politicians did not have to defend their own lavish appointments. Nobody seemed inclined to point out that movie actors were not to blame for the policies that put honest workadaddies out of work. The politicos were. But who wanted to fuss with niggling details?

All of a sudden, America saw sin everywhere. And Hollywood was Sin City. Even God was mad at us. I heard a preacher on a soapbox in Santa Monica rant about "the demonic hand at work in the immoral drama and motion-picture industry." And all Reverend Soapy was doing was parroting the message government and religious types were belting out on pulpits everywhere. No wonder I was tired. It was hard work corrupting the minds of Christian youth.

Just kidding! I, Fatty, remained a paragon of all that was good and decent in the entertainment industry. I had no choice—Jesse Lasky picked the scripts. He'd promised me artistic control, but that particular pledge never exactly panned out. What could I do? Sue? They'd have had me branded Red so fast I'd be playing canasta with Sacco and Vanzetti.

Not that Lasky didn't have an eye for what worked, movie-wise. By way of "classing" me up a tad, buying respectability for the studio, and—most important—hedging their bets by using material already beloved by the public, I was handed *The Round-Up*. A nice enough bit of fluff, *Round-Up* started out life as a popular Broadway play. And ended up as my first full-length movie vehicle.

In *Round-Up* I play Sheriff Slim Hoover. As a gag, Keaton, who had his own company by now, showed up to play an Injun. For my second epic, Lasky snapped up another popular fave, *The Life of the Party*, an award-winning *Saturday Evening Post* story. What I liked about both films—okay if I take myself serious here?—is that they gave me as much chance for characterization as slapstick. I was trying to be funny without being *fat* funny. They both turned out to be hits. But Adolph and Jesse seemed more glad that they were both wholesome.

A rash of scandals had been plaguing the movie business, beginning with Charlie Chaplin's marriage to his child bride, the pregnant and 16-year-old Mildred Harris. Then Mary Pickford divorced her movie-star hubby, Owen Moore, and married Doug Fairbanks five minutes later. AMERICA'S SWEETHEART A HUSSY, the headlines screamed.

Meanwhile, at Famous Players–Lasky, Mary's baby brother,

Jack, was implicated when his lovely wife, Olive Thomas, swallowed arsenic and killed herself. Unable, according to rumors, to tolerate another day of her husband's out-of-control cocaine addiction. To make matters worse for the Lasky lot, the police arrested the notorious "Captain Spaulding, Drug Dispenser to the Stars." The Captain, no fool, threatened to name names if charges weren't dropped. Nobody questioned that Zukor himself had shelled out half a million in hush money to keep his studio's reputation from sinking even further.

The door, of course, swung both ways. When a motorcycle cop caught Bebe Daniels blasting 72 miles an hour through Santa Ana—with Jack Dempsey and her mother in the car—the judge threw her in jail for days. Instead of hushing it up, Paramount spreads the word around, alerts the papers. And before you know it, the big department store up there, Barker Brothers, is furnishing her cell with carpets, divan, and curtains. Restaurants are competing to see who can provide her meals. And somebody shells out for Abe Lyman and his Orchestra to bus up from Los Angeles and serenade her on the prison lawn.

And how did the moral giants at Paramount respond to Bebe's misbehavior? They cranked out a flyspeck of a film called *Speedgirl*. And starred her in it.

Paragon of All That's Good

Somehow, in the midst of this "Epidemic Immorality," this "lecherous lair of debauchery," as the tabloids loved to call my hometown, I managed to maintain a sterling reputation. Lovable Fatty drew kudos from the very publications who were railing the loudest against the evils of moviedom.

Not to toot my own horn—it doesn't really toot anymore—but listen to this, from a humble exhibitor in Billings, Montana, after *The Life of the Party* knocked 'em dead up there. "How do you spell family entertainment? A-R-B-U-C-K-L-E, that's how. At a time when so many movies glorify lust, adultery and drugs, luring countless young Americans into the gutter, we wish more Hollywood actors made good, clean fun-for-the-kids photoplays like *The Life of the Party*."

Would I be shoving this at you if what happened later hadn't happened? Of course not. I wouldn't have bothered to save this scrapbook. The second *Party* wrapped, I got going on *The Traveling Salesman*. I finished that on a Tuesday morning in July and started *Brewster's Millions* that afternoon. By then the public couldn't get enough, and I couldn't see straight.

Trust me on this, making movies wears you out. Which didn't stop Lasky and Zukor from cracking the whip. With my contract inching to a close, these two slave drivers decided I could make three pictures at the same time. So, in January 1921, before I even had my *Brewster* pants off, I jumped straight into *Gasoline Gus, Leap Year*, and *Freight*. By the end of the summer, all three were completed.

In *Leap Year*, I played an innocent, rich little rollo who just can't shake the passel of females who want to get their clutches on him. At one point these women crowd into my house, all but smothering me with love. Needless to say, they never released it. Considering what transpired, the subject matter might have seemed a little—let's just say "ill-conceived."

I'd worked 15 hours a day, pretty much seven days a week, since signing with Famous Players. When Lasky had the money-saving notion of having me shoot three movies simultaneously, I went along. I need a nap just thinking about it.

A Dream Ride to Frisco

In September, on the last afternoon of shooting the last picture, *Freight Prepaid*, the Pierce-Arrow folks showed up with the $25,000 extra-large custom convertible I'd ordered. It had a flush toilet and a full cocktail bar. I don't think I've loved a person as much as I loved that car. I immediately took it for a spin, inspired to go on a buying spree, and returned home with a pocketful of diamonds, cases of perfume, and imported shoes. That's the strangest thing about having big money: when you can finally afford to pay cash on the table for everything, everybody wants to give you credit.

All *I* wanted to do was drive that car, and the only time I could do it was Labor Day weekend. That's how I came up with the idea of San Francisco. Ever since my Portola days—and my gratitude over not getting pancaked in the quake—I've had a soft spot for the place. A lot of us did. Hollywood loved San Francisco, even if Frisco didn't exactly return the affection. I even had an editorial from the *Chronicle* framed and mounted in my guest toilet. To our northern cousins, we were "Rogues and Ruffians from Hollywood . . . children who had not yet experienced the back hand of a parent," et cetera . . . But what the heck. Outside of the *Chronicle*'s city desk, the rest of the town was happy to take our money. And we were happy to give it. Frisco liquor made our L.A. swill taste like cat drip.

Buster and I'd been up north a million times, and I was hoping he'd come along for the Labor Day jaunt. But Buster'd become a fishing nut. He and the missus were boating to Catalina to do some angling. They invited me to sail along, but I declined. Then the brass got involved. Still battling to make the film business look wholesome, Zukor and Lasky had organized something called Paramount Week. During P Week, stars were ordered to show up and entertain the folks, to show what a happy, whole-some, just-like-the-family-back-in-Wichita batch of Joes and Josephines we really were.

That's what these dog-and-pony shows were all about. Book the studio movies into some showplace theater, then have some muttonhead actor give a speech on what a fine, moral place Hollywood, California, was. Tickets were free with purchase of laundry detergent or cold cream.

Giving the audience a free peek at their big names, Zukor banked on buying goodwill in hopes that Mr. and Mrs. Normal would stop their nasty boycotts and see how decent we showbiz types could be. That was a big thing with Zukor—maybe because so many of the scandals that made people think Holly-wood was Sodom and Gomorrah happened at his studio. He was always having us do stuff to make the magazines think we were basically outsized Boy Scouts. Three weeks before I packed the Pierce-Arrow and headed north, Adolph made me sit down with Adela Rogers St. John for *Photoplay*.

I must have talked to her for 20 minutes tops, but from the way her article read—"Love Confessions of a Fat Man!"—you'd have thought she and I had lollygagged for a month in Naples. Her style was what you fancypants would call louche: "*We were lunching together in his bedroom . . . I'd never interviewed anyone in pongee pajamas before.*"

As if that weren't ridiculous enough, she went on to quote "*a couple of schoolgirls—of the cut-his-picture-out-and-sleep-with-it-under-the-pillow age.*" This is what we're dealing with, fellow earthlings. Listen: "*After admitting that Wally Reid was un-doubtedly the handsomest man in the world—one girl said, 'But I just adore Roscoe Arbuckle.'*"

Then it gets really peculiar. I mean, listen to me: "*A woman today has got to have a good-natured husband. Statistics show that there have been more love murders, marriage murders and suicide love pacts in the last few years than ever before in the history of the world. It is very hard either to murder or to be murdered by a fat man."*

Sure. That's exactly the kind of thing I say. You want to talk about how good that was gonna look a couple of weeks later? Hand me the rat poison while I get a glass of arsenic.

Angering the Gods of Hollywood

I don't know who snitched. But when Zukor got wind I wasn't going to show up at Grauman's for a Labor Day showing of my latest, *Gasoline Gus*, he blew up. El Jefe wanted me there, extolling the virtues of Bible study before the movie. After Grauman's, I was slated to appear with Wallace Reid and Conrad Nagel downtown, for another showing of *Gasoline*. I ask you, is there no rest for the wholesome?

Zukor and Lasky both fired off telegrams to Schenck. Zukor's had steam coming off it. He was furious. Called me uncooperative. Called me ungrateful. Schenck, the lunk, thought he could play to Zukor's sympathies. "Roscoe's taking a holiday in San Francisco," he tells him. "He's been working like a coolie, he deserves time off."

Joe's words, big surprise, had the opposite effect. Schenck calls me up to tell me this while I'm packing. "First time Adolph ever hung up on me. Actually, he didn't hang up. He threw the phone against the wall. I could hear plaster shattering. I bet he bills the contractor who fixes the hole to the studio."

Meanwhile, I was still trying to snag somebody to caravan up the Coast. Bebe Daniels said she'd show up later. Alf Goulding, my director chum, had a film go long. Rocky Joe Rock, the producer, and my drinking buddy Lew Cody—neither could make it. No knock, but Rock and Cody would drive for a week if there was a free drink at the other end. I should have known then something was hinky. But that's my problem, folks. I'm the innocent type. A husky dunce from the heartland.

Only Lowell Sherman, who had so much contempt for the profession of acting he had to stay drunk to tolerate it, agreed to take a ride north in my Arrow. Now don't get me wrong. I liked Lowell. But he was the kind of drinker who just got quieter and quieter the more he drank. By the bottom of a bottle he could be scintillating as a corpse. Lowell'd just appeared in Griffith's latest, *Way Down East*, earning raves as the smoothie who ravishes the wide-eyed Lillian Gish. Naturally, success made him even more morose.

Still, when Fred Fischbach called on Friday to say he heard I was "wheeling to San Fran" and invited himself along, I can't say I was thrilled. I knew Fred from Sennett. He was a good enough director, but in my early days at Keystone, when Lehrman was busy telling Mack what a no-talent lout I was, Fred was always ready to back him up. Lehrman was still boring bartenders in Manhattan about how he got shafted by Mack. And Fred remained his great good friend. "Going north to scout some locations," he said.

I don't like saying no to anybody, so I booked rooms next to mine at the St. Francis for Lowell and Fred: 1219, 1220, and 1221. I figured once the party got started, people would start showing up. Anybody in vaudeville passing through would come. And, most weekends, a batch of actors and actresses on the lam from Los Angeles were generally banging around. The thing was just to get going.

I started to pack, and every time the phone rang I knew it

was probably Zukor or Lasky. So I had my butler answer. Somehow, Okie knew even less English now than he did when Minta and I hired him eight years ago. I leaned over his shoulder to eavesdrop, and when Zukor started yelling we both jumped. "You remind that ingrate I'm giving him a million goddamn dollars a year. He can cooperate for one goddamn free afternoon!"

It was Daddy all over again. I was so shook up I kind of wandered outside, where Puddy, my mechanic, was under the hood of the new Pierce-Arrow. He'd just finished doing something to the batteries. Still reeling from the Zukor call, I dropped down on a bench—and jumped straight up again, my ass on fire. Pardon my Spanish. *AI-EEEE!!*

"Gee, Mr. Roscoe, you musta sat on your battery acid!"

An hour later, the pain was making me chew my lip. I finally called my doctor, who came over with something to kill the burn-sting. He left me some morphine pills to hold me if the pain came back. Minta says I rang her up at three a.m., New York time, and told her I had a funny feeling about Fischbach. I don't remember talking to her, but the phone was in my hand when I woke up on the carpet, wearing one shoe I never saw before. In my experience, morphine and whiskey will generally introduce a man to his carpet.

I thought it was morning, but it turned out to be 10 at night. That's when I decided to track down Lowell and Fred and cancel the trip. Lowell was fine with it. He could get sullen and drunk anywhere. But Fred—you'd have thought I'd violated a deathbed pledge. He absolutely *had* to go to San Francisco! He was counting on me. I gave him my word. And a few more guilt inducers along those lines. Fine, I said, if it's that important . . . I called back Lowell and he said he'd go wherever I wanted, as long I stopped calling him.

St. Francis

The St. Francis was *la cramp de la cramp* of San Francisco hotels. Presidents and opera stars stayed there. It's where Barrymore was sleeping one off when the earthquake hit. (Along with a couple of underage acquaintances who, being younger and still in the possession of reflexes, were out of John's room and through the lobby while Barrymore was still trying to figure out what kind of hangover made the building shake.)

I wanted to go right to sleep when we checked in to the hotel on Saturday. I'd driven the whole way with a doggy pillow under my leg, and I was twisted up. The painkillers kept me dull anyway. I just wanted to soak in a tub and start fresh Sunday morning. But Fischbach, who'd been acting weird the whole trip, wouldn't hear of turning in early. He called a bootlegger he knew, who sent a case up under a tablecloth, rolled in by a bellboy.

I never liked to waste good drink, but whatever was good about the spratwater Fischbach poured was pretty hard to remember the next morning. I'd have probably slept till after lunch, but some friend of Fischbach's, a lingerie salesman by the name of Art Fortlois, called to say he heard Fred was in town, so he invited himself over. Banged on the door at noon.

"Lingerie salesman" covered a lot of territory, and I wasn't too thrilled about having Fred's friend on the premises. In person Fortlois looked like the kind of skeezix who talked little girls into coming to his "office" to "model underwear." Which, unhappily, we discovered he actually did when we met him 15 minutes later.

Mr. Fortlois, it seemed, was staying at the Palace, at the bottom of Market and Montgomery. A lovely stroll from the St. Francis. And wouldn't you know, he was enjoying that very stroll when who does he run into but Al Semnacher, Virginia Rappe, and Maude Delmont.

My thigh was still fried from the battery acid, so I answered the door in my pajamas. Fred, looking more sweaty than usual, was standing there with this unsavory crew behind him. "Roscoe, I'd, uh, like you to meet some friends of mine." "Oh, Roscoe and I have met," Virginia tee-heed. She liked to play the ditzy little girl. "Sure, I know Virginia," I replied, with as much courtesy as I could muster. It was like trying to be nice to a disease. For a guy who'd just run into old friends, Fred didn't look too friendly.

Being the gentlemanly type, I could say that everybody at Keystone knew Virginia. I could be polite and tell you she'd gazed into at least half their eyes from inches away. But maybe it's best to come out and say she'd given half the boys gonorrhea and the other half lice. Sennett even had to shut down the studio, to fumigate the dressing room on account of Virginia's generosity. You could call her a prostitute, but Virginia never came out and charged, she just happened to have a lot of crises in her life, dire straits that only one semiwhite knight or another could lift her out of.

The last man to have been publicly linked with Virginia was none other than Henry "Pathé" Lehrman. Henry's the one who brought her to Hollywood in the first place. Knowing the girl's story, Minta always thought Virginia was part of a white-slavery racket. Whatever the explanation, the sloe-eyed brunette was not shy about bestowing physical affection. But somehow, from what I could gather, everyone who shared her affections ended up shelling out a little something for the privilege. I never dove into that pool, myself. For a lot of reasons. But mostly 'cause I was afraid she'd tell the other fellas if I couldn't, you know, get the sausage in the grinder. In which case she'd probably ask me to slip her 50 frogskins a month to keep from selling the lowdown to the *Motion Picture News.*

But that's not even what made her dangerous. Prostitution and blackmail you can see coming—but Virginia had another habit. She swallowed cocktails as fast as she could grab them. After she hit double figures, she had a tendency to tear off her clothes and start screaming gibberish at the top of her lungs. Gibberish that usually involved some nastiness at the hands of whatever man was handy.

More than once some fellow who'd just gone on a belly ride was so startled by Virginia's mouth he'd smack it and back out the door. Since Virginia was a blackout drinker, most of these swells were safe once they escaped. Unless they were unfortunate enough to have company when they were having their way with her. A witness, in the soon-to-explode controversy, provided by the malevolent Maude Delmont.

If Virginia was trouble, Maude was like having the Devil's homely sister show up for snacks. Fortlois introduced her as a "dress model." Maybe he actually believed that. In Hollywood, the lady was known as a "helpful witness"—a fancy way of saying she made her living supplying incriminating photos for wannabe divorcées. I didn't know then that she'd already had 50 counts filed against her. I just knew you didn't want her anywhere near your private life. Or it wouldn't stay private for very long.

So this is what's going through my mind as I'm standing in room 1221, at half past noon on a blurry Sunday, wondering why everything Fred said made him sweatier. Watching these two sally-girls throw back the drinks, I wanted to call the hotel dick myself.

It was an open secret that Al Semnacher had been trying to get a divorce, so it didn't take Sherlock Holmes to figure out why a man of his stature would be traveling with Maude. Later, when he got sloshed, he confided before puking on my slippers that he needed evidence his wife was making hanky-panky. "For a fair price," he explained, the lovely Maude would provide it. This was a new one on me. As far as I knew, Delmont's bread-and-butter, was making sure a troubled wife would have a living witness to her husband's misbehavior—usually by supplying the girl he misbehaved with. She'd obviously branched out and was now supplying hubbys with evidence. Maude herself was going to appear as witness to Mrs. Semnacher's immoral behavior. The case was scheduled for September 9, in the court of one Judge Sommerfeld, on the bench in San Francisco. "She's gonna make me a free man," Al groggled later when he was rubber-legged. "Maudie's gonna make me a free man."

All of which explains why when Lowell stumbled in, wrapped in a cigarette-burned silk lounging jacket, I took Fischbach aside to tell him that under no circumstances did I want Virginia and Maude Delmont on the premises. I didn't care how he did it, but I wanted them out. Fred acted confused and said he had a bad hangover. I'm the gullible type—I always believe a man who blames his problems on booze.

The Wrong Party

We'd rented a Victrola, which Lowell insisted on cranking up the second he arrived. While other guests started drifting in, I did my polite best to prevail on Fred, to enlighten his hung-over brain as to why I needed him to remove Maudie and Virginia. I could have thrown them out myself, but when you're twice as big as everybody else you have to be careful about getting physical. Things can happen.

Trying to be gentlemanly, I filled Fred in on how Henry "Pathé" Lehrman blamed me for his reversal of fortune. I was probably more long-winded than I had to be. The thing was, Chaplin's the one who actually got Lehrman fired. But since eggheads loved Charlie, and Pathé was always trying to look classier than he was, it was easier for him to hate me. So in Lehrman's version—marched out in every gin mill from Beverly Hills to the Bowery—he'd been thrown out of Keystone for refusing to debase his art with my "crude and low-end antics."

Of course, what really debased old Pathé was the fact that the flatback whose career he'd invented, his "girl," was known to have fornicated with anything in pants. Pretty galling, when you consider all the favors Henry called in to get Virginia what few credits she had. Her face graced the cover of the sheet music to "Let Me Call You Sweetheart," because the publisher owed Pathé 50 fishskins from a pinochle debt.

I went on and on, working myself up in the process. The more I talked, the more uncomfortable Fred looked. The reason didn't hit me till later—Fred had gambling debts, too. *Maybe somebody was paying him to set me up with these professional ruiners.* The only thing that works slower than my brain is my digestion. And they both usually result in a load of crap.

By the time I finished telling Fischbach why I wanted Maude and Virginia gone, a few more guests had already ambled in. Alice Blake and Zey Prevon, a couple of fresh-minted actresses up from Los Angeles, marched in arm-in-arm between a couple of nervous bellboys with grub. Alice, a slinky brunette, kissed the little pimply one who was pushing the steam table. The poor kid blushed down to his ankles. Then she stole his hat and I thought he was going to cry. She danced around him and lifted the lids off the sausage and egg buckets, oohing and aahing like the Girl with the Blue Ribbon Grits Recipe at the Yokel Flats

County Fair. Then an older, unshaven "bellhop" knocked on the door and wheeled in a doghouse of rotgut. When Fred saw him, he stopped me in mid-sentence, ran over, and exchanged a few furtive words. If this hard case was a real bellboy, I'm a professional bird-feeder.

In minutes, the pretend bellhop lined up bottles on the wet bar, piled ice cubes in the bucket, and set out a chilled bowl of oranges and a hand squeezer like he'd done it a thousand times. Naturally, Maude and Virginia were on him like piglets on porker teats. The fellow did not exactly seem to be a stranger to them. I cupped my hand over my ear for a second to eavesdrop. It was tough to hear over the Victrola. Maude kept playing "I'm Just Wild About Harry." But over the chorus I heard the saucy grifter cooing, "Jack Lawrence, you handsome bootlegger!" And watched Virginia, pretending to drop an ice cube, waggle her backside in front of the handsome criminal as she bent to pick it up.

Finally, I pulled Fred into a corner and gave him my ultimatum: Eighty-six Delmont and Rappe or the party's over. Fred forgot his hangover blur and responded fiercely, as if I'd slandered his mother. "Virginia's had some tough breaks, but she's a fine little actress."

"Fred," I said, "you're not talking to *Photoplay* here! The girl's had more crabs than the Fulton Street Fish Market. I don't wanna have to worry about using my towels." But Fischbach couldn't even look at me. His eyes kept darting to the bar, to the door, down to his wingtips, then back up to the ceiling like he was reading hieroglyphics.

"You want them gone, you get rid of them," he blurted finally. "I came up here to scout locations. I'm going to borrow your car and go find some seals. Besides—"

"I know," I finished for him, "you have a hangover."

"Right!"

With that Fred dashed out of the room before I could stop him. I galloped down the hall, bellowing, "You're not taking my Pierce-Arrow!"

I was just fleet of foot enough to see him fly through the closing elevator doors. I pounded the buttons, thinking I'd ride down to the lobby in the other car and corral him. But when car two arrived, a dozen revelers spilled out. Two showgirls, Dollie Clark and Bet Campbell, still in their matinee-wear; Victor, the hotel chef, accompanied by a quartet of waiters, and a handful of San Francisco denizens who happened to be in the hotel and heard about the Hollywood party on 12. There was enough clinking when they moved to know somebody'd brought their own refreshments. Either that or they'd been pilfering glassware.

I wanted to just blast past them, but I never liked to be rude. Everyone seemed delighted to see me in my PJs. So, swept up by this merry band, I let myself be led back to my suite, where the party was definitely in full swing. And, speaking of pajamas, Maude Delmont was now wearing Lowell Sherman's jammies and smoking like a coal-mine fire. While Virginia, laughing raucously, leaned on the piano, tossing back orange blossoms as fast as Art Fortlois, that rancid underwear salesman, could slip them to her.

"Less blossom and more gin!" Virginia kept screaming, laughing hysterically at her own joke, then repeating it and laughing again. A swarthy Italian in shiny gold tights had obviously entranced her, and between drinks she draped herself on the foreigner, pointedly ignoring the nervous customer who'd brought her, Art the Undie Peddler.

Shiny Tights turned out to headline at Barnum and Bailey. He was an aerialist. What's more, in a couple of hours, Banini, the Flying Tuscan, was going to walk on a wire from the penthouse of the St. Francis to the roof of a building across from it. The circus was famous for publicity stunts, which explained why he was wearing gold tights in public. As a gag, I asked him if they came in my size.

I was considering changing into day clothes when Art Fortlois, in the grips of jealous pique, hit the Flying Tuscan in the head with an orange squeezer. At that point the aerialist's mother strode in. She was a six-foot store-dyed redhead packed in a lady sheriff's costume, complete with six-shooters and spurs the size of tiny wagon wheels. Mommy dragged the boy tightrope walker out by his ear, screaming at him in front of the whole party.

"You wanta to die? *Stupido!*"

She had the thickest Italian accent I'd ever heard outside the vaudeville stage. Everybody felt embarrassed for the kid, even Fortlois, who'd just brained him.

"You wanta to fall and ruin the good name of your father and grandfather? That'sa why you want to inhale this movie whore?"

Her English was flawed but her sentiment unmistakable. Then again, maybe Moms Banini said exactly what she meant to say. Turns out she was right about the danger of her boy breathing Virginia's gin fumes. The Flying Tuscan turned out to have a worse day than I did. Two hours after leaving the festivities, he slipped off the high wire. Fell 12 stories in front of a good crowd. He crashed through the roof of a fruit stand and landed on a bachelor Chinee who'd stowed away from Peking two weeks ago.

The Chinee broke his back. Banini died on the spot. It was a perfect front-page death. But nobody got to see it on the front page on account of another catastrophe—the one that was about to happen under my nose.

A Calamity

Virginia had been in hysterics since Handsome Highwire's Mother dragged him out of the party. She slammed down another four drinks before Art stopped her. He tried to shush her and she laughed in his face. And that, friends and neighbors, is the very moment her good friend Maude chose to go off with Lowell.

Perhaps the impressionable Miss Delmont was overcome by a sudden desire to sneak into the bathroom with Lowell Sherman—or, more likely, she knew what was coming.

Either way, as soon as her sweet Virginia started showing her "symptoms"—giggling hysterically, hiccuping, whipping her head from side to side like a dizzy show pony—Maude quickly got Lowell to disappear with her. Lucky for Maude, Lowell was never particular. He didn't care if a woman was 18 and plum-lipped or 50 with back hair. All Lowell wanted was to get her in a bathtub, in her underpants. That's what did it for him.

I'd witnessed the panty-bath routine the last time we shared a hotel, down in Tijuana. Lowell would fill a nice tub for a lady—his thoughtfulness almost shocking—then break into his patented "*Oh, honey, I almost forgot. For a shot I'm working on, would you mind leaving your drawers on when you step into the tub? I just need a few pictures . . .*"

So now Fred Fischbach's gone, and Maude and Lowell are locked in Lowell's bathroom, in soggy heaven. It's just me, a paralytic Art Fortlois, and a bevy of showgirls dancing with slumming society types and Hollywood drunks—along with a bootlegger or two and the odd hophead. None of whom do a thing but stare when Virginia drops her glass to the carpet and screams. Her hands flail at the air in front of her, then she begins tearing at herself, ripping at her own throat, her hair, her clothes. In seconds she's torn her dress to shreds. One breast dangles over the torn cotton, the nipple bleeding where she'd scratched it.

I'd seen Virginia's drink-and-rip routine before. At Keystone. That's why I wasn't worried when she hit the ground and started to convulse. "Get some ice!" I hollered to no one in particular. While a pair of showgirls attended to that, I saw my chance to slip out. I wanted to take a shower and get dressed.

Just before I stepped into the hall, Virginia suddenly jumped up and staggered to Lowell's bathroom. She began pounding on the door and shrieking that she was dying. Maybe Lowell and Maude were underwater and couldn't hear. After she gave up pounding, Virginia collapsed again. I closed the door to the suite as Alice and Dollie, both well armed with towel-wrapped ice, descended on Virginia's naked frame.

What happened next—and what didn't happen—would haunt me through every dark night for the rest of my life. Retiring to my suite, I made a call to Minta. I still did that sometimes, when I felt unhinged. But Minta wasn't home, so I decided to get my clothes out before I took a shower. As I hadn't even unpacked my bags, I had to dig through my suitcase to find fresh shorts. It was slightly inconvenient, but the way people were running around I was scared somebody might walk in later, after my shower, when I was in the altogether. There were plenty of cases where some chickie flew in a guy's hotel room, planted a hot one on his lips, and held it till some slimy shutterbug showed up and snapped it. So I wasn't taking any chances—I wanted to get everything ready now.

This must have been when Virginia slipped in, when I was busy excavating my boxers. Clothes in hand, I tried to open the bathroom door. It was blocked. Finally I shoved it open enough to pop my head in—and spy Virginia, on hands and knees, worshiping at the white altar. I shouldered through the door, held her steady while she upchucked, then propped her on the seat and cleaned her mouth. At one point she tipped sideways and I barely caught her, by the throat, before her head hit the tub. I figured the best thing for the girl was rest, so I put her in one of my shirts, stretched her out on my bed, and ducked back in for a quick shower.

Five minutes later, I'm wrapped in a towel, still soaking, and I decide to check on my ill and unwanted guest. At first I don't see her. Then I hear—the hoarking, the grunts. Virginia's curled on the floor between bed and wall, puking like a seasick sailor and writhing in agony. Disgusting, but I've been there, so I don't judge.

My first thought was that ice might help. What else can get a drunk undrunk better than ice? But first I peeled my shirt off trembly Virginia and used it to clean her soiled body. Then I lifted her back on the bed. I made sure she looked comfortable, and I made a decision. A bad one, naturally.

That Sinking Feeling

I did not even realize how upset the whole episode had got me until I ran into Fortlois. The undie drummer was lounging on the ice chest, a showgirl curled on his lap, strumming a ukulele. I grabbed the instrument and pushed him out of the way. Art wanted the instrument back, so I said, "Leave now and take your two ladyfriends with you, you can have the uke."

It annoyed me how Fortlois, and everybody else, had started drinking and laughing again after Virginia ran off. Not for the first time, it struck me that I didn't know half the people at my own party. I just knew they were drinking my liquor.

Fortlois puffed himself up and said he wasn't responsible for Maude or Virginia. He said Fischbach was the one who introduced them a day ago. This news was so alarming, I decided not to think about it, and to focus on the hell at hand. Ice. I needed ice. But when I opened the ice chest, there was no ice. Thinking fast, I grabbed a bottle of ice-cold champagne instead.

Buster once told me, if you ever have to wake up a Dumb Dora, some dizzy drunkette so prestoned you don't even know if she's alive—you ring her doorbell. I didn't know the term, so Buster explained: you find her vulva and place an ice cube square *on* the little buzzer. Then push.

I don't know if it's bragging or complaining, at this juncture, to confide that I had no idea exactly what a vulva looked like, or where it was. I knew, in a general way. But this was hardly the time for basic anatomy lessons. Laying the icy bottle to one side, I gathered up my gumption and dove in, feeling a little bit like a miner without his miner's light. I parted Virginia's lady-lips as best I could and searched for my quarry. Virginia, in turn, began to squirm at my ministrations.

Pleasuring the girl was hardly my intent. And though it would have been hard to look—or breathe—beyond the horrid young woman's bile-marinated torso, the all-white of her rolled-back eyes, I confess that for one instant, to my own surprise, I felt reeling desire. Excitement like I'd never known. When Virginia groaned, I groaned. Our own little call-and-response.

Then I remembered what I was doing. Under her rouge, Virginia was pale as thin ice. I placed my hand chastely on her forehead and recoiled from the burning heat. Her fever must have been massive. It was like touching a Dutch oven. That's when, remembering my duty, I fumbled to expose the vulval bump—or doorbell, as Buster called it—and pressed the wide bottom of the bottle against it, the business end pointing up to her breasts.

Virginia's head, which had begun to loll unnaturally, seemed to jolt forward on contact with the icy glass. Still working the bottle, which had slipped somewhat lower between her thighs, I leaned over to press my ear to Virginia's breast, listening for a heartbeat. What with the clamor and blaring Victrola down the hall, hearing anything was near impossible. I had to close my eyes to concentrate, hefting my bulk sort of above and diagonal to her nude body.

One ear, and half my face, were pressed to Virginia's naked breast. My left hand squeezed around her neck, checking for pulse. My right wrapped around that chilled champagne, urging it—as medically proscribed by Doctor Keaton—firmly along the nub of what, to the best of my knowledge, you would call the vulva. When, from out of nowhere, shocking myself, I heard myself think: *I can see why so many men want her.*

I immediately felt nauseous and, with a hot rush of panic, suffered another jolting thought: *This would look pretty bad if somebody saw.*

No sooner did this occur to me than I heard voices in the hallway. Someone started banging on my door. And then, before I had the chance to hoist myself off the exposed Virginia, in stormed Maude Delmont. Her gasp, looking back, was probably more happiness than shock.

I could feel Maude taking in my massive anatomy—clad only in boxer shorts—and the sweating bottle wedged between Virginia's parted thighs. Then she raised her eyes to my mouth, still poised within suckling distance of Virginia's beefy nipple, and screamed.

*　　*　　*

It was all accidental, of course. But I could feel the thoughts taking shape in Maude's brain even before she shrieked, bringing in Lowell and the others. I quickly gathered myself up on the bed. Tried to look respectable—but how? I was a fatso in his boxers on top of a naked girl. I turned my head to see Maude's face, aghast, then watched, with the gorge rising in my gullet, as Fred Fischbach stormed in. Before he was through the door he was already hollering, demanding to know what the hell happened when he was away. Self-righteous as a parson.

Maude's plate-shattering screams did more to wake up Virginia than my ill-fated champagne bottle. She leaned over the obviously febrile girl and whispered in her ear. A second later, Virginia bolted upright, eyes wide as a zombie doll's. She began flailing at the air in front of her, as though fighting off an invisible ogre.

Maude grabbed Virginia and whispered in her ear again. The girl snapped out of it long enough to jabber what sounded like "No, Daddy, no!" Then Virginia pointed at me, shaking wildly. She began shrieking, in a deranged voice, "Don't touch me! Maudie, please, don't let him hurt me anymore!"

Maude, now trying to look virtuous in Lowell Sherman's striped pajamas, scooped Virginia up from under me, as if saving her from the jaws of hell. I had Fischbach to thank for the presence of this professional blackmailer and the hysterical young psychotic in her arms. But you wouldn't have known that from his reaction.

"Fred, you saw what happened," I piped up lamely, "somebody yelled ice." But Fischbach just stared past me, towards the bathroom. Where the newly noble Maude held Virginia across her lap, in *Pietà*-like fashion, plunked atop the closed toilet seat.

Alice Blake and Zey Prevon rushed back in with buckets of ice and dumped them in the tub. Then Fischbach, in full hearing of all the women, let out a hollow little laugh. "Fatty, old boy, I guess you got what you wanted, eh?"

I was too shocked to respond. Did he really think that? Just to do something until my face stopped burning, I announced that I would see to it Virginia got her own room, and find her a doctor. Before I closed the door Virginia was at it again, mewling insanely, *"He did this! I'm bleeding, Maudie . . . He did this to me!"*

Who thinks, in moments of panic, about the import of their actions—or the actions of others?

Still in a daze, I ducked out to track down the hotel manager and the physician on duty. After much back-and-forthing, I finally corraled a nervous fellow in wire-rims, one Harry J. Boyle, assistant manager. He informed me, with visible distaste, that the hotel's regular physician, Dr. Beardslee, preferred not to "attend to improprieties." I went back upstairs, where one of the guests, a local entertainer named Mae Taub, summoned her own doctor, a fellow with the odd name of Olav Kaarboe. Minutes later, Kaarboe stepped in with a black bag and monocle. He observed Miss Rappe, tongue lolling out of her mouth as she soaked in the ice bath, and declared—with the full weight of medical knowledge behind him—that she'd "overindulged." Deep.

Before Doc Kaarboe departed, another fellow showed up, a stolid citizen who introduced himself as Glennon, the hotel dick. This Glennon, who had the demeanor of a cinder-block wall, took stock of the situation. He decided it was nothing too out of the ordinary, and—taking me aside by the door—asked if I'd mind if he "stopped in for a taste" before leaving. I told him I didn't mind at all, though I confess I found the request a little peculiar.

The second the doctor and the house detective were gone,

Virginia started yelping again. By then I'd just about had it. "I can't have her screaming bloody murder in my suite!" I snapped at Fischbach. "Can't you keep her quiet? She's your friend."

"Oh, but she's much more than a friend to you," Fischbach sneered. Meanwhile, Maude, who'd been guzzling moonshine nonstop since arriving, had passed out at the head of the bathtub and was snoring like a stalled Ford.

"Look, Fred," I said, trying to stay calm. Once I started blathering I couldn't stop. "I don't know what you're getting at, but you know damn well all I did with that girl was try to help, to get her to stop convulsing. Everybody's seen how Virginia gets when she drinks. At Keystone she'd get crocked and rip her clothes off every other week. She looked fit to die when I saw her, so I tried to help. End of story. Now give me a hand while I carry her down to 1227. I made arrangements with the management. She can stay until she feels better."

Fischbach listened, but didn't bother to reply. He just kept looking at me with that rotten sneer. We lifted Virginia's soaking cold body out of the tub. I wrapped it in my dressing gown and together we carried her down the hall and put her to bed. By this time, I don't mind telling you, I needed a drink. Who'm I kidding? By now I needed a lot of drinks.

Back in the party suite, people were carrying on like nothing had happened. Fully dressed now, I walked back in time to see Lowell Sherman doing his famous chicken walk between two obviously polluted showgirls. He was trying to "peck" their tops off with his gums—a trick at which, for whatever ungodly reason, he was adept—and soon enough he had the first girl naked down to her bra. Swinging her blouse from side to side in his mouth, an unsavory spectacle, the middle-aged Lowell then dropped it and began to chicken-peck at the giggling dancer's brassiere. "Get hot! Get hot!" someone yelled from the other side of the room, and I finally put my foot down.

"Keep it up, Lowell, and I'm going to stick you in a tub full of ice cubes with Virginia. I don't want any bootleg orgies on my nickel, okay?"

I hated feeling like the party poop, so I decided now was a good time to get some air. The truth was, my leg-burn was killing me, and I figured I could kill three birds with one stone—get out of the hotel, line up some morphine if I was lucky, and stash the car on the Frisco–to–Los Angeles ferry, the Harvard Steamer. You had to hit the steamer early to get a spot. And there was no way I could drive back with that kind of pain in my clutch leg. Ever the optimist, I figured the whole mess with Virginia would blow over by the time I ambled back. I could not have been more wrong if I'd bet the farm on the Kaiser.

I got back to the hotel after dark. Riding up the elevator, I could hear the screams before the car even got to 12. When the doors opened, I leaped out and ran down the fleur-de-lis-carpeted hall. I remember the fleur-de-lis 'cause Daddy owned a tie, his only one, of the same pattern. He used to strangle me with it.

I clambered straight into 1227. Virginia's room. Banged through the door just as a silver-haired gent wielding a syringe was leaning over the patient. He dabbed a cotton ball to her exposed buttock—was I the only one who saw bite marks?—then plunged the morphine home. Don't ask how I knew it was morphine. Hopheads are funny that way. Like piggies snuffling truffles in the mud.

"Dr. Beardslee," the silver fox announced, like I ought to recognize the name. He shook my hand after he unscrewed the syringe and packed it back in his bag. Apparently, the St. Francis physician had finally seen fit to make an appearance. "Roscoe Arbuckle," I said, "glad you could take a peek at her." The doctor gave me an odd look, then asked, in the most somber tone imaginable, "What happened to this child?" "*Child?*" I wanted to say. "*She's had more bones buried inside her than Forest Lawn!*" But instead I inquired politely, "What do you mean?"

Before our chat could progress further, Maude Delmont, wide awake now and dressed in what to her demented way of thinking must have passed for schoolmarm garb, grabbed the doctor's arm and led him urgently towards the door.

"I'll tell you what happened!" she cried, casting a backward glance in my direction. "I'll tell you *exactly* what happened."

For an instant I had the jitters, then caught myself and almost laughed. What can she possibly say that would put me in Dutch? Why would she bother? Sure, Maude was a bad bag of applesauce, but really, why would she do anything to me? *Roscoe*, I thought a second later, *don't be a feeb*. For a price, Maude would do anything to anybody. Then again, I *was* paying for her room—and Virginia's. Digs weren't cheap at the St. Francis. And let's not even talk about the five bathtubs of antifreeze Maude guzzled in the course of her stay. I could not imagine she'd want to annoy me and risk getting stuck with the bill. Why look a gift Clydesdale in the mouth? I figured it was the pain in my acid-burned thigh, or the painkillers I'd just bought to kill it, that made my thinking so cloudy.

By now my whole leg was throbbing. I felt like a bear dragging around the trap he stepped in. So I gulped more painkillers, then limped back to the party. I was thirsty for a nightcap. But what I really wanted was to forget all about the alarming Bambina

Maude Delmont and the hapless Virginia Rappe. It was my party, wasn't it? Those two were just the flies who buzzed in and gunked up the ointment.

The next morning, a Tuesday, we were slated to check out and head south, back to work. I showered and stepped into the hall in time to see Dr. Beardslee again, flat-footing his way down to Virginia's room. Better him than me was how I figured it. Like I say, I was paying for her room—as well as the lovely Maude Delmont's—and the way those two drank that was no small stack of cabbage. They might as well have run a hose from the still straight to Maudie's tonsils. On the elevator going down, I noticed a pleasant-looking lady, a nurse, giving me the once-over.

"Aren't you . . . Roscoe Arbuckle?"

"Well," I said, "I'd hate to look like this and *not* be Roscoe Arbuckle."

She managed a polite chuckle, started to talk, then stopped, then started back in again. I think the phrase is "cute as a button." "You know, Mr. Arbuckle, I'm a nurse. My name's Meg Jameson, and I have to tell you, this Virginia Rappe, she's . . . she's not well."

"You're telling me," I said.

She wanted to know if I'd noticed any symptoms—itching, burning, redness . . . I realized where she was going—by now we were stopped on seven—and asked her straight out, "You mean she's got the clap?"

"Gonorrhea," she whispered, aiming her eyes at the little lit-up numbers over the door. "Plus she was bleeding. Not fresh blood, though. Like she had some wound that opened up. If I were you I'd get . . . looked over."

I could tell this was as awkward for her as it was for me, so I

just held up my hand for her to stop. "Lady . . . I mean Nurse
. . . you got it all wrong. I never touched that girl. She collapsed
after too much firewater and I tried to help her."

Nurse Jameson squinted at me. "But Miss Delmont, she's
saying you . . ." She straightened her uniform and stared down
at her white shoes. "She's saying things about you."

"Maude Delmont will say anything about anybody," I told
her, trying to keep it pleasant. Two respectable people having a
chat. "That's how she makes her living."

The nurse and I parted with a handshake in the lobby. But just
to be safe, I called Dr. Beardslee back. He said the patient was
doing fine. He'd had to catheterize her, as she'd had some kind
of bladder problem and hadn't relieved herself in over 24 hours.
"Near as I could tell," he said, "that could be why she had the
stomach pain."

"No other complications, then?"

I didn't want to ask about the gonorrhea. Then *he'd* think I
was worried about pissing razor blades.

"Nothing to fret about, Mr. Arbuckle."

I left a $50 bill with the doc's name in an envelope at the desk,
another 50 for Nurse Jameson, and set off to find Fred and
Lowell for the ride to the ferry. The more time I spent in San
Francisco, the less I wanted to spend. Everything was painful,
starting with my leg, and I had the insane notion that if I just got
back to Los Angeles, everything would be better. Or maybe I just
wanted to panic in familiar surroundings.

My mind still hadn't wrapped itself around the unfolding
drama. But my ass was already sweating.

Los Angeles Bounce

By Wednesday I'm back at the studio, working. Glad to jump in with both of my size 12 quadruple D's. *Freight Prepaid*, our last gem, was in need of editing. And I had some story ideas I wanted to sketch out for our next one, *The Melancholy Spirit*. How's this sound? There's a spirit named Ek that comes down and takes possession of a mild-mannered professor. Whenever Professor Milquetoast's in the grip of Ek, he gets drunk and goes wild. Doing all kinds of stuff the professor wouldn't do. Pretty philosophical, huh? Was Ek making the professor into something he wasn't—or was the spirit just showing the professor for who he was?

I met a real nice girl named Doris Deane on the ferry home. Since Minta—minus a couple of hooch-fueled smooches with Alice Lake—I hadn't really been too involved with the fair sex. But something about this Doris got me. I even mentioned her to Schenck, on Thursday, when we met to catch up on production. "Just make sure she doesn't meet Adolph Zukor" was all Joe had to say. "Right now you're on his disloyal employees list."

In all the hubbub with Virginia, I forgot all about Paramount Week. "He's still eatin' bugs over that, huh?"

Schenck bobbed his head up and down. "Oh yeah, the boss doesn't forget stuff like that." Then we got on the subject of the party up north, and when I told him that Fischbach, Maude, and Virginia had showed up, Joe started playing with his tie. He did that when he was nervous. "I thought I saw Fischbach talking to Zukor at the Formosa. Last week."

Schenck did not have to say why that would seem odd. How often does the King of England slop rashers and mash with a chimney sweep? But I didn't give it much thought. "Maude and Virginia," Schenck went on, in that wrong way of talking he had. "Those two dames . . ."

When I told him, "Yeah, and Fischbach found the bootlegger, so they were all pretty well oiled," Schenck got that spooked expression again. Did everything but strangle himself with his tie. For a sec I misted up thinking about Daddy.

"Roscoe," Schenck said, bringing me back. "I know Fischbach. Fred is not the go-get-the-bootlegger type."

"Uh-oh" was all that came out of my mouth.

That Thursday night I got a weird call. Somebody from a place called Wakefield Sanitarium, in San Francisco. A shaky-sounding guy who called himself Dr. Rumwell asked if I knew a certain Virginia Rappe. At first I thought it was Buster. "Dr. Rumwell" was his style. He'd once woken me up pretending to be Chief Wannaspankee, asking for a donation for the Fat Little Navajo Fund.

I didn't recognize Buster's voice, but for all I knew he could have hauled some rummy off a bar stool to call me. When I said, "Sure, I know Virginia, who doesn't?" the shaky guy kind of cleared his throat and said, "Are you the father?" "This isn't Buster, is it?" I asked. But the way Dr. Rumwell replied, gathering all his shaky dignity together to inform me, "I assure you, sir, there are no Busters in my family!" made me think the call was legit. It sounded so much like something Keaton would say I just knew it wasn't him.

"So, are you the father?" Rumwell repeated nervously.

I told him I may be no spring chicken, but I'm not *that* old. "I think I'd know if I had a daughter 10 years younger than me. I'd be in *Ripley's Believe It or Not*." I figured 10 years was just about what I had on young Virginia.

I could hear the doctor not saying anything for a second of two. Then he sputtered an anxious "Thank you, sir" and hung up.

On Friday, I told Buster about the call, and he gave me a big fake slap across the face. "Wakefield's an abortion clinic. Rumwell wasn't asking if you were Virginia's father, numbnuts. He was asking if you're the spud who made her a mother."

When *that* sank in—us big lovable galoots can be naïve—all I could do was shake my head. I told Buster about Maude Delmont, and we both figured maybe she was trying to shake me down on a paternity suit. Buster stroked his chin and made that deathbed-serious face of his, and we both burst out laughing.

Buster knew about my problems south of the border. I could always tell him anything. I mean, we were both raised on the stage. We'd been put—and kicked—through the same paces. There was nothing either of us could do that the other would judge. Pretty soon, I'd realize that's the definition of a friend. And that Buster was the only one I had.

That Friday was pretty much the last day of my life. The last day of it as *me*, anyway. The me who thinks about gags, and movie plots, and funny angles, as opposed to the "fanged lard-monster" or "sex-crazed blimp" I was about to be labeled. Chatting with Buster, I was already on the slide from "beloved family entertainer" to "lock-up-your-daughters monstrosity." I just didn't know it.

Branded

There were lots of things I should have known but didn't. But what, really, do you ever know about the future? If you're lucky, you never have to see how wrong you were about everything . . .

Friday morning, at 10 a.m., Virginia's bladder ruptured.

Right in time for the nurse's coffee break, she went into a coma. Her bladder popped, then she got the peritonitis. By Friday afternoon, infection had spread inside her body. By nighttime, it was about to spread outside of it. Courtesy of Maude Delmont, my personal Typhoid Mary, it was going to spread to me.

While I was spending the day sketching out plot gags for *Are You a Mason?* and *The Man from Mexico*, Maude was still in San Francisco spinning her own funny tale.

See, Virginia died at one-thirty in the afternoon, and by two o'clock Maude had already made two phone calls: one to the San Francisco Police Department, one to the *San Francisco Examiner*. I didn't know any of this, of course, until I got a knock on the door. A couple of mugs in sheriff's outfits—San Francisco sheriffs—handed me a summons. The littlest monkey, who owned jug ears that would have held up a gravy boat, pulled out an official envelope. He got his dirty prints all over it trying to get the letter out, then read, in a halting tone, "By the powers vested in me by the Police Department of the City of San Francisco, I am hereby authorized to remand you to the care of said department, and return you for questioning, on charges of murder in the first degree."

"You gonna tell me who I murdered," I quipped, "or should I ask Buster, since he's the one paying you?" I snipped the butt off a cigar and sipped a brandy while they pondered their reply. His practical jokes were getting to be masterpieces.

"Not just murder," the other cop, a real hatchet-face, declared after they'd conferred. "Murder and rape."

At that point I stepped outside and yelled into the yard, "Very funny, Buster." But Buster didn't answer. So I stepped back in. I didn't know what to think. You hear people say, "Oh, such-and-such felt like a bad dream." But that's not how it is. It's just the opposite! When the worst thing in the world actually happens, it feels absolutely real. That's what makes it so bad. It's everything else that feels like a dream.

"How'd you like it, crushing that little girl?" the hatchet-faced cop asked me. His expression was nakedly hateful.

Slow as I am, it finally started to dawn on me. "Maude Delmont." My voice came out like a croak. "That's who's saying this?"

Both cops just looked grim. The little one piped up again, making fists at his sides as he talked. "Virginia was Maude's best friend. And you made Maude watch while you took your sweaty way with Virginia. That tiny beauty. That *angel!*"

"Easy, Floyd," said the bigger cop, putting his hand on emotional young Floyd's shoulder. "Easy there, partner."

Floyd made a manly face and soldiered on with his story. "Maude said Virginia was a virgin."

"She said *what?*" Should I have laughed or cried?

"You heard me!" the cop snapped back. The little fireplug kept hopping from foot to foot, like he was going to either wet his pants or punch me in the face. He was *that* indignant. "You kept screaming at Virginia, 'I've waited five years for you!' You acted like a pre-vert."

"Maude said *that?*" I was flabbergasted. I knew the woman was capable of lies, but why *these* lies? And why, by the way, was I talking to the police? "Who'd she say it to?" was the one question I managed to ask.

Hatchet-face pulled a rolled-up newspaper from his back pocket and slapped it in my hand. I unrolled it and saw the Page One headline: DYING GIRL LAID BLAME ON COMEDIAN! Then, just below, "*So Charges Woman at Bedside of Orgy Victim to SF Police.*"

The first thought I had was "*Orgy victim?*" Where was the orgy? My heart felt pumped full of bad air. What was going on?

I looked up at the policemen, but their eyes were dead. If I were a balloon, I'd have flown backward around the room and sputtered to the floor. It was that wrong. The picture on the front page showed a "Miss Rappe" I'd certainly never seen. Her hair was cut like a Sunday-school teacher's, falling demurely above the shoulder straps of a humble gingham dress she might have made herself, with a matching bonnet.

"She was mad at me," I heard myself say to the cops. I'd polished off a snifter of brandy, but the drunk was sucked right out of me. My own voice sounded tinny and faraway.

Even though it was horrible, it seemed silly. That was the way things felt, for the next day or so. Horrible and silly. The idea that I'd killed Virginia, the idea that people believed I'd raped her to death—one second it would make me lose my breath and nearly upchuck, the next I'd start laughing, *then* lose my breath and nearly upchuck. Why would anybody have to rape Virginia Rappe?

"So you did crush her?" one of the cops said.

"Not Virginia," I said. "Maude. The one who made this up. She was mad. She thought I insulted her."

"Whyzzat?"

"Not to tell tales out of school," I told the boys from Frisco, "but I had to 86 Mademoiselle Delmont when she started showing her breasts to the bellboys."

Did I mention that before? Lowell's pajama bottoms hid her well enough, but his tops were missing all the buttons, and Maude kept finding an excuse to lean over and pick up nickels. Real class.

"*These people were a breed unseen by churchgoers . . .*" That was the one line I read in the papers I agreed with. When I told Maude to play ladylike or vacate the premises, Lowell got to be the White Knight—the reward for which, in this case, was getting to toss her in the tub with her knickers on. Lowell even thanked me later for getting Maude riled up. "Gave me the chance to play tough guy," he winked. "Maudie likes tough guys."

After that, I could not stop contemplating how I'd riled Maude up. It got me thinking, had I spent a lifetime riling people up and not knowing it? Making folks so mad that they wanted to do things to me? Was my Dad just first in a line that stretched to Adolph Zukor, Maude Delmont, and a cast of thousands I'm just too dense to have noticed?

When the sheriffs announced that we'd be leaving for San Francisco tomorrow at seven, I felt like I was trapped in a script that needed a rewrite. I figured it wouldn't hurt to improvise, so I said the first thing that came to mind. "Ever ride in a Pierce-Arrow? It's got a toilet."

Red Meat

So it was that I was tooling north at the wheel of my trusty Big Man–mobile, the pair of San Francisco's Finest wedged between Frank Dominguez, the lawyer Schenck lined up, and Al Semnacher, Virginia's manager. Al said he'd be happy to ride up and vouch for me. Schenck didn't tell me Semnacher's next call was going to be to Zukor and Lasky. I'd find that out later. For now, my pariah status was still in its fetal stages. Horrifying as it all seemed to be—the headlines, the lies—I could not help treat it, at least partly, as a joke. I dressed as if for a formal occasion. Minta had once bought me a set of emerald plus-fours, with jacket and hat of the same material. I figured I'd march them out.

My part-scared, part-larky outlook was altered after Schenck called and told me not to talk to anybody on the drive north. He hung up before I could ask him why. He called back later to say that no hotel in San Francisco would take us. We'd have to check in at the Olympic Club, a rooming house outside the city, under pseudonyms. I said I'd sign in "Will B. Good." Joe didn't laugh. "Remember," he said, with what sounded like genuine dread, "San Francisco already hates us. You're going to be red meat."

Well, how do you prepare for that? With a helmet, if you're smart. But we already know I wasn't smart.

We were three blocks from the Olympic when the first rock hit the car. A swarm of women, upper-crust and angry, waved posters in front of the car: FATTY WILL FIT IN THE GAS CHAMBER! VIRGINIA—THE BEAST WILL PAY!

Maybe that's when it *really* hit me. This was worse than I'd imagined—though I hadn't imagined much. It still seemed ridiculous. In the abstract. But not when a young lady who looked about Virginia's age, in a starched collar and Salvation Army cape, rammed her face right over the windshield and spat. There's nothing abstract about spitting women. Not when they look at you like you're missing a noose.

Photographers were everywhere when we pulled in. Dominguez and Sherman had to make a wedge so I could squeeze into the lobby. Ever since I could actually afford to stay in them. I'd loved walking into hotels. The way the 'hops run over, the manager's smile when he offers you cigars and a handshake. Or when some shy kid with his dad wants an autograph. I could never stay unhappy about anything in a hotel lobby. Until today.

The Olympic desk clerk looked so uncomfortable, I felt bad for *him*. I slid a 50 his way on the counter and said, "It's going to be okay," though maybe I was talking to myself. The clerk just stink-eyed the greenback, then inched it back to me with the nub of a fountain pen, like he didn't even want to touch it. After that he threw the check-in card across the counter and said, as coldly as he could, "Sign here."

The bellboys had scattered, so our bags were still sitting in the Pierce-Arrow, unfetched. I slipped the 50 back in his direction, left it there, and gave him my biggest smile. "Buy your mother something nice. She deserves it."

I called up Buster long distance and said, "J'accuse!" He said, "Gesundheit," and told me to be careful. "There's blood in the water, Roscoe. Don't take your trunks off." That's how Buster and I spoke to each other. Every conversation was half gag.

The deal was, I would check in to the Olympic Club—where I'd been so warmly welcomed—then drive with my lawyers down to the Hall of Justice. This was Dominguez's idea. Don't act guilty! But the two S.F. assistant DAs who met me at the curb were not impressed. In time I'd get to know Izzie Golden and Milton U'Ren pretty well. Golden was a ham-loving Jew. U'Ren was a tough guy who must've taken a lot of poot about his sissy name. In a way it must have been a lot like being a fat kid.

The Laws of Nature, Gone

It all happened so fast. But since nothing like it had ever happened before, I could not believe it was happening now. If you saw an apple fall up, you wouldn't believe that, either. Until you fell up after it. And knew gravity no longer applied. Think how that would feel, and you have an inkling of my days and nights.

This was unprecedented madness. One minute I'm still a movie star, the next I'm plunked behind a battered desk, 100 watts in my face, and these DAs are walking around cracking white folders off the table. "We got three affidavits, Arbuckle. Maude Delmont, Zey Prevon, and Alice Blake. They all say you dragged Virginia into the bedroom, you overpowered her when she resisted, and you tried to rape her."

Dominguez interrupted. "Tried to?"

I thought this was an odd time for my lawyer to speak up. And an odd thing to speak up about. I squirmed for reasons I hoped I would not have to go into. You know what I'm talking about. Then my swarthy attorney asked the DAs if we might have a moment. Muttering openly, they agreed. Dominguez led me into a corner, turned his back on U'Ren and Golden, and whispered in my ear, "Don't give 'em anything." I whispered back, "Why not?" And then, more urgently, "How can they know I'm innocent if I never tell them what happened?"

Dominguez sighed and put his hands on my shoulders like you would a 5-year-old. "Roscoe, they know you didn't murder her. If you give your story, they'll just think you're trying to snow them and think maybe you did!"

It didn't make any sense, but nothing that was happening made any sense. So I went along. What did I know?

For the next three hours, my high-powered attorney did not say boo while the two district attorneys grilled me like a salmon. Ten minutes in, they were joined by a trio of big micks in shirtsleeves: Harry McGrath, John Dolan, and Griffy Kennedy. The homicide dicks. The Fighting Irish took turns trying to trip me up. It was like trying to remember whether they said "Simon says" or not. Finally I had to go to the bathroom, and U'Ren and the Jew told me they were done anyway. A couple of peach-fuzzed deputies then led me down the hall to the Little Suspects' Room. We turned a corner and I could see the reporters pressed against the glass doors of the Homicide Office. The pack came alive when they saw me. By instinct I shot 'em a smile and wave, and the flashes popped like fireworks. Smoke leaked under the door. Then I caught Dominguez's eye, and he looked over my shoulder when he talked. "I wouldn't look too chipper, Roscoe. The last thing you want to look right now is chipper."

Ten minutes later, the DAs had two homicide bulls wrap me in handcuffs. Then they signaled for some uniformed string bean to open the doors and let the press mob in. The newshounds started barking questions. String Bean pulled out his pistol to shut them up. Then, in suitably hammy fashion, DA U'Ren began to read his official statement. "Roscoe Arbuckle, I am arresting you in the name of the State of California, County of San Francisco, City of San Francisco, on the count of Murder in the First Degree."

And that was that. It wasn't even me trudging down the stairs to processing. It was somebody I didn't know. Never met. At the same time, the fear that grabbed my throat was completely familiar. I was wet-undie scared. The way I used to be. All the time. So I did what I did when Daddy'd march me behind the shed, woken out of a dead sleep, to whip me with the rake handle. I looked at the ground. I kept my eyes down and counted spittoons. I shuffled where they pointed me, and didn't look up till we came to a high counter manned by a baldie in green eyeshades.

The baldie said, "Processing." I shrugged. He droned on about section 189 of the City Penal Code. "Life taken in rape or attempted rape is considered murder."

That damp, strangling fear was almost comforting now. Like family. Even if it was horrible, it was *familiar*. From the moment they dipped my thumb in ink, rolled it around on the pad, and planted it over a line below my misspelled name, "ROSCO

'FATTY' ARGUCKLE," the fear shut off my thoughts. I couldn't let myself think anything, because every thought was impossible. What was happening was impossible. I was on Pineapple Upside-Down Cake Planet. The place Buster and I pretended to send bad gags when they popped into our heads. The place where everything too wrong to happen happens. Where things that should be funny aren't, and things that shouldn't be aren't, either.

On top of all that, where the booze and narcotics had been I felt an enormous, buzzing silence, as though a phone had been left off the hook inside my skull. The stuff had provided a kind of cushion between what was happening behind my eyeballs and what was playing out in front of them. But now the buffer was gone. My nerves were stripped. My heart was naked . . .

PART 6

May You Never Have to Learn What I Am Telling You Now

HERE'S WHAT you find out when the world turns on you. You see things differently. You take a telephone book full of people you once thought liked you, people you thought were your friends—or at least not your enemies, not out to *get* you—and you listen to them, one after the other, say things about you that you couldn't imagine your worst enemy even thinking, let alone voicing out loud. I'm talking about awful, hateful, *personal* things . . . And they're saying them to newspapers.

And as soul-crushing as the behavior of people you know is the behavior of people you *don't*. Characters you haven't seen for 20 years crop up to detail your monstrous qualities. A guy named MacIntyre, some dodo who used to beat me up when we were boys back in Smith Center, told the *Kansas City Star*, "As a child, Roscoe was prone to pick the wings off ladybugs." I could barely remember MacIntyre's face. Now he was getting back at me. But for *what*? And why?

Of course the fans turned, too. Suddenly, in the eyes of Bobs and Betties who used to love me, nothing but murder. Former Fatty devotees now glared at me and saw someone they didn't know. Someone they hated! Everyone, strangers and friends—by now there was no difference—they all had the same dark question in their eyes . . .

All at once, seeing the whorl of fingerprints in that dripping ink, I felt my knees go watery and my bowels begin to flood. I cracked a freezing sweat. The floor was flying toward my face. Dolan the homicide cop grabbed me in a fireman's carry and hauled me to a door marked ADMINISTRATION. Dolan turned the knob, tried jiggling it, then banged it open with the butt of his gun. The door opened on a bare, seatless toilet in a closet.

"Think you can fit in there?" Dolan asked.

Prime slapstick material. I made a note to work up a man-stuck-in-toilet gag as I squeezed past him. But I couldn't even make a joke. That scared me in a way nothing else had so far. I managed to tug down my pants and lower myself on the freezing bowl. Then I saw a soggy-old *Examiner* on the floor. GIRL STRICKEN IN ARBUCKLE ROOMS.

Can I talk to you about sitting alone in the can, dazed from bright lights and unending surprise, perusing a newspaper story in which you're portrayed as a raping, drug-using, virgin-crushing monster? All you're trying to do is take a crap. But that's over. No more mindless little craps for you, Roscoe. From now on, every minute, every day, you're guilty. You got that, you big fat sap? Millions of human beings you don't know now want you to die. The ones that don't want you to die want to meet you in person—so they can kill you themselves.

At that moment I could almost feel my mind go off the tracks. And yet, I'd be lying if I didn't admit to catching myself, in the high drama of my sudden, humiliating parade, thinking out loud: "If I knew I was gonna go through all this, I wish I *had* rolled on top of the little wench." A thought for which I am not proud, but one I confess in hopes any honest Joe who puts himself in my loafers will admit that under similar circumstances, he'd likely feel the exact same way.

Here's what I know now that I did not know then: from a certain angle, anyone looks capable of evil. (Ever been slapped by a nun?) I may not have done what they accused me of doing—but every man on the jury knew in his heart that, in similar circumstances, *he* could have. Unlikely maybe, but not unimaginable. To find me innocent would be to find me, somehow, better than them. And who the hell did I think I was?

The Life of the Newly Despised

By the time Dolan led me out, clinking the cuffs over the backs of my unwashed hands, another crowd had made their way inside and up the stairs of the station. MOTHERS OF INNOCENT DAUGH-TERS, a hand-painted banner read. These haggard women seemed to gain color at the sight of me. It dawned on me, with terrible clarity, *I've given them a reason to live.* I am the thrill of true hate they will get to savor in lieu of true love. Or so it occurred to me then.

Was I that drunk for the past 10 years, not to see all this hate? That possibility was as scary as what was actually happening. *You actually believed everybody liked you, Roscoe.* How could I have been such a nincompoop? Success and adulation turned out to be just a vacation from the jeers and ire I'd known before. And now I'd been brought back home. It was as if the entire world had come together to say, "Daddy was right. You ARE disgusting!"

Crowbar Hotel

Minutes after being shunted into my cell on Felony Row, I fell asleep. But I was soon awakened by a menagerie of thugs and drool cases, violent-crime types who poked at my clothes like I was a window display. I thought of Minta's wedding gown, on the mannequin in the window at Buffums for a week before the ceremony, Long Beach. Then my new pals grew bored. Perhaps sensing my condition—utter ruin—they soon left me alone, and I recollapsed. I awoke in pale light. Two words sum up what you don't know about jail until you get there: unventilated flatulence. I blinked at the gaggle of men on the damp concrete around me. Bodies were strewn about as if shot, and I suddenly knew, as surely as I knew the sky was out there even if I couldn't see it, that it no longer mattered if my hands were bloody as Cain's or clean as Moses'. How had I ever thought it did? It had taken me this long to discover what the dumbest prisoner on the block knew instinctively. Even if I was never convicted, I was already a convict.

For a Man Scared of His Own Good Luck, Calamity Can Be Relief

Even now, I have a difficult time capturing the quality of my distress. Surprise was gone. My sadness was massive. Mostly, what roiled through me was a horrible confusion. But if I can make you feel only one sensation, it would be that of sudden, total loss. The whoosh of your own life disappearing.

I don't know how else to say it: everything goes away, and you're still there. Left behind. *Daddy's never coming to the train station*. Everything you took for granted—from cars to friend-ships—is either gone or different in a bad way. You don't know why exactly, you just know it's bad.

Imagine waking up one morning, and the life you've been living has been rolled up, the scenery taken away, and suddenly you're onstage in a new drama. In the new play, whatever used to make you lovable makes you hateful. Every line you spoke that got laughs now gets you hisses. Every word is used against you. And still, you're stuck with the old script.

Once you're condemned, there is nothing you have ever done in the past that does not make you suspicious. And nothing you can say or do in the present that does not, somehow, prove all suspicions justified.

My attorney told me I was the symbol of everything perceived as evil or depraved in Hollywood itself. I'd never thought of Hollywood as evil or depraved. Just overpaid . . . But those screaming headlines in the papers weren't just savaging Fatty Arbuckle—they were savaging the movies. Show business was being denied bail. Maybe Hollywood was so wicked, Buster wrote in a letter, it needed a 300-pound Jesus to die for its sins.

Which explains why, before the cell door was even locked, steps were being taken by my superiors 500 miles away. Afraid the lynch mob would come for them, these pillars of the industry formed their own mob and lynched me first. Just to show their hearts were in the right place. To show that, damn it, they were clean livers, too . . .

Not that I knew any of this then. Mostly, during my time in stir, what I was really trying to figure out was how I could get my hands on a drink.

Before I even picked up my state-issued towel and toothbrush, my good friend Sid Grauman pulled *Gasoline Gus* from his premiere venue, the Million Dollar Theatre, down on Broadway in Los Angeles. By Sunday, the "witnesses" that District Attorney Matthew Brady and his assistants had rounded up were already cooking up the stew Brady wanted.

Fred Fischbach started off by telling the DA's office he was not a drinking man. So right off, thanks to my friend Fred's testimony, *I* was the lawbreaker, for breaking the Volstead Act, Fred having forgotten that he's the one who knew the bootlegger's number. Then a chambermaid confessed to hearing Virginia scream "Oh God, please don't!" through the door. After the maid, Zey Prevon and Alice Blake both claimed they'd seen me take Virginia in my room, that I "had" her for a half hour or so, during which the screams were terrifying. When I emerged, the budding starlet was crushed, and I was a sweating, grunting monster.

Just talking about this makes me go clammy. Shame you feel for no reason is excruciating. Shame you feel because people are inventing reasons that don't exist—that makes "excruciating" a feeling you remember fondly. Knowing some of these are people you used to quaintly call "friends"? Forget it. Excruciation is five flights up from being accused—and knowing your near and dear believe what you're accused of. I know I've said this already, but so what? Go through what I went through and see if you don't get a little repeaty. Repeaty's the best thing you're going to get.

Pathé Cashes In

I don't think Virginia Rappe's body was cool before Henry Lehrman hit the headlines. As far as I could tell his career of late consisted of sitting at Tony Roma's on 49th and squawking about the injustice Hollywood had dealt him. A major director-ial talent, bum-rushed from the industry . . .

When word got out I'd sex-murdered Virginia, Henry used the event to crawl back into the limelight. Buster, who'd actually read a book, gave me a good one from Jonathan Swift when he heard about Lehrman: "Crawling is performed in the same position as climbing." Never mind that Henry'd called his beloved a drunken nympho in front of the studio medical staff. Never mind that he dumped her and hightailed it east when he heard his betrothed had gotten pregnant. He didn't just dump her, either, according to Minta; he took all the jewels he'd given her back, and some he hadn't given her.

Now "Pathé" was playing the role of wronged romantic. His honor was at stake! From his perch in Manhattan, he used his fiancée's calamity to eviscerate me. To get even, I guess, for being shoved out of Keystone by Chaplin and me. Come to think of it, I'm surprised Henry didn't crawl out of the cobwebs to claim the 16-year-old Charlie married as *his* "beloved." Except, of course, it would have implied Henry'd had her when she was 15. Which might impugn—a new word I picked up in the trial coverage—his credibility. Say what you will, getting tried for murder is a real vocabulary builder. Mama taught me to look for the silver lining.

Henry's photo was now popping up in the *New York Times*, in what looked like rented hair. You learn to spot a toupee after 10 years in the theater. Lehrman was claiming he could not come west to view Virginia's body because he'd have to kill me! I wondered if he had trouble keeping a straight face, discussing his virginal, sweet-natured beauty. Don't get me wrong—I was sorry Virginia died. And I feel bad for her family, assuming she had any. But, come on! They should have interviewed the crabs she gave the crew at Keystone. Though Brady would have probably strong-armed them like he did all the other witnesses. *"Shut up or I'll fumigate ya, ya little bloodsuckers!"*

I just realized that I haven't mentioned Matthew Brady's problem. See, two years ago he beat the incumbent DA, a fellow named Fickert, by criticizing Fickert's ho-hum record in prosecuting big-time criminals. Since taking office, though, he hadn't done much.

More than anything, the San Francisco DA wanted to snag the governor's seat, so when Maude Delmont waltzed into his office with her St. Francis fairy tale it was like God said, "Here, Matty me boy, a gift from political-hack heaven!"

Clapping the biggest comedian in the country in shackles, convicting him of the city's biggest crime, would make Brady famous, beloved, and bulletproof. It would also make the public forget the two years he did absolutely nothing.

There was a problem, however. Even before the trial started, word leaked out that Maude was packing a rap sheet longer than Al Capone's. She was, among other things, a grifter, panderer, and blackmailer with a string of aliases from Rothberg to Montez. For some reason she always kept the same first name. When not busy corset-modeling, the enterprising Miss Delmont-Rothberg-Montez spent her free time being convicted for fraud and racketeering. And there was still a warrant out for a bigamy charge. She was a busy woman.

Testament to his skill at chicanery, Brady managed to keep his star witness from testifying before the Grand Jury. As far as the good people of San Francisco were concerned, Maude Delmont's word was gold. When it came to the Coroner's Jury, convened to determine cause of death, Brady pulled off another hat trick. The coroner apparently agreed with the esteemed Dr. Rumwell that the cause of Virginia's untimely demise was peritonitis, due to a crushed bladder, along with a smorgasbord of other fat-man-inflicted internal injuries.

The niggling detail Brady successfully suppressed: Rumwell had not only performed an illegal autopsy, but removed Virginia's internal organs and disposed of them. In return for Brady letting the Wakefield Sanitarium stay in the abortion business, all its director, Doc Rumwell, had to do was not mention that he'd just given Virginia Rappe an abortion—and tried to hide it by slicing out her parts. Something he was understandably happy to do.

I almost wished my own attorney had not seen fit to tell me these details. It drove me crazy, sitting there for an entire trial, knowing the one fact that could spare me was not going to be mentioned: *Virginia Rappe would have died anyway.* With or without coming to my party. She'd been fatally penetrated before our paths ever crossed.

But I'm leapfrogging again. Barkeep, a shot of lead and a bicarbonate of soda.

Fatty Behind Bars

Thank God I knew how to juggle. Every time one of the inmates tried to sneak up and steal my shoes—handmade, ostrich and soft leather—I'd grab three of whatever was handy and start throwing them in the air. One time I even punched myself in the head, which had my fellow reprobates roaring. I'd played to harder crowds in Tucson.

Despite the DA's edict to the contrary, Dominguez pulled enough strings to get himself into the jail for a meeting. We used a laundry room, which smelled about like I did after 36 hours in the same socks and boxers. Checking the door to see if we were monitored, Dominguez laid out the abortion situation. Maybe I *was* a little cheered to hear about Virginia's illegal surgery. I'm not without feeling, but it now seemed clear that she walked into the St. Francis a dead woman, victim of Rumwell's butchery.

Again and again I wanted to know why we couldn't use the abortion info in court. "Because," my good Catholic lawyer kept explaining, "we bring up the girl's misfortunes—shame a dead girl publicly—it makes us look heartless, like we're exploiting her. We'd lose whatever sympathy we got."

"B-but . . . but it's *true!*" I could hear myself sputter, trying to keep from tearing open the two Baby Ruths Dominguez had smuggled past the guards. I'd have preferred a couple of short dogs, but the warden frowned on that.

"Doesn't matter, Roscoe." Dominguez was a patient man. "They already think you're a brute. You go with she-just-had-an-abortion as your defense, it's gonna make you sound more brutal. If Virginia was pregnant, then that means you murdered a girl in *a family way!*"

"But that proves I *didn't* murder her!" My brain felt like a jar full of flies.

"Defense has a different strategy," Dominguez shrugged.

"And what's that?"

But just then the warden broke in and said it was time to wrap things up. "This ain't a rooming house for famous blubber-guts," he cackled, yukking it up at his own joke. Everybody was a comedian.

Except, at this point, me.

Zombie Wisdom

Let me admit something right here. I marched through the days after my arrest—through all three trials, actually—like Ten-Carat Carmichael in *Zombie Island*. I think that was his name. Maybe it was Two-Carat Louie. At this point, I can't remember Jack, so don't hold me to it if I'm wrong. (What are you going to do, throw me in Fact Jail?) I never had much truck for zombie pics. But now I understood 'em better: zombies were people whose lives had gotten so agonizing, the only way to keep living was to ape the dead. As the days wore on, each one bringing more had news, more stinging displays of public hate, I continued to walk and talk but inside I was numb. I was a junior zombie, waiting for his wings.

Speaking of zombies, I'd like to thank the safecrackers who gave me moonshine my second night in stir. You want to get zombified, jailhouse hooch is your ticket. The prune-juice-and-paint-thinner left me fairly ding-dong the next morning, but I was almost glad of the hangover. Compared to the pain and sadness, the betrayal and surprise and flat-out scared-dripless insanity of what was happening, a pruno headache was pleasant—like a neighbor you never liked, but are glad to bump into in Siberia.

Since my rearrival in San Francisco, after all, I'd suffered a nonstop stream of awfulness. A Venom Marathon. The only time people opened their mouths to me, it was to say something hellacious. I'd hardly ever heard the word "pervert" before; now people shouted it in my face. Even some inmates shunned me. A guy who'd flim-flammed widows out of their pension money actually called *me* scum. Worse than the insults, though, was having to listen to the list of heinous new developments.

"Fatty, you hear about them cowpokes up in Wyoming? 'Bout 150 of 'em, in a town called Thermopolis, busted into the movie

house and shot up the screen where one of your films was playing." This from the same malicious screw who slipped me news that the MPTO, Motion Picture Theater Owners of Southern California, had banned my movies, from now until Jesus Christ came back in a gas mask and Panama hat.

In the midst of it all, I did have one chuckle. An Irish rummy in my cell realized I was famous, but was too soused to figure exactly what I did to get that way. "You're Leroy Haynes, aintcha!" he kept saying. "Boy who sat on a flagpole for 18 days in Denver?" The other fellows had a guffaw over that. Imagine my meat wagon fitting on top of a flagpole for two minutes, let alone a record-breaking two and a half weeks.

It really hurt that nobody came to see me in jail but my lawyer. I didn't know Zukor and Lasky had talked to the other studio heads, that they'd issued a decree forbidding any actor from visiting. *I* may have been done for, but they were gonna make damn sure no other talent brought down the wrath of Hollywood haters by taking my side. Not knowing this, all I could figure was the obvious. Everybody in the known universe thought I did it. Cheery thought.

Hell doesn't always wait for you to die before it invites you inside. Sometimes it wants your life above ground to get so bad you bang on the gates to get let in early.

Expect the Worst, You Won't Be Disappointed

I knew from the papers, and the ever-helpful guards, that my films had been pulled. And I'd gotten a telegram from Zukor saying I was in breach for pulling a no-show on *The Melancholy Spirit*. This way he could suspend my salary until the matter at hand was cleared up. But Dominguez and Cohen kept telling me that was just window dressing, part of a plan. At three in the morning, listening to the snores and Mommy-whines of the other prisoners, I'd think, *Maybe Zukor's plan is to keep me from spouting off about what a cesspool of drugs and debauchery Paramount and Famous Players–Lasky are . . . Maybe my own lawyers aren't on my side . . . Maybe they're getting pressure from Zukor and Lasky*. But presure to do what? Then, just so I could let myself sleep, I'd entertain the zaniest thought of all: *Maybe Zukor and company are actually men of honor. Maybe those boys will come to the aid of a friend and colleague who's made them all more rich and powerful than they were when we met . . .*

I just had to believe. 'Cause, like I said, deep down I'm just a wide-eyed optimist.

Mostly, I confess, I just wasn't used to accommodating such weighty matters between my ears. The constant fretting and figuring blew some fuse in my brainpan. Shorted me out. Take it from me, being thrown in jail is almost more than your mind can accommodate. See, it's not where you are that's so disorienting. It's where you're *not*.

Namely, in your own life.

Your home, your work, the view out your back door—all the things you never even think about, they're gone. You're now *in another* life. Another world you didn't even know existed, let alone see coming. If this happens to you, get ready. The suddenness of the drop from movie star to slammer—from the planet you take for granted to one you never imagined—will give anyone the bends.

Absorbing the shock of what was happening to my body was

ordeal enough. The damp, the cold, the grubs in the oatmeal. Grasping the savagery being done to my name and my career was more than I could begin to contemplate.

I'd be lying if I said I remembered the chronological details of this period. You don't remember the chronology of an earthquake—you remember flashes, moments, random heart-grabbing impressions. The time between and during my trials is a jagged blur: endless minutes and weeks when just walking into a diner or stepping out of a car in front of the courtroom was like having your skin flayed. Reporters, haters, baiters, more reporters, and always the police. Brady kept me surrounded by cops, so it looked like I was Public Enemy Number One—someone from whom the God-fearing citizens of his decent city required protection.

The days and nights bleed together like eggs cracked over a skillet. Still, even in my haze during that first week of confinement, I was aware enough to know Dominguez was killing me by not letting me tell my story. The shame and terror were still novelties then. So I remember my shock, my sense that Brady—this will sound so corny—*was not playing fair!* Every other word out of the DA's mouth at the deposition was "murder." All I could do was listen and try not to fly out of my chair and pound my fists on the floor when he said it.

The whole strategy felt wrong—but everything was so wrong I thought I had to let my lawyer tell me what to do. Dominguez was hanging everything on getting Maude Delmont in front of the grand jury. He kept saying that's how we were going to get her. The problem was, Brady finessed him every time, going so far as to insist that the subject of "forced and violent intercourse" was not one on which any lady should be asked to ruminate, let alone one as refined and delicate as Maude Delmont.

Even with my bug-juice hangover, I almost laughed. If the wannabe governor had seen Lady Maude gallivanting in Lowell Sherman's unbuttoned pajamas, he might have had to rethink his notion of "refined."

Here's something else from the early days of my damnation. Have I told you about the warden yet? Listen to this. The man was a Bible-reading teetotaler in a string tie who told me he hated my "kind" and poked me in the stomach with a shoehorn the first time we met. "Your type are ruining this country, but not for long!"

"My type?" I managed to ask him. "You mean fat guys?"

"*Owff!*" Another poke with that ivory shoehorn.

I'd wondered why the goons who marched me up to the Warden's office shoved me so far forward I almost butted heads with the guy. Now I understood. He wanted the screws to drag me into shoehorn range.

After he jabbed me in the breadbasket, the warden snickered. "Whatever you were out there, Two-Ton, in here rat turds got more value than you."

Every few hours, for my entire state vacation, the warden visited my cell, popping his waxy face between the bars to remind me that no one was coming to my defense. That I was the most hated man since the Kaiser. Warden Meers is the one who told me about Grauman. When Zukor and Lasky announced that the studio was suspending my salary, pending the outcome of my trial, the warden cackled at that, too. "See, you get in a Jew business, you're going to get jewed."

The esteemed warden took great delight in showing up with a folded newspaper, key passages circled carefully in red ink. I thought he might keel over from delight the day he told me I'd been condemned by the League of Nations. Seems the ambassadors were gathered in Geneva to discuss the White-Slave traffic, and the Danish delegate declared that Fatty's party contributed to a steep rise in the business of sex. On top of everything else, I was now banned in Switzerland, Denmark, and England. The French, on the other hand, ordered more prints of my movies.

In between the international news, the Warden reeled off all those juicy quotations from Lehrman. Who'd have expected to see Pathé's pointy kisser on anything but a mug shot? But there it was, slapped on front pages from Bangor to San Berdoo. I was in the prison barbershop receiving my regulation snippage when Meers pushed his way in between two Dempsey-sized bulls and told me he had something I'd want to hear.

The barber kept trimming, for which I was unaccountably grateful. But I can still smell the Warden's rancid aftershave. In close quarters he gave off the scent of lavender soaked in bacon grease.

If I close my eyes, I can still hear the Warden's reedy, wheedling voice—not unlike my old man's—as he held his bifocals over the page and read to me from Lehrman's rant: "*For a year and a half I was Arbuckle's director. He is merely a beast. He made a boast to me that he had torn the clothing from a girl who sought to repulse his attentions. This is what results from making idols and millionaires out of people that you take from the gutter. Arbuckle was a spittoon cleaner in a barroom when he came into the movies.*" Here the Warden looked up from his dramatic reading, smiled, then resumed, savoring Lehrman's last sentence: "*I would kill him if I had the chance.*" He smiled with glee. "Well, *he* won't get to do it, Fatty boy, but I will. Your fat ass is gonna get the gas."

"After five days of jail food, my ass already has gas," I responded, and let loose a clapping fart that just happened to be sitting idle in my guts, waiting for the go-ahead. The Warden was so shocked he dropped his bifocals. But the convict barber laughed and I told him to resume his ministrations. It probably wasn't the wisest move: cracking wise and risking the wrath of the man who had my life—not to mention my bodily comforts—in his hands. But nature provided the punch line, and I used it.

By way of retaliation, the Warden produced yet another newspaper, and recited a list of cities: "Fresno, Memphis, Toledo, Medford, Massachusetts, Pittsburgh, Butte, Montana, Des Moines . . ." And so on. He then proceeded to tell me that these were cities whose theaters had canceled my films. *Gasoline Gus* was pulled at once. And my next one, *Crazy to Marry*, was canceled while it was still in the can.

"The thing's been snuffed," I replied, without thinking. "Snuffed as surely as the demon child Virginia was carrying after the butchers at Wakefield Sanitarium got to it."

I occasionally get dramatic when nervous, and this was one of those times. A doughy vein in the Warden's temple swelled up so fast I thought he was going to have a stroke. "That is beneath despicable," he hissed at me. "To slander a dead girl that way!" Which half-convinced me Dominguez was right about not announcing the event to a jury. But only half.

On account of my wrists were too thick for regular handcuffs, I was late getting to the arraignment on September 16. When Police Chief O'Brien apprised Brady of the situation, Brady was livid. He screamed through the telephone that he wanted "that bastard restrained" if they had to hogtie me and roll me up the courthouse steps in a wheelbarrow.

By the time I picked a pair of leg shackles off the table and snapped them on my own wrists—"Anything else I can do to help, fellas? You want me to drive?"—the forces of good were already marshaled at Superior Court.

Members of the frothy-lipped San Francisco Women's Vigilante Group crowded the sidewalk. None of the 250 females on hand were shy about expressing their desire that I pay with my wretched life for my treachery. Thanks to Zukor and Lasky's order that no one from the studio show any public support for me whatsoever, no pro-Arbuckle brigade was there to counter my henhouse of detractors. I was alone.

Trials and Permutations

On the suggestion of my second attorney, Milton Cohen—again supplied by the studio on condition they not be linked—Minta was induced to brave the pack of reporters camped outside her apartment and make her way to Grand Central for the train to Frisco. Importing Minta was a gamble. Her presence at my side would look good to a jury of married people. But it would be disastrous if some roving reporter had the chance to ask why she kept a residence in Manhattan while her husband resided in California.

The sea of hateful ladies reserved their special wrath for Minta. This was painful to observe. One young harridan pulled out a harmonica, accompanying a scarecrow I presume was her mother through "Carry Me Back to Old Virginny." The other women picked up the tune. I wanted to die for my poor wife. She bore herself with stoic dignity as the police parted the crush of females before us like Moses dividing the Red Sea. But I knew enough about Minta's face to know the set of her jaw meant she was squeezing back tears, fighting them off with every shred of strength she had.

Inside the court, I felt my mind career in and out of awareness.

One second I was watching Matthew Brady preen with his thumbs tucked in his vest like a bantam rooster, the next I was back in Kansas, jerking awake when Daddy urinated on my head, as he was wont to do when the amount of beer he'd gulped caught up to the amount of hate available for release. I juked back to consciousness when Holy Ladies began standing on their chairs and chanting "KILLER! KILLER! KILLER!" I turned around to see how Minta was taking this. Oddly, she looked almost happy. She said she was glad I needed her.

Judge Shortfall banged his gavel and declared that the trial would commence in November. Then I tapped Dominguez on the arm. What was I being tried for? The attorney just mopped a handkerchief across his brow and shook his head.

"I asked to dismiss all the charges, Roscoe, but two old ladies wanted you hung. Rape and murder have been dropped down to manslaughter."

It's hard to fathom a planet where being wrongly accused of manslaughter is cause for celebration. And yet I seemed to be living on one.

For this break—and please forgive the digression—I always meant to thank Jim Richardson, a newshound with the *Evening Herald*. Richardson, with a judicious combination of skill and martinis, had gotten Maude Delmont to brag that not only did she plan on changing her testimony, but, and I quote, "it's going to help the prosecution, you can be sure of that!" This was pretty much gold for the defense. Brady declared a conspiracy by the studios—which, as it turned out, could have been my defense. As if anything the studios did could explain Maude Delmont. The jurors all wanted to let me go, except, as mentioned, for the two church secretaries who wouldn't sleep again until I was neutered.

For $5,000 in bail—which Schenck produced on condition it

not be announced that Paramount contributed in any way—I was free until the start of the trial in November.

Manslaughtered

If I had any doubts left as to why I'd become a prize pariah, the first paper I bought back in Union Station helped remind me. I tipped the newsie a five-spot and he looked at me like the world had gone purple.

The screaming headline said it all: FLESHPOTS OF BABYLON! Then came the good word from Reverend Bob Shuler of Trinity Methodist Church in downtown Los Angeles. Reverend Bob declared "the death of poor Virginia was God's way of waking America up!" The Almighty was saying that it was high time to end the moral decay of show business. Here's the line burned into my brain for all time: "Movies, dancing, jazz, evolution, Jews and Catholics are all destroying this fine nation."

The article left no doubt that movies and Jews were the worst. And I was but their monstrous tool. I, Roscoe Arbuckle, had gone from humble slap-and-tumble man to Tool of the Hebrews.

Los Angeles Greeting

The longest minutes of my life were spent wading through those legions of God's Army assembled outside the train station to shout my damnation. It was one thing in San Francisco, where hatred of all things Los Angeles is the perpetual *plat de jour*. But in my own town! Even though I'd seen the headlines I hadn't expected it. Somehow—and I know how nuts this must sound—the headlines seemed like props. No more real than a breakaway dinner chair. But that sensation was shattered fast. There was no escaping the massed wrath of the folks who turned out to curse me. Not when they were staring me in the face, screaming that I should die, waving banners calling for this portly lad from Kansas to be lynched, axed, castrated, or gassed. Maybe all at once.

More of these hate fans were lined up on Adams Boulevard, outside my house. A curious thing—at first glance they bore no discernible difference from the devoted who once showed up because they loved me. The reason they looked the same, it finally occurred to me, is that they were. Their expressions were different—rageful instead of delighted—but that was all. "The sad part is," Minta remarked, when Okie had to step out of the Pierce-Arrow and clear them bodily off the driveway, "if they hadn't loved you so much before, they wouldn't hate you so much now."

No time to mull on love gone wrong, though. We'd arrived right in time to meet a phalanx of deputies from the L.A. Sheriff's Department. Call me sentimental, I was beginning to feel lonely without men in uniform around. The burly sheriffs were doing double duty as furniture removers. A line of them were busy removing couches, tables, chairs, doilies, and anything else not nailed down and worth more than a nickel from inside my house. Or what I, nostalgically, continued to refer to as my house.

My mug must have looked particularly hangdog when the policeman-in-chief approached me with a bill of lading. "Sorry, Fatty, says here you owe the, uh, California Furniture Company $6,500." A Boggsy loveseat happened by us at that moment, followed by a satin couch and a pair of lounge chairs. "That's all right, Officer," I managed to chuckle, "all the stuff gives me backaches anyway."

"You got heart, I'll give you that," the top cop said to me. This may have been my proudest moment. If Daddy was watching from purgatory, at least he couldn't say I whined.

The next weeks were spent consolidating whatever assets I had, scraping up money to wage a legal defense, and trying not to think of what would happen if the trial went on more than a week and a half. After that, I'd have to find lawyers who didn't mind being paid in old suits and shoes.

Right off I cashed in my shares of Comique. Keaton's Metro shorts were produced there, so that brought some moola. Then I unloaded the Vernon Tigers. They'd been on a losing streak, anyway.

Domestic Derangements

Besides finances, there remained a more delicate matter: Minta. She and I had not lived together in a while—yet here we were, man and wife, reunited under one roof. We decided on separate bedrooms without really discussing it. I appreciated her coming back, but at the same time the way she kept talking to me—"I don't care what you did to me, I forgive you"—made me almost wish I'd taken my chances going solo. She was happy to be needed, like she said. That, or she was anxious not to pass up a chance to rub my nose in what a "bottom-heavy bastard" (her words) I was for ending our marriage. For banishing a selfless specimen like her to Manhattan while I sashayed around neck-deep in debt and splendor on West Adams.

Oddly, Minta never asked me if I did the deed with Miss

Rappe. A state of affairs I found alternately gratifying and eerie. Mind you, I still loved the woman. (Minta, not Virginia.) Even now, I have nothing bad to say about the Durfees' baby daughter. These were just stranger-than-strange times, so the usual strains were, you might say, amplified.

Sometimes, when Buster, Bebe Daniels, or Mabel dropped by—they were the only ones uncowed by Zukor's keep-away commandment—we'd find the most horrific headlines and read them out loud. Buster's favorite was a Hearst sidebar in the *Examiner* claiming that I had actually held "dog weddings" on my property. The tone of the piece lent the whole activity an unsavory implication, as if, somehow, dog nuptials were one rung up the Heinous Behavior Ladder from bestiality. A fact duly noted by Buster. "You don't read too careful, devil-boy, they make it sound like you're bangin' poodles."

Once my blood was in the water, tabloid-wise, no evidence of my depravity was too far-fetched. Four-legged romance was the least of it. In truth, the dog-wedding gag had its origin in some two-reeler I can't even remember. Luke took a bride, a saucy little schnauzer, which made for a moment or two of comic business. Maybe we rehearsed it a couple of times at a party. Did that make me a pagan? "*Caninus Foulupalus Disgustus Nono*," Buster intoned dolorously. Translating, in his trademark deadpan mode: "There is none more foul than he who stages dog weddings in his driveway." It was funny, but the laughter always rang a bit hollow during these visits. It was like trying to enjoy the coffee cake at a wake. You can't really savor a single bite, because someone has died.

Not even madcap Mabel could counter the air of doom. Gone were the days of fun and frolic. On her last visit, the once-vivacious beauty was so toasted on coke that all she did was babble about some one-legged jockey she claimed was her latest paramour. Pretty soon her babbling turned manic. She began laughing and sobbing at the same time. We had to hold her down and ply her with brandy. I still had a stash in the trunk of my Model T, the one car the feds hadn't towed. Nothing else could stop her from chatting to the shrubs all night. With all those reporters staked out, there's no telling what Hearst would have made of Mabel's rantings.

Most evenings, during that pretrial madness, it was just Minta and me. After another day of scrambling for cash to cover my legal bills, we'd have some newspapers delivered and size up the day's damage. Leaving the house, by now, was out of the question. Holding each other on my bed—hers we hocked, along with everything else—we'd take turns perusing the newest twist in my public dismemberment. Minta tried to act like we were generals manning strategy as the battle waged, but that never lasted. We were both so scared I think we had no choice but to hold on to each other. I was in this alone, and she had chosen to come to me, at considerable cost to her own career on the New York stage—and, let's face it, to her reputation.

People threw stones at the house at all hours. When we did have to go somewhere, getting from driveway to street involved a gauntlet of screaming, hate-crazed lunatics convinced that I was the source of evil, lust, and ungodly behavior in Christian America. At first I would just stare straight ahead. Once the abuse became routine, I took to finding the most livid maniac and staring at them full-on—a move which, for reasons I myself am helpless to explain, would silence even the most shrill and violent.

What I'm about to tell you sounds straight out of a two-reeler in Hades. You see, only in this crisis, gripped by the most hopeless, incomprehensible despair you can imagine, when our future together seemed so bleak Minta and I felt like trench-bound soldiers, blinking out at No-Man's-Land as the haze of gas drifts slowly towards them . . . only when we both felt absolutely *doomed*, was I finally able to perform. *To be a husband.*

Imagine! What if you knew, every morning of your life, that something horrible was going to happen that day? Or no—that something horrible had already happened, and it was only going to get worse?

This was a perfect description of my post-Virginia existence. Yet this is when "it" happened. Slandered daily in the press, attacked in public, shunned by friends, drummed out of the profession I loved, and awaiting a future so tainted it promised to be worse than today—which is saying something—only in the midst of this nightmare was I able to accomplish, with Minta, what I never could when life was a dream.

Strange but true, ladies and jugglers. In the good times, the act was like trying to push linguine through a keyhole. Success gave me plenty. But ruin left us with something those drunk and famous days had denied us. Each other.

PART 7

Purgatory

SORRY IF I'M getting windy here, but I feel—how can I say this?—*immodest* even talking about these things. Only I have to, darn it! Because this is what saved my life. Temporarily, at least. See, it took falling through the trap door—from legend to leper—to let me be a man. If Freud's couch was wide enough, I'd have liked to hop on and hear what the old coker had to say on the subject. Call it the silver lining. Sort of. All that public humiliation made fears of any private humiliation downright niggling. Which meant I could finally relax. From abjection, erection. Once in a while, anyway. I didn't have to be anything for anybody. That was over. The Fatty star had fallen out of the firmament, hauled off with the other props of a show that closed fast in the middle of a good run. All that was left now was me. A stripped-down, ham-cheeked, got-nothin', got-nothin'-comin' hoo-boy any woman would have to be crazy—or crazy in love—to be with.

The night I achieved the miracle of coitus with Minta stone cold sober, the mailman had brought a note from the government. More good news! The IRS had hit me with another 100 G's in back taxes.

It was my lucky day. "I don't know what else can they can do," I told Minta. "I feel like Job!" She was in her nightie, and I was resting my head in her lap. Minta shifted a little and repositioned herself. "Well, I bet I know what kept Job going," she giggled. The joy in that *giggle*. How long had it been since I'd felt joy? Then she batted her lashes in a way she hadn't done since our early days on the Long Beach Pier, outside the Bide-A-Wee.

We had just retired to the bedroom. After dark we always went upstairs, since reporters would sneak right up to the first-floor windows and try to peek in or take pictures. At least upstairs you could hear the ladders hit the house, if they were trying to get a shot of you—or just shoot you. Minta's room still had a plush Persian carpet on the floor. Luke had ripped a hole in it, so it wasn't worth much.

There we were, on the floor, my head on her little thigh. When suddenly, like I'd gotten a shot of he-man serum, I found myself wanting her like I'd never wanted anything. Even lunch. It was almost frightening. I was scared to do anything—how could she possibly want me? How could anybody? Then, in spite of myself, I kissed her. To my surprise Minta kissed me back. Pretty soon she was ripping her unmentionables off. Even then, I couldn't help but think to myself: *Thank God she's not screaming and bleeding!* Couldn't help but remember Virginia peeling off *her* chemise like it was made of burning rags.

As Minta and I kissed, a rock smashed the gable window of her bedroom. The hole in the glass let the voices outside rush in even louder. Cries of "Satan!" "Jew-lover!" and "Rapist!" echoed from the mob. But what should have distressed me somehow goaded me on instead. At last—with "Fatty, you monster, you deserve to die" ringing in my ears—I began to experience that mystery known to most but, up till then, more or less foreign to me.

And after that—I will go into no detail, except to say, when it was over, Minta and I were at last man and wife. I was careful to settle my bulk alongside, as opposed to on top of, her. (I could already imagine *that* headline: FATTY ARBUCKLE BREAKS WIFE'S RIBS IN LUST-CRAZED FRENZY!) It still warms me to recall how Minta snuggled her tiny body into mine under our old Navajo blanket.

McNab to the Rescue

A couple of weeks before going back to court, Joe Schenck dropped by to say Zukor was kicking in 50 grand to hire another lawyer. "It's only because you got some films in the can," Schenck confided, shaking his head over the lox and bagels he brought. Schenck preferred to eat when he talked. And I was happy for the food. "The good news is you're back on the payroll," Joe said, licking a shmear of cream cheese off his pinky.

I nearly spit my lox out on the card table. "You mean I can work again?"

"Not exactly," Joe sighed. "You're on the payroll so he can garnish your pay and use it toward the legal bills. That way it's a tax writeoff."

I nearly smiled. Leave it to Adolph to find a way to help you and screw you at the same time.

Schenck also wanted to let me know how he'd tried to get Clarence Darrow to defend me. He was proud about that one. But Darrow was busy defending himself against charges of jury tampering. So instead Joe roped in Gavin McNab, the sheister who smoothed out Mary Pickford's divorce from Owen Moore so she could marry Douglas Fairbanks. McNab hailed from Frisco. He had friends there—a big help defusing the San Francisco–Los Angeles hate party now raging full-tilt. Dominguez, whose say-nothing strategy blew up, had fired himself.

The first thing McNab and his team did was start digging up the real Virginia. Not that anybody was surprised to find out she wasn't a choir girl. Choir girls didn't usually require fumigation. But the facts McNab's man unearthed in Chicago, her hometown, were as sad as they were shocking. My alleged victim had endured a handful of abortions, along with a battery of treatments for chronic cystitis, all due to her penchant for copious intercourse. A nice lady who ran a home for unwed mothers confirmed that Miss Rappe had been a frequent visitor—dropping by five times for treatment of venereal warts alone. Which, as McNab described it in his first phone call, put her in line for some kind of Venereal Wart Olympic record. Where was Guinness when you needed him?

But there's more. While nude modeling, Virginia met a sculptor by the name of Sample who proposed to her, then threw himself off his roof a week later and died. After that she moved in with a one-armed dress manufacturer named Robert Muscovitz. Poor Muscovitz "fell" in front of a trolley car and expired shortly thereafter, in the Granada Sanitarium.

Then Virginia turned 18.

If her juvenile résumé wasn't damning enough, there was some scuttlebutt that, prior to her illustrious career as bit player in Henry Lehrman epics, she'd worked for her family's business in Los Angeles—as a prostitute in a whorehouse run by her mother.

When Minta heard all this she said she felt sorry for the girl. I'm generally inclined to compassion myself, but in Virginia's case I found it tough sledding. Did I mention that her funeral, at

St. Stephen's Episcopalian in East Hollywood, attracted 8,000 panting strangers? Unknown in life, Virginia attained a brief spate of stardom after her demise. Ever noble, the studios made sure the three or four movies in which Miss Rappe's sloe-eyed gaze graced the screen were rereleased. Maybe, I told Buster, if all else fails, I could arrange for agents to pay me to look suspicious when a client dies. Anybody the public thinks I killed was bound to be box office gold.

Slander

While McNab and company were busy digging up dirt on dead Virginia, Maude, Rumwell, and the rest of them, Brady pressed his compadres to the south to clamp down in Los Angeles. Arrests for lewd and immoral behavior, and prostitution in particular, suddenly skyrocketed. And I was to blame. The degenerate reputation of my hometown was surely as big a factor in my trial as the doctored photos Randolph Hearst had begun to run. The most appalling of these depicted your friend Fatty, looking lewd and greasy-lipped, guzzling a bottle of bug juice over the nightie-clad, pure-as-the-driven-snow figure of the virgin Virginia. If one reader in the country still had doubts, that picture would convince them I'd done what they said I'd done—and probably worse.

I've saved this happy concoction from Page One of the *Examiner*, which just happened to hit the stands the day of Virginia's funeral. I keep it folded in my wallet. Fake calfskin, thanks for asking. Somehow, until I read this I really didn't know what I was up against. Somehow, in spite of myself, I could not stop believing that the truth still meant something.

I know, I'm an idiot. But I saw the paper and my pants went damp. Listen: *"Would not this dead girl now, whose every impulse is said to have been wholesome and kindly, whose life is said to have been given to defend her honor, would she not feel that her life and death had not been in vain if those who read her story would be influenced to saner, simpler living, would see as she saw at the end how futile it is to seek gaiety and pleasure which are not 'within the law'?"*

Be still my heart. The sheer size of the lie was staggering. But no lie was too big for Randolph Hearst! That was the secret of his success. The truth was, McNab had proof that Rumwell had left a nurse's finding of "severe alcoholic poisoning" off his death report. But, just to really help me sleep at night, my lawyer let slip that they—as in Zukor and Lasky—did not want to press the good doctor too hard on this point, on account of he'd done some "work" for Paramount.

"What kind of work?" your friendly bumpkin asked.

"What kind do you think?" McNab snapped. "Rumwell performed abortions on a couple of stars, and the last thing the studio needs is him blabbing about it. The public's already itching to dig a big pit, throw Hollywood in, and burn it till there's nothing left but false teeth and mascara ash." McNab was a colorful man with a phrase.

Of course, if Rumwell *did* list alcohol poisoning as a contributing factor, that raised another hoary beast. Who supplied the hooch? Fischbach, now playing teetotaler, wanted the authorities to know that the illegal drinks were Mr. Arbuckle's idea. McNab spotted my reaction to that whopper. After some prodding, I admitted that it was Fischbach who provided the antifreeze—but under no circumstances was I going to rat him out. The way I looked at it, if Fred cooked up that story, it's because he had to. This may sound simpy after what he did to me, but deep down I knew Fred wasn't a bad guy. He just had gambling debts.

"Yeah, I know all about those *debts*," McNab scoffed. He always liked to let you know he was two steps ahead of you. "Lehrman paid them off."

That was news. Turns out Fishbach had lost a bundle at the track, and Lehrman offered to pay him if he'd take a trip to San Francisco and "check up" on Virginia. Apparently Henry'd met a rich debutante at the Waldorf he wanted to marry, but he had to make sure Miss Rappe was sufficiently blotto she wouldn't remember that he'd asked *her* to marry him first—and make a stink before Henry could get the deb to the altar. Fred was supposed to spy on Virginia and report back, but after he spent a little time with her, he came up with a different plan. Virginia had poor Fred's nose wide open. Or, as the ever highbrow Mack Sennett liked to say, "she gave him a midget leg."

So much info! So many backstories! Trying to follow it was like trying to juggle clawhammers and do geometry at the same time. All I knew, I told McNab, was that Fred Fischbach said he was coming to San Francisco to scout locations. "He wanted to find some seal pelt or something."

McNab gave a snort. "The only pelt he laid eyes on was Virginia's—right before she got delirious. Oh, and Fred didn't just say the liquor was your idea—he told the feds you supplied it, Tiny."

I didn't see how that mattered much, considering the rest of my calamities. In the grand scheme of personal betrayals, this one hardly registered. But it made the government perk right up.

Around lunchtime, October 7, the federales showed up again. Where's Pancho Villa when you need him? Minta and I were just walking in the Japanese garden when three agents in matching fedoras introduced themselves from behind a bamboo thicket. "Roscoe Arbuckle, we're here to inform you that you have been found to be in violation of the Volstead Act." Then they asked for $500, bail money, and I called Gavin McNab to see about getting it. He showed up in 40 minutes with Joe Schenck, who brought a bag of deli. After the feds left with half a grand, Joe, Gavin, and I sat down to smoked whitefish.

"Not good," Joe sighed, pulling bones out of his teeth. "Jury thinks you're a bootlegger on top of a rapist and murderer. Not good at all."

McNab picked at his fish like it had scabies. "You already owe 100 grand in back taxes. Violating the 18th Amendment is going to cost you another 50 long. And, just for the record, your friend Fred fingered you good." He showed me the transcript, obliging me to put down my kosher nourishment and read. Sure enough, Fred had declared that, being a law-abiding nonimbiber himself, he was shocked at the ease with which I had procured demon beverages. He even hinted that I was part of an underworld combine that shunted booze up from Tijuana to Frisco, along with bales of Mexican marijuana and "foreign painkillers."

"At least he left out white slavery," I quipped, to no one's amusement but my own.

Hearst kept expanding on the pills-and-maryjane angle. The *Examiner* even ran a "Police Insider" on the subject of my status as Drug Kingpin, fat-ass pasha of a ring that polluted the youth of California—"*quite possibly paving a path to prostitution and debauchery and death for angels like Virginia Rappe.*" That same afternoon I read a story in the *Times* describing the late Miss Rappe as "a descendant of Belgian royalty." Hearst had a genius for juicy libel, but his fake praise was just as amazing.

Either way, it no longer seemed strange to be sitting at a card table in an empty living room, kicking around the subject of my future on a municpal farm. When I said I still wouldn't fink on Fred, Joe waggled a pickle in my face and shouted, "Roscoe, you putz! You may be the nicest white man I ever met—but you're also the stupidest!"

Then Gavin clapped me on the back, hard enough to let me know he'd have liked to have hit me harder. "Use your thinker, buddy boy. Lehrman used Fischbach to set you up. Fischbach used you to keep Lehrman from knowing he gave Virginia a doggy bath. Maude Delmont's gonna get rich helping Diamond Matt Brady use you to get his butt in the governor's chair—*and you're telling me you won't say who gave you the damn booze?*"

McNab slammed the table for emphasis, then changed gears and rocked back on his chair. I was too frazzled to say any-thing—no doubt the exact effect my attorney wanted. Having achieved it, he smiled crookedly. "Speaking of damned booze . . ."

McNab mimed smacking his thin lips, and I explained that the feds had absconded with my liquor cabinet. He'd have to settle for ginger ale. "Just as well," he said, with no sincerity whatso-ever. "We have more work to do."

As Gavin and Schenck were leaving—having started to school me on matters of strategy, defense, and how not to look like a slob on the stand—Gavin turned and announced that I wasn't the only one with troubles. "This might cheer you up," he chirped from the doorway. By now I'd gotten used to standing to one side when the door was opened, to dodge photographers. "Your pal Lehrman's in a little hot water, too. He sent $1,100 worth of flowers to be placed on Virginia's casket. Now he's being sued by the florist for nonpayment. They won't find him, though."

Gavin liked to brag about dabbling in vaudeville as a youth, so I played straight man. "Why won't they find him, Mister?"

McNab beamed and rushed the punch line like an amateur. "Because—he's on his honeymoon!"

As a comedian he was a great lawyer.

Jury Performance

Being on trial for murder is just like appearing onstage—except that if the audience hates you, they don't throw tomatoes, they kill you. The IRS had already garnished the Pierce-Arrow, and my Model T was riding on axles, so I hitched a lift to Frisco with McNab. On the ride up he explained how he and Brady had already pored through 207 potential jurors to settle on 12. He said he was pretty happy about all of them. But when we stopped for coffee and sinkers at a Barstow diner, he dunked his cruller and confessed that he still had his doubts about one Mrs. Hubbard, a feisty old haybag he was certain had secret links to the DA.

I put down my milk shake, not sure I'd heard right. "Secret *links?* Then why let her on the jury?"

"Because!"

Then McNab shut up and—I'll never forget—swung his coffee-logged cruller from his cup to his mouth without losing a drop. I almost clapped. Whenever I tried that, I got a lapful of mush, and had to walk around with a sugar-glazed crotch till I could change pants.

"Because what?" I asked when he was done dunking.

"Because maybe we got a few ringers of our own the DA doesn't know about."

I could tell this was supposed to make him sound cagey. But all it did was make me more nervous than I was already. I was so upset I could barely finish my third milk shake.

Round Two

The first day of the retrial, on November 22, my attorney braced me on the way into the courtroom and said he had two words of advice: *Don't fiddle.*

He looked so solemn when he said this I tried to look solemn back. "Don't fiddle," I repeated, nodding my head. "I'm not sure I—"

"*Fiddle, fidget, fuss!*" McNab hissed, wiggling his fingers and darting his eyes around to show what he meant. "Remember, no matter who's on the stand, the jury's going to be staring at you. And if there's one principle of criminal law that's proved consistently true, it's this: juries respond unfavorably to fiddling. Death Row's full of fiddlers."

Before I could respond to this bit of wisdom, the courtroom doors swung open. I was flanked by two large uniforms, billy clubs at the ready, as though poised to protect the women of the jury in case I was feeling rapey.

An hour into the trial, I was no longer worried about fiddling. I worried about staying awake. The courtroom was hot and stuffy. It felt just like being in grade school in Santa Ana, except the boys all shaved. And I couldn't drop out.

The Assistant DA, a handsome fellow named Friedman, started his opening arguments by talking about Virginia's bladder. Then everybody started talking about it. In fact, for the first three days the attorneys did nothing *but* tangle over Virginia's bladder. Both sides trotted out a string of medicos like show ponies. Doctors Rumwell and Beardslee, Nurse Jamison, some other bonebreakers I forget. Each M.D. or doctor's helper was asked whether, in their professional opinion, the late Miss Rappe's pee pump was already badly damaged or it was Roscoe Arbuckle's savagery that so badly damaged it.

The day after the final bladderfest, Zey Prevon and Alice Blake were marched in to support Maude's story that I'd viciously attacked Virginia in a fit of drunken lust. Both starlets looked so stricken, even though what they were saying could have killed me, I found myself feeling terrible for them. Terrible that on account of me coming to San Francisco in the first place, they'd been made to show up looking hollow-eyed and telling lies.

Miss Delmont herself would not be present to testify. Brady wanted her story. He just didn't want her to tell it. So the DA kept Maude in jail on an old bigamy charge for the entire trial. Though that would not come out till later.

"Imagine a sweating beast," Friedman implored the jury, glaring my way with righteous disgust. He turned to aim a dewy-eyed photo of Virginia looking nunly at the jury, then pointed a well-manicured forefinger back again in my direction. "Imagine *this* enormous, sweating beast, in all his nakedness, throwing himself atop the innocent and fragile victim you see here. Imagine this outsized *actor* slaking his massive appetites on her tender frame."

After five minutes of this, I was almost ready to hang me myself. But it got worse. Guided by the swarthy Friedman, Zey recited the by-now-famous scenario: hearing screams in room 1219, she and Maude Delmont rushed in to find Virginia sprawled on the bed, "panting that she was dying, and pointing to HIM . . ."

With that damning word—that "HIM"—every head in the courtroom swiveled my way. I could feel their eyes on me like leeches, as Zey mimicked Virginia's dramatic moan. *"He hurt me! He hurt me inside!"*

Poor Zey, normally a sprightly girl, shook so much during her interrogation I thought springs were going to fly out of her ears. When Gavin grilled her, it became clear why. Under questioning she broke right down and admitted that she'd been held captive, a veritable prisoner, by the DA's staff. She'd been reprimanded, over and over, until she got her story straight. "What story would that be?" McNab wondered aloud. Shoulders heaving with sobs, Zey replied in a tiny voice, *"The one Mr. Brady wanted me to tell . . ."*

Well, you could have tossed mice in all the open mouths Zey's revelation inspired. When Alice Blake was called, McNab got her to admit that she, too, had been held against her will. And people's mouseholes fell open all over again.

Having dragged these admissions out of the prosecution's key witnesses, McNab puffed himself up. He addressed the jury with respect, but conviviality. Like you would a stranger you've said hello to at the bus stop for 20 years. "Personally, folks, I gotta tell you, I *like* the district attorney. I even *admire* him. And yet, as good citizens we have to ask, has Matthew Brady the right to take away the liberty of two girls that they might swear with him to take away the liberty of an innocent man?" Here he paused dramatically, as though overcome, then bravely soldiered on. "Is this not why we sent two million good men overseas, to put an end to this sort of thing?"

I'd been tutored for my own time on the stand, but after McNab's stellar performance I thought the prosecution was just going to give up. So when Friedman started to cross-examine me, his spewing tone and vile implications rattled me down to my curled toes. "Mr. *Arbuckle*—" he even made my name sound vaguely unsavory—"did you at any time hear Miss Rappe say, 'You hurt me'? Did you hear her say, 'Please stop!'? Were you in any condition to have heard her if she did say these things?"

"No—yes . . . no," I sputtered, not sure which question I was answering. Then I repeated the version of events that I'd worked out with McNab and Dominguez before him—which happened to be the truth. "Miss Rappe was sitting up and tearing at her clothes. She was frothing at the mouth. I saw her tear her waist. She had one sleeve almost off. She was prone to fits!"

Friedman stepped so close I could see the pores on his forehead. He wrinkled his nose, as though my nearness sickened him, and I could see the Black Forest in his nostrils. "Mr. Arbuckle," he sneered, "the fairy tale you just told the Court, would it surprise you to know that I have seven versions of the story, told to different people by you?"

"That's the true story," I said as calmly as I could. Busily not fiddling with every muscle in my body.

For a long time, Friedman stared at the ceiling. He made a show of straightening his tie, pursing his lips, placing his hands together briefly at his chest—no doubt to let us all know he was a praying man. I knew a thing or two about stage business, and had to grudgingly admit he was a master. When the prosecutor whipped himself back in my direction, he lashed out with such ferocity I jerked backward in my chair, nearly toppling it. His words hit me like spume.

"Virginia Rappe had a few drinks and you lusted after her. You pulled her into the bedroom, locked the door, threw her on the bed despite her protestations. You tore her clothes off and practiced Lord knows what manner of perversions on a helpless girl. You tore her inside out and she screamed for mercy."

Would someone please tell me the right expression to wear on your face when a man is calling you a rapist in front of your wife? In front of God? In front of a roomful of angry females whose hate for you is like a *smell*? A fly buzzed continually around my head, and I dared not swat it, for fear of appearing violent. The airless tang of perspiration, stale perfume, and floor wax made it hard to breathe. I felt myself flush up. My knee hurt and my thighs itched. More than anything I had to fight back the urge to cry.

In his closing argument, Friedman harangued the jury to render a guilty verdict—"*To show the Arbuckles of the world that American womanhood is not their plaything!*"

In spite of being disemboweled in cross-examination, I was optimistic. McNab had so thoroughly exposed the prosecution witnesses as frauds and weaklings, nothing he had to say would matter anyway. Or so it seemed to me. The galoot's galoot.

We thought the jury would make up their mind fast. For two or three hours I felt almost cocky. Even called Buster and told him to round up the boys when I came back. Call me naïve. In my mind, once 12 reasonable humans come back with a Not Guilty, I'd be able to hop back on the movie train and toddle on like nothing happened. Isn't that the way things happen in a just world?

After 10 hours, my mouth was so dry I was spitting feathers. By 24 I was seeing spots. The walls in the Hall of Justice lobby started to look wet, *spongy*, like the whole place was made of dingy angel's food cake. Maybe I was just hungry. The whole night ended up like one long smoking and pie-eating contest. And I was the only contestant. I even paid the men's room Negro to go out and scare up some firewater. "What kind?" he wanted to know.

I liked the way he folded my 10 spot and tucked it in a slot on the inside of his red attendant's jacket in one clean move.

"The kind that works," I said, without thinking about it.

The attendant nodded and stuck out his hand again. "For that, gonna be another 10, boss." So I gave him my Paramount watch, the one inscribed, TO ROSCOE — ONE OF THE TEAM, FROM YOUR FRIEND ADOLPH.

"What's 'at writin' say?" the Negro asked.

" 'Hello, Sucker,' " I told him.

The thought of what might happen—and the realization that it actually could—unnerved me so much I had to eat, pace, or roll cigarettes to keep from running out in front of a train. Don't forget, I'd been inside already. Before you go to jail, you think it's going to be like in the movies, full of crusty-but-lovable old cons and gangsters with good teeth. But now I'd been there. I *knew*.

How could you not get plastered knowing that one wrong move, one slip-up, and you'd spend the rest of your life in a circus full of vicious pea-brains who'd kill you for your comb?

It took the jury 41 hours and 22 ballots before it finally gave up. The foreman, pink-eyed with fatigue, blinked into the lights and announced that one juror had declined to consider any evidence, had declared that she knew a guilty fat man when she saw one. Said juror, skip the drumroll, was Mother Hubbard, the ringer McNab had spotted right off.

A screaming mob surrounded our car and started rocking it until a policeman cleared a path. For one bad moment I wondered if jail might have been the safer bet, until the driver gave it the gas and got us away from the courthouse.

The trip back to Hollywood is kind of patchy. But I had the biggest crying jag of my adult life the second Minta and I made it past the bottle-wielding mob at Union Station. When I remarked that all the bottles were Coca-Cola, Minta looked pained. I'd stopped reading the papers halfway through the trial. The headlines ruined my digestion. Now here were these red-faced queen bees, waving Coke bottles and screaming "Die Fatty Die!" I got the screaming—what else was new?—but the empty Coca-Colas had me stumped.

I wish I'd never lived to see the sad wonder on Minta's face as she tried to explain. "It's that Hearst, honey. He says that you, um, you used a bottle—either Coca-Cola or champagne—to, you know, to penetrate Virginia."

When Minta couldn't look at me anymore, she reached in her wallet. She unfolded the actual article she'd neatly clipped from the paper, and began to read. " '*My manly equipment would not do my bidding,*' *Arbuckle cracked to guests,* '*so I did what I always do, I grabbed a bottle.*' "

That was as far as she got before I started crying. *Why?* Why do you think? Because worse than the lies in the paper were the accidental truths. Imagine being accused of something, and in the process of proving that you didn't do it, you have to parade all the secret, shameful things you actually *did*. Not crimes, exactly. Just . . . *behavior*. Details you wouldn't want to read about yourself—or your manly equipment—on the front page of the *Los Angeles Examiner*.

The shame was like a knife that cut deeper the more you tried to pull it out. But bad as it was for me, what I was really bawling about was how this must be for Minta. What was it like to be the monster's better half?

"*Abandoned then reunited with the man she loves only because he's been charged with a sex murder.*" Hearst again. To have to not just read these lies—but *live* with them. Because of me, Minta had to suffer the soul-killing scrutiny. Because of me, she was the subject of the lowest jokes. Because of me. That was the awful truth. It wasn't Virginia Rappe I ripped apart, it was my own wife. Because one day I got snockered with the wrong bunch of degenerates.

Like the man said, inside every fat man is a really fat one who's stuck.

The red-faced truth: I'd pressed a cold bottle to the dying girl's pudendum to wake her up, not get inside her. But I was too uncomfortable to relate such facts to my own wife, let alone an entire courtroom. To say I tried to save a girl by icing her privates is to admit her privates were there in front of me to be iced. Guilty by virtue of innocence. Or vicey versey. What a gag.

Devastated as I was at the notion I'd stuck a bottle up Virginia Rappe, when I looked out that car window and studied the haggard faces of the women who fervently believed it, I couldn't help but observe to Minta, "These biddies are too hard up for champagne, so they're waggling Cokes."

Minta gave me a peculiar smile. "If I were a Russian revolutionary, I'd say they were really mad 'cause you had champagne and they didn't."

"Don't tell me you've gone Red," I said. Now that was funny. *She can always surprise me!*

This was the last coherent thought before they scraped me off the lawn in Los Angeles and dumped me inside.

Purgatory

Brady immediately demanded a retrial, slated for January 12. I spent the intervening weeks with my friends Mr. Morphine and Monsieur Brandy, and didn't care to leave their company no matter how much Minta implored me. Whatever faith I had, not just in humanity (who thinks about humanity?) but in right and wrong, loyalty and trust, truth and fibbery, went up in flames with the empty liquor crates and unread newspapers we burned in the backyard. We had no maids now, no staff but Okie, who stayed on, without pay, not out of loyalty, I suspected, but because he had nowhere to go—and no one would hire him after they got wind he'd worked for me. He never complained about the cot he slept on in the three-car garage he'd converted to his new living quarters.

The first day of my second trial, my other old friends, the Women's Vigilante Committee, were back at the courthouse to greet us. When they saw the ladies, my police protectors—a trio of shifty flatfeet recruited from their beat on the Tenderloin—stepped quickly away. Leaving 50-odd morally outraged females to encircle me. They kept about a one-yard distance. And when the righteous grayhair who reigned over the ladies stepped forward and cried, "*America, Do your duty!*" all 50 spat in unison. The throngs on hand cheered them on.

"*Fatty made a most impressive centerpiece in the fountain.*" That's what the *Examiner* said. I felt like a punch line trapped in a bad joke. But as long as Hearst could make money telling it, I was stuck.

When I was thoroughly soaked—it's unnerving how warm saliva is—the Tenderloin bluebirds stepped back to their positions, politely letting the Vigilantes pass. I said, "Thank you, ladies," and took my hat off to wring it out. Then we continued on to the courthouse.

I didn't talk much to anybody after the spitting incident. I preferred to keep things muffled, and the right cocktail of moonshine and needle juice kept me what you might call *pillowy*.

For Trial Two, Alice Blake and Zey Prevon were back in center stage. Zey tearfully admitted she "couldn't remember" if she'd lied or not during the first trial. Then McNab took her further. What nearly got me fried last time was Zey's claim that Virginia screamed, "*He hurt me! He nearly killed me!*" Now McNab had her thinking she wasn't so sure . . .

DA Friedman was incensed. "So, Miss Rappe did not say what you claimed?" he chided Zey. "You have heard of the crime of perjury, haven't you?"

Zey looked at me like she wanted a splash of holy water. "No, you don't understand," she pleaded. "Virginia *said* it, but she wasn't talking about Roscoe. She was talking about Fred Fischbach."

Even the bailiff gasped. McNab grabbed my hand and whispered, "We got him!" But Friedman, the trouper, didn't flinch. He just waited for the courtroom to calm down, then casually asked his crumbling witness, "All right, dear. And what *did* the defendant, Mr. Arbuckle, reply when he heard Virginia's explanations?"

Zey looked panicked again. "He, Mr. Arbuckle, said, 'Someone shut that monkey up. I'll throw her out the window if she doesn't stop yelling!'"

Friedman smiled like the cat that ate the cat that ate the canary. McNab grew old in front of me. Why couldn't I just leap up and tell them the truth? "*She was a bughouse slut! Every time she got bombed she started screaming and tearing her drapes off. How was I supposed to know this time she was dying?"*

But the damage was done. Friedman came flying out of his corner and pinched his brow in front of the jury box. "Ladies and gentlemen"—big sigh, like what he was about to say pained him, but doggone it, he *had* to say it—"ladies and gentlemen of the jury, I am *ashamed* at what you've had to hear today! It offends the ears of decent people. But I must ask you all to look in your hearts, and to ask yourselves, 'What kind of beast could ever utter such foulness in the presence of a young woman, no matter her station in life?' I bow my head at the depths to which this defendant—and other so-called movie stars in that Gomorrah called Hollywood—have descended. And pray that you will all look in your hearts and decide whether this defendant deserves to walk free. Free to force himself upon your daughter. Free to thrust his unnatural bulk upon your little sister."

McNab was apoplectic. He must have interrupted the Assistant DA with objections five times. To no avail. Zey's statement had proved my innocence—and the sermon it unleashed from Friedman tarnished me worse than guilt.

Everything that happened after Friedman's speech is a whirling blur: gasps, gavel banging, reporters slamming through swinging doors out to the phone booths. Judge Louderback—who boasted the complexion of a rum-soaked sponge—chose this juncture to announce a recess. When McNab pressed him—"Your Honor, why now?"—the judge admitted it was so that he could perform a wedding in his chambers. McNab objected to this, too, and Brady, who'd been waiting all day for something to say, tugged his suspenders out and winked at the jury. "A lawful ceremony between decent people—of *course* Mr. Arbuckle's lawyer would object." The decent folk ate it up.

From that instant on, our fate seemed sealed. The very

morning the jury was sequestered, my good friend William Desmond Taylor, the suave Brit Paramount director, was found shot to death in his home on Alvarado. Old Billy DTs, as a select few liked to call him, was either a wily fruit or a world-class ladies' man, depending on who you talked to. One of his ladies happened to be another great friend, Mabel Normand. But more important than any of this, Taylor was an industry darling: a leading proponent of censorship and head of the Motion Picture Directors Association.

Within a day, you'd have had to pull a blanket over your head not to hear the screaming headlines. Splattered over front pages everywhere was poor coke-addled Mabel Normand, alongside Henry Peavey, Taylor's pansy, drug-dealing butler. Most damning, for the dead director's reputation, were details of his famous 500-plus panty collection—all dated, rated, named, and stashed in a custom humidor in his lavish boudoir. (Scuttlebutt had it some of the panties were boxers, but not even Hearst saw fit to slap that in 12-point type and see if it stuck.)

Had Taylor consulted me, I'd have encouraged him to postpone his murder till after my trial. Or at least hide his undie stash with a little more care. Only he didn't consult me . . .

But where was I? Right. So even though the facts showed me innocent, the jurors were inclined to convict on general principle. To send those heathens down in Sin City a message. Faced with such public outrage, McNab decided to forgo a final argument. The less they see of us the better, was his thinking. But the jury—and the papers—took this concession as evidence he'd given up.

Years later, I found out from Buster Keaton's sister-in-law, Norma Talmadge, that Zukor had actually wired 10 grand to Brady during the second trial. I also found out that Zukor arranged for McNab to get the plum job—immediately after dispensing with me—of representing Mary Pickford before the Nevada Supreme Court. The movie star's movie star was trying to quash an attempt by disgruntled hubby Owen Moore to keep her from trading up to marry Douglas Fairbanks. Norma claimed McNab acted like he couldn't wait to blow San Francisco and set up shop in Reno. But I'll never know, will I?

Only a fluke holdout prevented the jury from going 12–0 for conviction. A fellow named Lee Dolson was my savior. Dolson happened to have accompanied his pretty girlfriend, Doris Deane, to the ferry at the start of this fiasco, the very day I met her myself on deck. Thanks to Doris telling her sweetie I was a good egg, Lee promised on the sly that he wouldn't vote to convict. He might have changed his vote if he'd known I was going to make the girl of his dreams my second wife. Which I did, on May 16, 1925, in San Moreno, after parting amicably with Minta. (Could you see it coming?) Doris and I only stayed married till '28, but still, that's three years—and a lifetime—that poor Dolson didn't have with her. Stop me if I'm getting mushy.

But wait! I neglected to mention the stern fellow with the slicked-down Princeton who showed up every day of the second trial, scribbling furiously, his beady eyes fixed on mine with vivid hate. That beady-eyed scribbler was Will Hays. Zukor, Lasky, Selznick, and a bunch of the other big boys had finally corraled him to run the censorship board—and keep the craven goyim in Washington from closing down Hollywood and locking up all the studio heads' kosher behinds for rank immorality and onscreen heathen behavior.

Ex–postmaster generals didn't come cheap. Along with a tidy $150,000 a year, the Movie Jews sweetened Hays's pot with two million in life insurance, an expense account with no top, and complete discretion over what was moral and what wasn't.

Officially, Will Hays did not unchain his brainchild, the

decency-defending Motion Picture Producers and Distributors Association of America, until March 14. But he accepted on January 14—just in time to tackle his first boil on the festering cheeks of the movie business: me.

In the meantime, Matthew Brady, knowing his chances at landing the governor's seat were nil if he didn't put me on ice, finagled a third trial, beginning on March 6. By the time they dragged my carcass back to San Francisco for *that* tea party, I felt like I had a new calling in life: Professional Murder and Rape Defendant. If you can concoct a more unpleasant occupation, wire me and I'll send you a dressed turkey.

In case William Desmond Taylor's rubout and Mary Pickford's wanton divorce had not yet cemented the notion of movie folks as moral lepers, word that Wally Reid had to be diapered and strapped down in the throes of narcotic withdrawal hit the papers. I thank my lucky stars—and the ever-discreet Okie—that my own hayride on the needle was never leaked to the press. Wouldn't *that* be the perfect trifecta: *Killer, Rapist, Drug Addict.* And worse than all three—*ACTOR!* Hearst would have died and gone to slander heaven.

Not every Filmtown dope fiend was so lucky. One enterprising pen pusher bribed Wally Reid's doctor so he could sneak into the dope ward and tantalize a hungry public with grainy candids and a screaming lead: "*Drooling and diaper-clad, the one-time heart-throb now sits rocking in a corner, mewling like a kitten and spewing teary gibberish . . .*" I always pictured Hearst's stringers panting when they typed.

In San Francisco, Brady started mewling himself when word came down there might not be a third trial. The DA pleaded his case to Will Hays. Hays promised him that he'd have his chance. Holy Will, as it happened, needed something to counter criticism that all the chicanery the moral public loved to hate—the murders, divorces, and godless narcotic mayhem—had continued unabated on his watch. This gave Hays's enemies—the Democrats who hated him and the Harding he rode in on—plenty of ammo to mock him as a high-paid shill for the studios. Translation: Slave of the Hebes. FATTY GETS GAS was the one headline that could save the DA and the Morality Czar. And at least it was a half-decent gag.

Zukor had lifted the idea for a Movie Morality Czar from baseball. Studio heads have to lift their ideas from somewhere, otherwise they wouldn't have any. After the Black Sox Scandal of 1919, baseball execs had been in the same spot Hollywood was now: they needed to show folks their sport was *clean* again. To this end they enlisted Illinois's own Kenesaw Mountain Landis, a Red-baiting judge famed for sentencing Big Bill Haywood, number-one labor man in the country, to 20 years. As baseball's morality Czar, Landis made the game wholesome again. Exactly what wholesome and sanitary Will Hays was brought in to accomplish for the movie business.

On the dismal eve of Trial Three, Hays staged an event to pledge publicly that "no longer would stars be allowed to act as hooligans with little regard for the American public." That I was the hooligan in question was no surprise. What surprised me was Gavin McNab showing up unannounced at West Adams—mortgaged but not abandoned—and admitting over a glass of hair tonic that he'd made a gaffe by passing up his closing argument in the last trial. "*Right here and now*," he said, taking my hand in his over the card table, "*I'll make you a pledge.*" This time, he promised, he would cut the legs off the prosecution once and for all. Which, to the dismay of right-thinking citizens everywhere, he did.

*   *   *

Gavin McNab, "a veritable terrier of truth," as he liked to call himself, dug up a crusty old gal named Josephine Roth, matron of a "maternity home" in Virginia's hometown. The heavily powdered Miss Roth testified to Virginia stopping in to "become a mother" when she was 14—and leaving her baby boy behind when she left.

After this winning maneuver, McNab hammered away at the continued absence of the prosecution's chief witness—their chief accuser—the bigamist chiseler Maude Delmont. For his *pièce de résistance*, McNab announced that he could prove once and for all that the alleged damage I'd caused Miss Rappe's bladder was the result of prior misbehavior. And plenty of it. This he did— get the children out of the room—by producing the *actual organ*.

Put down your sandwich, Happy Lips. McNab had Virginia's bladder floating in the same kind of jar you'd reach into for a penny dill pickle at the deli. To the untrained eye, the dead girl's bladder looked like a blob of rotten gefilte fish. (I'd eaten gefilte, when Joe had poker night, and it *always* tasted a little rotten.) When the bailiff lugged the thing in, the poor lunk was so nauseated he nearly tripped and dumped the stippled dumpling in Friedman's lap. I suspected my attorney had greased the man handily for his pratfall, but when I asked, Gavin held his mud.

After the near bladder-spill, the Assistant District Attorney went ashen, looking dangerously close to presenting his breakfast as evidence. During closing arguments Friedman was pallid and rambling. This left McNab to stand in front of the court-room, an avenging prophet, and address the jury in high moral dither.

For the first time since my trial had begun, my *first* trial, I felt myself come alive and listen. "Did the state illustrate how Roscoe hurt Virginia Rappe? Nobody saw it. There was no proof of it. Because he never did hurt her!"

Then, while I tried 11 different expressions on my face, McNab wrapped up with a recitation of my good works and accomplishments. He summed the whole thing up: "Roscoe Arbuckle has made millions of people happy. Brought joy to the world. Never hurt a living soul. And this has been his reward."

I get the weeps just thinking about it! And the jury felt the same way.

Six minutes after the case was submitted to them, on the afternoon of April 12, the 12 souls who controlled my fate shocked the masses on hand by returning a verdict. More than a verdict. The foreman, a square-jawed, bespectacled, retired tractor salesman, requested permission to read a statement to the court. I knew enough not to get my hopes up. But Minta, who'd stayed by my side in court despite the fact that we barely spoke, grabbed my face and kissed me before he even got the square of paper out of his pocket and unfolded it. The spark of sex ignited by my calamity had long since fizzled, but my future ex-wife was still glad I'd managed to stay out of the gas chamber.

"Acquittal," the foreman read in a thin voice unaccustomed to public presentation, "is not enough for Roscoe Arbuckle."

Before he could continue, the courtroom exploded with happy yips and hoots. These surprised me as much as the verdict itself. Much as I longed for acquittal, I was afraid the backlash among the vigilantes on hand would set off a lynch mob. My worse fear was that they wouldn't be able to find a branch that could hold me, so they'd try stringing me up to trees all over town, and I'd keep breaking them. Set free, only to survive with a crushed voice box and permanent rope burn around my neck.

When the cheers died down, the foreman continued. "We feel that a great injustice has been done. We feel also that it was only our plain duty to give him this exoneration . . .

"He was manly throughout the case and told a straightforward story on the witness stand, which we all believed."

Manly! Feature that!

"The happening at the hotel was an unfortunate affair for which Arbuckle . . . was in no way responsible.

"We wish him success and hope that the American people will take the judgment of 14 men and women who have sat listening for 31 days to the evidence that Roscoe Arbuckle is entirely innocent and free from blame."

But I was not too manly to let the hot tears roll down my cheeks in front of everybody. This was my second adult crying jag. My first in public. Though this one was much more subdued. But those few hot tears were not from joy. Gratified as I was at being proved innocent, I wept from the crushing knowledge that it no longer mattered. Innocence and two bits would buy you a bowl of gruel but no crackers. I was 700 grand in the hole, I was still suspect and hated, and if there was any place on the map I could ever be funny again, it would probably take a safari to get there. Was any free man ever more condemned?

I'd won the case, and lost any reason for caring.

I reeled out of the courtroom and back to Los Angeles in a darker haze than any drug or panther piss had put me.

Buster and Chaplin came to meet me at the station. But I could barely wave when I saw them. My arms and legs were made of pig iron. Keaton and Charlie kept asking me, "What do you want to do now?"

So I finally told them. *"Pass out . . ."*

Aftershocks

Shall I even bother to tell you about the years that remained? The mug's game called redemption? I could have done talkies. I mean, I can do voices. I could do everybody's voice. Play the woman and the man. Man and wife, Dog and pony. But I couldn't play Adolph Zukor. Nobody could ever play Adolph.

Six days after the jury apologized, Zukor held a powwow in the Paramount bunker with Lasky and General Hays himself. Eager to finish off the job the Prosecution couldn't, the three wise men were meeting to cook up a statement for Hays to sign.

That afternoon, over Hays's signature, on off-white Famous Players–Lasky bonded paper, they issued my professional death sentence. Lemme play you the high notes:

> *After consulting at length with Blah, Blah, and Blah, Mr. Adolph Zukor and Mr. Jesse Lasky of the Famous Players–Lasky Corporation, the distributors, etc. . . . canceled all showings and all bookings of the Arbuckle films . . . notwithstanding the fact they had nearly ten thousand contracts in force for the Arbuckle pictures. Et cetera, et cetera . . .*
>
> *Will Hays*

Minta, who could do jigsaw puzzles in minutes, made no secret of her suspicion that Zukor was behind everything that happened. "That bastard never forgave you for skipping Paramount Week." She hardly ever swore. But when she was this upset, little Minta steamed with a kind of seriousness that was almost frightening. She glowered as she went on with her theory. "Plus which, Fischbach took money from Zukor, *and* from Lehrman, *and* flimflammed Lehrman's fiancée. Fishy used you to hide his grift from both of them. It's disgusting."

"So Hollywood's a cesspool. Stop the presses. Daddy needs a job."

And back and forth like that from the laugh-packed script we'd replay every night. Without an audience. No props but a bed, a bottle, and a broken man. It sounds like the title of a cowboy song. One night I actually jotted down our patter. Maybe I could sharp it up a little.

Scene from *Fun Night with Roscoe and Minta*:

M: I'm sick of all of it.
R: *I'm sick of you!*
M: I'm sick of you!
R: *No, no, I'm sorry, I'm sorry. I'm sick of myself.*
M: Oh, Roscoe, come here . . .

I went to Europe. Can you blame me? I went for the sheer fuck of it. (Now I cuss all the time—why not? I can't get sent to hell, I already get my mail there.) The Old Country treated me like a king—even more than on my first visit. Girls in Paris kept putting their pantaloons in my soup. I don't know if that's a tradition or if they were low on dinner rolls. Douglas Fairbanks and Chaplin also happened to be in Paree. Fairbanks was shilling for *The Three Musketeers*. The Frenchies kept screaming "Charlot!" at Charlie, like he was some kind of wine.

Those boys could cheer up a dead pigeon. But one night we went to the Crazy Horse with Mary Pickford, and I had the distinct feeling Mrs. Fairbanks would have rather been seen with Lincoln's corpse. Still, back in London, it buoyed me considerably when the Brits broke into one of those "hip-hip-hip hoorays"! on Piccadilly Circus. The English and the French had pretty much the same opinion about the trials: "What do you expect? You Americans are all Puritans."

I guess, like Oscar Wilde, another outsized, publicly shamed sex criminal, I emerged from the experience humbled and shunned.

And, in my own way, somewhat more spiritual. Wilde wrote *De Profundis*. I wrote a groveling letter to Will Hays begging to get my old job back.

And why not? Back in the States, still buzzing from the cocktail of "continental adulation" (as Buster called my reception overseas), I decided to compose a mash note to the ex-postmaster. I had, in fact, just lumbered through *De Profundis*, or as much of it as I could swallow, and probably tried too hard to ape Wilde's loftier style. "There is a higher law which deals with the spiritual side of mankind," I wrote, "and surely this Christmastime should not be a season when the voice of the Pharisee is heard in the land. No one ever saw a picture of mine that was not clean."

Hays, no doubt, kept the entreaty framed in silver and propped at his bedside, so he could see it before he laughed himself to sleep.

Too Much, Too Late

You might think redemption would be sweet. But when—after my pleas, countless letters from Minta, plus pressure from Keaton and Joe Schenck—Will Hays finally relented, the end result was less than stunning. Three days before Christmas the moral arbiter of the nation declared that I was "entitled to a chance to redeem" myself.

If I had any illusions that this meant I'd be returned to my former glory—or, at least, my former state of not being hated like a rabid, child-killing dog—the *New York Times* editorial the day after the jury's apology should have tipped me off. "Arbuckle was a scapegoat, and the only thing to do with a scapegoat, if you must have one, is to chase him off into the wilderness and never let him come back." The last line was even worse: "It will do the picture business no good to have him trotting back into the parlor bringing his aroma with him."

Did he say "aroma"? Roscoe Arbuckle, parlor skunk. Not exactly *We missed you, laddie, welcome back!*

There's no deodorant for desperation. And, apparently, no way to wash off that jailhouse cologne.

Not that everyone turned against me. I think I already mentioned that Joe Schenck showed surprising backbone. Joe was always simpatico. After Hays issued his half-baked retraction of my satanic status, Schenck stepped up to Zukor and said they had three scripts for me ready to go. The three I'd been slated to shoot during my unfortunate detainment had all gone to other actors. Will Rogers galloped off with *The Melancholy Spirit*. The great John Barrymore swordplayed *The Man from Mexico* into a bag-o'-laughs swashbuckler. And, before he rode his horse over the cliff, Wallace Reid smackled his handsome way through *Thirty Days*.

Naturally, this being my life, the very thing I thought would *relieve* my situation soon proved to be *the worst thing for it*. See, Schenck's plan was to release *Leap Year*, the last classic I'd made before the safe fell on my head. The movie would put me right back on the Happyland map. Mark my return as Much-Loved Funny Man. Or tank so badly I'd want to claw my eyes out and throw them at the projectionist.

If you picked the second possibility, you win the stuffed pink elephant. When *Leap Year* hit, the effect was quite the opposite of what I thought it would be. Moviegoers now found my hijinks more horrifying than funny. Since my arrest, my place in the world had backflipped. Gags once good for a sure chuckle— Roscoe the Coy Fat Boy making googoo eyes at a retiring violet, Roscoe as Chester Chubby-Money, the innocent tubbo being chased by a bevy of beauties—had been rendered nauseating.

I snuck into the back of a theater showing *Leap Year* in New York and heard the Mommykins in front of me whisper quiet as a buzzsaw to Daddykins: "*How can they let that fat rapist chase that little virgin!*"

It was terrifying. I staggered out of the movie house and took a cab around Central Park. Within two days the *Examiner* came back full-blast: FATTY'S FACE AGAIN STAINING NATION'S SCREENS.

What did I ever do to make Hearst love me so much?

After that headline there wasn't a civic leader worth his saltines who didn't cash in with a public statement protesting my return. "Just because he's innocent, he's still a monster" was a sentiment echoed by the mayors of Boston, Detroit, and Indianapolis. These civic giants joined a floating country club of suffragettes, pastors, and moral paragons of every stripe. So popular a topic was Roscoe Arbuckle in sermons, the Devil must have felt slighted for weeks after my acquittal.

Need I point out that this backlash was *encouraged*? The Anti-Fattyites were supported by Hays, whose off-the-record insistence that studio heads blacklist me was not even off-the-record. I knew my pork was roasted when William Jennings Bryan, of all people, published an open letter to Commissioner Hays. Via some trick of rhetoric, Bryan, the failed presidential candidate, managed to make the fact that I was found innocent the most damning aspect of my entire ordeal. "His acquittal only relieved him of the penalty that attaches to a crime. The evidence showed a depravity entirely independent of the question of actual murder."

Thanks for thinking of me, William!

I know, I shouldn't be bitter. Might as well pound nails into my kneecaps as dredge up the memory of my detractors. It's painful. But sometimes pain is the one thing left a man can feel. Maybe I stole that line from *De Profundis*. Or the three and a half pages I could decipher without dozing off. Or maybe it came out of the rye I just dumped down my gullet. What does it matter? *Wronged Fatsoes Of The World, Unite!*

Gainful Employment

Against all odds, Joe Schenck still took a chance and pitched me as a director to Zukor. Zukor had his eye on a circus act named Poodles Hanneford, and Schenck told him I might be the man to crank out some two-reelers with him. The shorts would take two weeks and cost 20 grand. I'd get a 20th of that, two weeks in a row. Schenck was so nice to me, I was starting to think he had a guilty conscience.

Except for Lew Cody—who had less clout than a canned ham—the only old-time pals who'd dare show their faces in public with me were Buster, Schenck, and Charlie.

Chaplin, truth be told, never saw fit to jeopardize his standing in the community by endorsing me for a job. Buster, on the other hand, did everything but walk a HIRE ROSCOE sandwich board up and down Hollywood Boulevard. Thanks to him, five studios—Keaton's, Metro, Paramount, Goldwyn, and Educational—tossed 33 G's into the hat to start Reel Productions and set me up again.

My Reel deal was not set up with prestige in mind. For my sins, I was signed on to direct the fellow professional lard-ass just mentioned in his gaggle of two-reelers. Poodles had made his name touring with Billy Sunday. But happily, the flask in his pants defused any tension I might have had about his God-fearing tendencies.

My big hits with Hanneford were *No Loafing* and *The Bonehead*, if that tells you anything. Circus people were always different than vaudeville people. Nights when we worked late, Poodles would lie right down on the ground and go to sleep. He was happy in sawdust. We'd shake him awake when the cameras were about to roll. All he'd need was a bang of rye and a cigarette and he was ready for his first take.

I wrote and directed the Poodles sorties. Not that you'd know it. I couldn't slap my own name on the marquee, so I opted for the moniker Will B. Good. Until Buster, in a moment of typically inspired Busterdom, decided over martinis at Musso and Frank's that it wasn't legit enough. He stared at me for a moment and then announced. "You're more of a 'William Goodrich' type. Now *that* son of a bitch is legit!"

So that's how I became William Goodrich. Though, thanks to Hays's continued harassment, it wouldn't have mattered if I'd called myself Puddin' the Wonder Chimp. The Front Office decided it was best to keep my name off the credits altogether. And after six weeks of yeomanlike effort, there was no getting around it: Roscoe Arbuckle was one more out-of-work fat actor.

"When in doubt, exit left." That's what old Poodles said every night before he fell off his bar stool. I took his advice to heart and signed on for eight weeks at the Marigold Gardens, a nightclub outside Chicago. Two grand a week beat anonymous directing gigs. And it was definitely a left turn.

I won't lie. I was nursing a case of wet-seat the first night I stepped onstage at the Marigold. *"Ladies and gentleman, I'd have been here sooner, but I had trouble checking out of my hotel in San Francisco."* BEAT. *"They thought I was stealing towels!"*

The standing O I got every night made me happy. But what really thrilled me was the sound of ice clinking in my glass offstage at the start of my last number, a joke version of "California, Here I Come": "California, here I come. Even though you want me hung . . ."

"Oh wait," I'd fake ad-lib, *"where's my head? They wanna hang me here, too, don't they? Did you read that editorial in the Trib?"*

Hard as it was to laugh at my trials, it was the only way to let the jakes in the audience know they could laugh, too. Since a quarter of the crowd were gawkers, it helped to cut right to the chase. When I got back to Los Angeles, I got a cameo in *Hollywood*, a movie biz satire Jimmy Cruze was directing for Paramount. It was one of those a-star-in-every-part vehicles the studio nabobs concoct to make sure their big names still know how to come when the front office whistles. I played a down-on-his-luck actor cooling his heels in a casting office. If I had had any pride left, it would have probably stung. But 500 bucks is 500 bucks. Then I went back to anonymity and directing again.

Did I relish punching a clock as a nameless director? The answer is yes and no. For a while I humped it as journeyman comedy hand for Educational, Metro, and Universal, directing whatever claptrap they threw at me. The good news was, at Educational I crossed paths with Doris Deane, the pretty thing I met on the ferry back from San Fran, right before I changed my profession from actor to pariah. Doris Deane, whose ex-boyfriend was the reason I was walking around in my own clothes.

Doris acted in a number of goofball efforts, including the

memorable *Stupid but Brave* and *Lovemania*. I guess you could say we fell in love. Or at least *I* fell in love, and she didn't seem to mind the attentions of a gin-soaked marshmallow. The hardest letter I ever had to write was the one to Minta, telling her I'd met someone, asking for a divorce. I had to get so polluted I could barely hold the pen.

The split was official on January 27, 1925. Despite everything, tiny Minta'd been my biggest champion since the acquittal. She hounded Hays with letters nearly every day, even when I was abroad. But she was kind—and classy—enough to wish me the best and start marriage-ending proceedings immediately. The last thing either of us wanted was another scandal, so she arranged to file the divorce papers in Providence, Rhode Island. During Christmas season. An unlikely time and place for celebrity snoops.

Then Keaton, God bless his porkpie hat, came through again. He snagged me a chance at my first credited directing job post-Virginia. I'd be filming him in *Sherlock Jr.* I left Educational to write and lay out the gags with him. I was excited, and so was he. It was great to be working together again. And, feet in the fire, I still couldn't tell you why it went south.

I guess, about one-third in, Buster and I both realized I was coming up with stuff *I* wanted to do—not what worked for him. And it was too painful to keep talking around the fact that I was not allowed to perform on camera. It's one thing to not act, another not to act when you're on the set, the camera's running, and you have a headful of great gags that no one can sell but you.

Little by little, I started getting touchy about everything. I heard grips whispering behind my back. I felt their judgment. The lighting man, I knew, was worried because his wife's folks, Four Square Church people, would throw the couple out of their house if word got out her husband worked with the blubber-thighed Antichrist Roscoe Arbuckle.

Then, of course, there was the drinking. Buster never came out and said it wasn't a good idea for a director to gulp out of the bottle between takes, but it was obviously a problem. Things ended before my best friend had to fire me outright. I knew it was over and left one morning in the middle of a gag involving Keaton's hat and a lovesick dove. The dove gag didn't make it into the movie, and neither did the directing credit.

After the *Sherlock* debacle I did a few more comedies back at Educational. On *The Iron Mule*, the last one I directed with Doris Deane, I asked her if she'd consider marrying me. I always say she looked like a bunny who saw a bear when I popped the question. Or semi-popped it.

I know I've mentioned this already, but indulge me. Here's the official version. I didn't want to be so bold as to assume Miss Deane would say yes. Minta had bandied Sigmund Freud around often enough for me to know I had some ego problems. (I was oral, too. But that's part of your job when you're a professional fat man.)

I suggested Doris take her time in deciding. In the meantime, I ran into Alexander Pantages, my champion from way back when, drying his hands in the men's room of Musso's. He asked me what I was doing and I went fag on him, "Not looking for phone numbers, *thailor*." Pantages laughed his way into a coughing fit and accidentally whacked Jackie Coogan, who was behind us, trying to see between our shoulders to wet-comb his hair in the mirror. After we dusted Coogan off, Pantages turned to me, with tears in his eyes, and said, "I'm gonna do something crazy and offer you a cross-country tour."

I didn't have to check my date book to say yes.

*   *   *

The show, a variety bill, was slated to open in Long Beach, at some dump catty-corner to the Bide-A-Wee, where Minta and I'd gotten married onstage a few centuries earlier. But your Long Beachers, it turns out, are not the nostalgic type. There was a petition in City Council to keep me out. So instead of a dump in Long Beach, I opened at the Cotton Club, a hop-skip-and-a-lawsuit from Goldwyn Studios in Culver City. The Cotton got raided occasionally, but Pantages assured me he'd paid off the cops.

All the big movie people in town turned out for the revue. They hadn't exactly been flocking to see me before now, but my guess is everybody was so relieved I was leaving movies, they came to show their support. On account of me, after all, any actor who sneezed on the Sabbath was bound to show up in a tabloid. An entire industry devoted to trailing the stars around, trying to catch 'em in some unsavory gaffes, had sprung up from my own phantom crime at the St. Francis. Gloria Swanson actually laid me out at a restaurant, "*Charlie Chaplin used to do underage girls by the bucketful. Now he's so scared* Photoplay *will find out he won't even drive by a grade school. And I nearly had to hide in a nunnery after my divorce. Thanks to you, Roscoe Pee-in-the-Soup Arbuckle, nobody in this town can have fun anymore . . .*"

What could I say but "Gee, sorry. I was framed. It could happen to anybody . . ."

The crowds were with me in every city, even if the local headlines steamed over the return of Beelzebub in Santa Claus's body. That's when the obvious sank in: *The people who buy the tickets aren't the ones who go to church.* In fact, the greater the commotion over my show, the greater the devotion of those who braved public opinion to take it in. Big lesson.

At Saxes's Strand Theater in Milwaukee, it was all I could do to get through the seething frenzy of women's clubs, Christian Youth Groups, and theater owners' association members, all in full, self-righteous rut under the marquee out front. The protesters' idea was to force any folks who wanted to attend my performance to walk a gauntlet from sidewalk to theater doors. But my theory held—and the people who walked in did not seem to mind the scoffs of the Fundamentalists. The fracas became part of the show.

Inside the theater, the foot stomping and whistling commenced the moment I stumbled onstage. The reception was more deafening than any I'd earned with an actual gag. What were they cheering for, really, but the happy fact that I hadn't been given the gas? It was bittersweet. Night after night, I got so choked up all I could do was pretend to slip and fall on my ass.

Opening night, as a joke, the management paid a 16-year-old to stand up in the first row and throw a pie at me. Much to everyone's surprise—but mostly mine—I caught the thing, Pancho Villa style, and hurled it back. The kid ducked, and the custard splatted square in the mascara of an elegant, middle-aged woman. Her husband was one of those industrialist types with iron pilings for hair. When he jumped out of his seat, I had visions of strike-breaking goons pinning my arms in the dressing room while hubby worked me over with a lead pipe.

I'd gotten so used to the worst that could happen actually happening, I was almost nervous when it didn't. In fact, after I hit her with the pie, the elegant lady froze for a moment, then ran a finger over the blob of whipped cream on her cheek, licked it off, and burst into the grandest horse laugh I ever heard. One of those laughs that make other people laugh. Till pretty soon the entire place was teary-eyed from laughing. It's the kind of moment you want to scoop up and lock in a vault, to pull out and savor when life returns to its usual ho-hum catastrophe.

And it was that moment I clung to a week later, in Dallas, when Ernie Young, the twitchy yokel who'd booked me for the Texas State Fair, burst into my room and blubbered that he had to bounce me for an Italo Muscle-man Act, The Amazing Corelli, before I ever hit the stage. "Technically, that means I can't cover your hotel bill, Roscoe, since you didn't actually perform. It's in the contract. You know how it is."

I knew how it was. The Dallas City Fathers, who ran the theaters, "just didn't want my kind." And they wouldn't want Twitchy Ernie Young's kind if he didn't get rid of me, either.

When the tour died, I stopped in to Atlantic City, where Minta was appearing, billed as "Mrs. Roscoe Arbuckle," at the Club Palais Royal. The Palais manager, a conniver named M. A. Williams, offered me six grand a week just to stay in his café—and not to wander onto the boardwalk where folks could see me for free. M. A. thought word of Mr. Arbuckle on the premises with Mrs. Arbuckle would reel them in the way grubs snag haddock. If grubs snag haddock. I was never one for fishing. A drunken fat man on a rowboat is a dangerous situation.

I admit it wasn't the brightest maneuver on my part to suggest that Minta and I book a suite together. I don't know why, I had a yen to go back and try it with her, maybe even start up an act together. Minta helped me come to my senses. With a slap.

Doris—did I mention this?—had been a friend of my wife's. I mean, of Minta's. And Minta, ever the definition of class on perfect pins, actually told me she was glad that if she had to lose me, it was to a wonderful girl like Doris. I know I said she filed for divorce in Providence. But she ended up making it legal in Paris. Parisians didn't care about niceties like nuptial fidelity. A faithful marriage—*mais non!* Nothing was more chic, in the '20s, than a Parisian divorce. Thank the God of the Jews, I somehow managed to make enough to keep my first wife in diamonds and dresses while I went about the business of trying to secure my second one.

Doris had considered my proposal—I haven't told this story more than five times, have I—and to my surprise decided that I was the man for her. What I'd realized, during my Atlantic City stint with Minta, was that I needed someone whose head was not full to bursting with images of me as a sniveling junkie, a sweaty accused criminal, a fall-down, boorish drunk. Somebody who couldn't drag my history out and whack me with it, the way Minta did. Not that I blamed her. I had not exactly made her life a celebrity paradise.

At first, Doris's parents seemed less than thrilled at the big surprise their daughter dragged home to San Moreno to ask for her hand. I've always liked old-fashioned girls. And really, what bride's daddy would not want a fat actor, accused killer and sex criminal, for a son-in-law? Whole chunks of the country still wanted to see me strung from a lamppost and deballed. What a catch!

Not Losing a Daughter, Gaining a Felon

Even if *they* had reservations, I liked the Deanes straightaway. Doris's dad, a natty little wisp of a man, asked me if I always drank like sobriety was a hanging offense. I told him a bit of whiskey dulled the pain in my leg. Then Daddy Deane pulled out a hip flask, said he reckoned he'd been havin' some leg pains of his own, and joined me on the back porch.

Joe Schenck, in a show of paternal concern that still gets me misty, made the wedding arrangements. Through the entire ceremony, he never failed to provide a Dad-like shoulder to lean on. The novelty of that alone made the experience special. Buster was best man. A commitment for which he paid in blood to his mother-in-law, Peg Talmadge, who found it disgraceful that her daughter's husband should even associate with a pervert villain like me, let alone host my wedding in his home.

Nothing could deter Buster, though. Even after the *Sherlock Jr.* fiasco, even after his wife's family locked him in the doghouse over the wedding, he came back with a still bigger demonstration of friendship. Behind my back—it would have to be behind my back!—Buster approached William Randolph Hearst about me directing his beloved better half, Marion Davies, in *The Red Mill*.

You heard me. William Randolph Hearst. The man who doubled his fortune spewing lies about my life and crimes in his personal birdcage liner. But forget that for a minute. (Not that I ever could.) Lest there be any misunderstanding, this was by no stretch a plum project. Marion was a natural comedienne. But Hearst was so sensitive about the fact that they'd met when she was 18 and he was 54, he always thought people were laughing at *him* when they laughed at *her*. So instead of comedy, he'd secure her dishrag dramas like *The Red Mill*, which began life as an operetta in 1906—and was every bit as musty 20 years later. He'd buy these cornballs and put them into production through Cosmopolitan, a company set up for no other reason than to make movies featuring Marion. Movies Hearst could control.

When I first heard that Hearst's secretary had called to invite me and Doris to San Simeon, I had the temporary bends. Hearst—can I say this too many times?—who had single-handedly created a lust-crazed, murderous version of me so awful even *I* didn't think I deserved to live. Hearst, who had made untold millions on the broken back of my career and reputation. *Hearst*, who had done everything but offer to pay for the cyanide to guarantee that I got the gas chamber for my so-called crimes.

Yes, that Hearst was inviting us for lunch.

Even though I swore I wouldn't, within two minutes of meeting my tormentor—who'd have guessed the man who could break other men had a squeaky voice?—I got him in a corner and asked him, straight out, "How can you just call like this, after what you said about me?"

The pallid giant had taken me out to his menagerie to feed his gorillas, Cain and Abel. "Son," Hearst said, throwing a handful of rotten apples to the caged apes, who seemed glad to get them, "you sold more papers than the sinking of the *Lusitania*. Least I can do is offer you a little job."

"So just like that, you're my friend?"

Hearst laughed, a high, whinnying titter that seemed even less worthy of a man of his gravity than his chirpy voice. "Son," he said, in a not unkindly matter, "let me save you a lot of trouble and explain something. The only difference between a friend and an enemy is five minutes and the right price."

He may have put his hand on my shoulder. I was too stunned by the whole situation to pay close attention. All I could think was, *So that's the kind of wisdom that snags you a castle with matching monkeys.*

Hearst made it clear that a number of directors had turned him down. Directors, he made no pains to conceal, he preferred to me. But since Buster spoke so highly of my work, he figured what the heck. He'd take a flyer. After all, we had history together . . .

Even while he was talking, I still couldn't believe I was standing in front of William Randolph Hearst. Something about his prim lips, and the way Marion and Doris looked at him like he was a wind-up doll, made it impossible to hate the man. Doris had told me he and Marion never slept together, which immediately made me wonder if Randolph had the same problem I had. Maybe his doctor told *him* to eat more bloodmeats.

At lunch, we sat at a table large enough to sail across the Atlantic. I realized, from the way he talked at me over the tureen of clam chowder, that Hearst believed I'd done everything I'd been charged with. And that, even more alarming, it didn't matter to him.

It mattered to me, though. And from the beginning—the very first shot—I could feel the shadow of the great man falling over my every step. By the third day, King Vidor, a young MGM director, had started hanging around the set. King didn't say much. When I introduced myself, he looked sheepish and said that Mr. Hearst had asked him to keep an eye on things. "That's it?" I asked him.

"Actually," said Vidor, doing his level best to keep things civilized, "Mr. Hearst wanted me to run every shot by him before you start rolling."

I believe I stroked my jowls for a minute, then sucked it up and said, "Fine, the more the merrier." Not that I meant it. But I had no beef with King, who could not have been more respectful. All I really wanted to know was how his parents happened to name him King. Did he have a sister named Queen and a little brother named Jack? But somehow, I never found the right angle of approach. Vidor was always staring, in that way people stare when they don't want you to know they're staring.

In a funny way, it was like Lehrman sending Fischbach to check up on Virginia all over again. Except I didn't think Vidor was mattressy with Marion. For all their disparity in age and sensibility—stodgy Hearst, sprightly Marion—the young lady seemed to genuinely care for the high-pitched old toad.

When it hit the screen, *The Red Mill* packed about as much impact as boiled broccoli. Without the flavor. Marion mouthed her lines as well as anyone could have, but the film as a whole sagged badly. A state of affairs Hearst himself wasted no time in blaming on the director.

After *The Red Mill* came and went, I was no longer just tainted—forced to work in the shadows, forever unnamed—I was also deemed incompetent. In the plus column, I was a former million-dollar talent who worked in a pinch. The perfect fall guy for problem projects. After *The Red Mill*, Joe Schenck secured me a directing slot on *Special Delivery*, a bit of fluff featuring Eddie Cantor and a dewy-cheeked William Powell in a comic mail-robbery caper.

Somehow, prior to my arrival on *Special Delivery*, it had not occurred to anyone that a heist comedy mocking the post office might not sit well with former Postmaster General Hays. Sure enough, Holy Will, expressing much umbrage about citizens not taking the business of mail delivery seriously, demanded a total rewrite. Which left the story good and butchered by the time Joe persuaded me to sign on and ride the barrel over the Falls.

Special Delivery went the same route as *The Red Mill*. Straight to Dudsville. Meanwhile, Cecil B. DeMille, that brainy hypocrite, was in all the papers talking about the strict moral code he maintained during shooting of *King of Kings*. "It would never do to have the Virgin Mary getting a divorce or Saint John cutting up in a nightclub . . ." DeMille never explained why Jesus turned water into wine if He didn't want people cutting up. And nobody asked him. Midway through *Kings*, the director began to see himself as a biblical figure. Buster said he heard

Cecil DeMille had hired the Pope to do punch-up—and paid so much the Pontiff kissed *DeMille's* ring.

The moral, ladles and geraniums, is that when one door closes, another swings open—and breaks your nose. But not always. I was ready to pawn my own ring—Doris and I were already on the rocks—when, out of the proverbial blue, Pantages offered me another 12 weeks. Back on the road, at $1,200 a week. A different hotel towel around my rumble seat every night. Nothing like wondering if an audience is going to hear your name and throw tomatoes with razor blades in them. Or leap to their feet and clap their hands bloody to show you how much they love you. Sometimes in the same night.

In Cleveland, when the crowd threatened to go native, a kid with a big forehead ambled onstage and started dishing the snappy platter. In a minute, he was passing the laughs off to me. He did a variation on the two-bit routine, where he taps me for two bits, I say I'm not sure I have two bits, and he says, "Okay, then, I'll take whatever you got—except advice about women. I was in jail once, Mr. Arbuckle, and it didn't agree with my complexion." There was, as they say, a gasp—then the laughs let loose in a torrent. Maybe a monsoon.

The kid with the big forehead had the phoniest handle I ever heard: Bob Hope. But he was as crafty with a setup as any comic I'd crossed paths with. I wired Joe Schenck about the kid and slipped him train fare to L.A. If you can't buy your friends, who can you buy?

Then I caught the sleeper to New York, where I'd just gotten the offer I wanted my whole life: a prime part in an honest-to-God play, on honest-to-God-Broadway no less. By now I didn't want to go home to Doris. This must sound abrupt, but I don't feel like going into it. Who wants to relive the days and nights with a woman he used to adore and now seems forever at war with? If you've been there, you know. If you haven't, pull up a bottle and hit yourself over the head. That'll give you a hint.

So when Broadway beckoned, I succumbed.

The Great White Whale

Baby Mine—a whimsical drama about motherhood, with some B plot about infant switching—ran for the first time in 1910, for 287 days. It wasn't what you'd call a great play. But still . . . My name would be on the marquee at Chanin's Theater on 46th, just above that of a junior phenom named Humphrey Bogart. Could anything be a bigger cinch? The backers were expecting another long run with me on board.

The rave in the *New York Telegram* was nice enough to say I was the best thing in the show. The *Tribune* went even further, quoting a batch of snappy patter I did after a curtain call. "*Ladies and gentlemen, I just want to tell you, a motorcycle policeman overtook me on the way to the theater this evening. I asked him how he was doing and he said. 'Fine—$25.'*"

That kind of run. Old vaudeville stuff. People seemed to eat it up. For a minute and a half.

Like I said, the backers were expecting another long run. They didn't get it . . . We closed before my name was dry on the dressing-room door.

Mae West bit the dust that year, too, in a play called *Sex*. Mae ended up doing 10 days and paying $500 in fines. But she wanted it that way. Nobody saw fit to throw me in the clink for acting in *Baby Mine*, but it wouldn't have surprised me.

If I had to come up with a slogan that captured my state of

mind after the St. Francis imbroglio, it would have been: *Dread everything, expect nothing.* Doris said that was no attitude for a man supposed to be in love with his wife, and I agreed.

The Coast I Left Behind

This time, when I rolled back to Hollywood, the prospect of reinventing myself once again seemed too daunting to even contemplate. I had a bit of money socked away. I knew a thing or two about saloons. So when the opportunity came to open up my very own watering hole in Culver City, I figured why not just go ahead and become what everyone already thought I was? A profligate lush who does nothing but drink and party.

After the tabloids ran me around the block in my funny underwear, the public demanded ever more scandalous stories about the famous. They even wanted to mingle with them, to feel famous and dangerous themselves—if only for an evening. Which is why so many speakeasies were owned or hosted by celebrities.

Gangsters were celebrities, too, and not all that removed from actors, who now had their own criminal tinge. A joint like Salon Royal in Manhattan got popular because regular folks wanted to rub elbows with the greeter, a colorful lady named Tex Guinan, who'd once been partners with real-life mobster Larry Fay at the El Fay Club. At the Salon, Tex heralded one and all with her trademark, "Hello sucker!" Since the joint charged $25 for a fifth of booze, and eight bits for a pitcher of tap water, the lady wasn't kidding. Jimmy Durante's Club Durant, on Broadway and 58th, was another spot—always packed. Helen Morgan's Chez Morgan did business at West 54th from fall to spring. Then the joint moved to West 52nd, in its incarnation as

Helen Morgan's Summer House. What brought the crowds to all these rub joints was the personality of the name on the door. Showbiz dives promised late hours, secret revelry. Real-life adventure. Slow learner that I am, it always took a while to register the obvious: I was never going to get respectable enough to make a decent living, so maybe I could make an indecent living by *not* being respectable. A career, if nothing else, with better hours.

With no better half to answer to, and no prospects on either side of a camera, I opened a playhouse with my name on it, Roscoe Arbuckle's Plantation Club.

Once the Plantation doors swung open, I took to living a life of all-night revels and all-day morphia nods. Why not? It's not like I needed to memorize lines to shake hands with the genuine imitation flappers and glamour boys who passed through the doors. I kept ROSCOE "FATTY" ARBUCKLE AND HIS MERRY GANG IN A SMART SET REVUE on the marquee. The folks like to know they're getting a show. Even if the show was just a fat souse who pumped your hand at the cash register.

Charlie Chaplin was as likely to roll into the joint as Clara Bow, Al Jolson as Janet Gaynor. In fact, Janet showed up with Charlie the night she won her Academy Award for Best Actress—the very first one ever given out. Janet said if she sharpened the statue's head she could use it to roast weenies. Otherwise, what good was it?

By way of after-hours entertainment, Chaplin invented the Coke Bottle Shuffle, in which he parodied a certain, *ahem*, alleged activity once attributed to me but long since discounted. Theoretically. With a willing lass before him, posterior posed *just so*, Charlie would rework some music-hall bit to current themes. Waggling the bottle in flagrante delicto, he'd sing and wiggle:

It's those darn cokeettes
With their darn darn coke . . .
Why, one thing leads to another
And pretty soon a girl's broke!

Broke he'd punctuate with a forward bump of his hips that sent the cokeette of the evening flying, usually into the bass drum.

I no longer cared who made carnival with my calamities. Or else I did. Or else I'd floated so much alcohol and good German painkiller through my veins I couldn't tell you the difference between please and thank you.

Most nights at the Plantation I started at the door, pressing flesh. More important than the biggos who showed up was how you treated the no-names who walked through the door behind them. And believe me, I hadn't reached the point where I'd lost sympathy for the little fella. Our friendly burg was rife with little guys trying to make it big. (I was one of the few big guys who got little again.)

In the beginning, the Plantation made so much money I couldn't believe it was possible. Feature drinking till dawn every night with your friends and getting paid handsomely for the privilege. A sizable chunk of the clientele were silent actors who never made their way into talkies. Professionals who, even if they hadn't exactly rallied round in my time of need, I still had feelings for. Poor old John Gilbert, a silent titan, spent so much time at the club I gave him his own bar stool. Sometimes he could go as long as an hour without falling off of it.

A lot of these erstwhile stars were broke, and Buster berated me nonstop about what an easy touch I was. One Saturday he dragged me onto a conga line. The dancers held up a banner that said THE "FATTY, LOAN ME A QUARTER" LINE. Everybody in the club had to dance past me with their hands out. And I gave everyone who showed me their palm a quarter. No lie. Some chiselers came by twice, but I let it slide. You think I don't remember what it was like being hungry? I'll tell you a secret: I don't remember what it's like *not* to be. Even when I'm not.

You figure it out.

Crash

Had I known the financial fate in store for the nation, I'd have hung on to some of those quarters. Black Tuesday hit in October '29 like a thug with a blackjack, and I was caught as flatfooted as any Wall Street sidewalk diver. The Plantation gasped along for another couple of months, but few folks had the money left to burn. And the ones who did did not want to spread it around. My last gesture as club owner was to rip out John Gilbert's bar stool from the floor and hand it to him. I don't think the old ham had anywhere to go when the doors closed. That stool was the closest thing he had to family.

Maybe I was the only man in America secretly glad when the market got kayoed. Now *everybody* was just trying to survive. I signed on with Educational Pictures, to do my part once more as William Goodrich. Considering the state of the union, I tried not to feel too badly about the dregs it was my lot to "direct." I could ride the streetcar to the hack factory every day and hold my head high. At least I had a job. And I wasn't wearing state-issue drawers.

Educational was the brainchild of an erstwhile idealist named Earl Hammol. Hammol began with the high-tone intent of supplying quality films to schools and churches. As the economy tanked, he saw his ideals go down the toilet, along with his life savings. To stay afloat, Earl stopped shooting history lessons and started cranking out cheesy one- and two-reelers, short subjects other studios snapped up as filler to run before their feature presentations. "More time to get their asses in their seats," explained Mr. Hammol, a formerly erudite man, when I asked him why exactly movie theaters would even *want* to run these lousy filmettes.

For the most part, Educational was the kind of place where nobody really met anybody else's eyes. It was the studio where you began working for the sole purpose of making enough money to stop working there. I met the very young Louise Brooks at Educational, while directing *Windy Riley Goes Hollywood*. Louise, like anybody with a thimble of ambition, was just passing through. Educational, it was common knowledge, stood out as last stop for many an older talent, and as the only stop for young ones with no talent at all. Both of which were fine with me.

Life passed by in a mist of pills and cocktail glasses. One day I realized I'd directed an entire reel of film without once raising my eyes from the toes of my brogans. In spite of that, RKO Studios asked me to bang out some stories to direct for Louie Bartels, a quirky comic who starred, if that's the word, in a series of Traveling Salesman Comedies. My first was called *That's My Line*—the tale of a nightie salesman who stumbles into Olde Mexico, where he gets set up by a married matron and seduced by a young woman. The two females also have a couple of men friends, who try to ventilate Señor Lingerie's forehead with fireplace pokers.

It felt strangely nice to mine the hackmeat I'd tumbled into, molding it for hammy Louie Bartels instead of myself. I followed *That's My Line* up with *Beach Pajamas*. In this one our salesman steps into the web of a conniving lady who cons him into mucking up her niece's wedding engagement. Pretending to try on a bathing suit, the evil aunt arranges for her niece, the sweet fiancée, to crash in and catch her in the altogether with her intended, our friend the flummoxed salesman. Another innocent sinner bites the dust.

While I wasn't paying attention, something else happened. I started to care again about what I was doing. Maybe it's because in my shorts, so to speak, I was trying to capture a feeling, not just set up a gag. Each little movie asked the same question life had left me asking myself every waking hour: *What do you do when the world thinks you're a monster, and you know it's the world that's monstrous?*

You try and make good movies, that's what you do. What you don't do is kid yourself that it matters.

Somehow things felt lighter now. I couldn't tell peaceful from numb with a burp gun to my head, but so what? Maybe this was neither. Maybe, I know it sounds sappy, maybe it was just my heart unclenching. Not completely, mind you. Just enough to let a sliver of light into the blackness. A little ray of sunshine called Addie Oakley Dukes McPhail, a sweet-eyed Hollywood up-and-comer who, for reasons I myself could not explain, decided she liked my company. I don't remember meeting Addie, I remember feeling like I knew her. Sure, I was older, and the size of an ice wagon. But Addie laughed like she was falling backwards. It was intoxicating. I could tell her whatever story I was broiling for a Bartels shorty and she'd guffaw. How many girls guffaw?

To my surprise, Addie replied "I wouldn't mind" when I got up the gumption to ask "Would you?" Even after I gave her the ring, I kept thinking she was going to jump up in the middle of dinner somewhere and say, "Just kidding! I wouldn't marry you if your head was a slot machine and your nose spit nickels." But she never did. Say that.

Number Three

Call me a romantic. Addie and I tied the knot on June 21, 1931. I picked the longest day of the year. But I didn't believe in long courtships, and pretty much proposed a week after I met her. Why not? Do you think, in this life, there is one right way and one wrong way to do anything? Maybe the idea is to fuck up as many ways as we can before we die. Maybe the gag is you weren't fucking up after all. In Pittsburgh, I met a midget who juggled sardines. When I asked him "Why sardines?" he said, "Shark won't fit in the suitcase." You got a better explanation for your stellar performance on this planet? Or am I going Oriental?

In 1932, I brought my blushing bride to Broadway. I'd been asked to join an all-star bill in New York with Jack Whiting, Milton Berle, and a pipsqueak named Peter Lind Hayes, making his onstage debut. I only signed on the dotted line 'cause I knew my new girl would be coming with me. I know what you're thinking. What about sex? Well, what about it? Of all the free sleigh rides in the world, what good had sex ever done me? You figure it out.

Addie and I took a big old apartment over Central Park. I used to like just sitting there and staring at the trees. The way the light played on the leaves—dark one second, bright the the next. Somehow it's not a view you get in Los Angeles. Addie would sit beside me and we'd both stare until dusk turned the elms and maples to blurs. I was happiest when things got blurry. I'd do my shows, have dinner with my better half, and go back to Central Park West. That was enough.

Then, out of nowhere, at the end of the Whiting-and-Berle run, Jack Warner called: Would I be available to do *Hey, Pop!*, a two-reeler with child star Billy Heye?

I told Warner I hadn't directed in a while and he got mad,

asked if I was trying to aggravate him. "I'm not talking about directing. This is about you, and little Billy. Starring in the film. That's what I'm talking about."

I couldn't believe I would be appearing on-screen again. "Under my own name?" I asked Warner, at least twice.

"Unless, for some reason, you want to use mine, yeah," Warner said. "If you and the kid click, it'll be the first in a series of two-reelers. Then we move to features."

Just like that. Eleven years after he was so rudely interrupted, Roscoe "Fatty" Arbuckle was back. In fact, by now I'd become such a moral paragon, little Billy's dad left his son in my care for the entire two weeks of shooting. I made it my job to take him to Coney Island every day and teach him manners. We were great copy, and the magazines sent teams of photographers and writers to cover us. "The beach is good, clean, wholesome fun, just like my pictures," I'd say to that now friendly scribe on hand, as he'd write my words down on his little pad. I won't name names, but he was the same fellow who'd printed scurrilous rumors about me and a certain container of bubbly cola. But now he was beaming, grateful for both of us I'd become fit for human consumption again.

"Roscoe," the reporter said, and the way his eyes wet up I think he really meant it, "in this town you're either corn or firecrackers. Well, now you're pure corn, buddy boy."

When *Hey Pop!* came out, the story that ran about my two weeks as little Billy Heye's sorta-Dad made me out to be a cross between scoutmaster and a wacky uncle.

I took time off from work at Warner-Brooklyn to walk on-stage at the Strand before the opening of *Hey, Pop!* It had been 10 years since my name had appeared on a film. The decade had ridden me to the curb. It opened with *Finally I've Made It* and ended with *What Difference Does It Make Anyway?*

Life Is the Pie That Hits You in the Face and Kills You

After *Hey, Pop!* I signed with Vitaphone, a Warner Bros. holding company, for five more two-reelers: *How You Been?*, *Buzzin' Around, Tomalio, Close Relations,* and *In the Dough.* I worked like a man being chased. You spend a few dusk-to-dawns contemplating death by chemical asphyxiation, and tell me how long it takes *your* eyeballs to stop rattling.

In the Dough wrapped around 9 p.m., June 28. It almost wrapped about nine hours earlier, when I ran down a hill top speed for a chase sequence and got so winded I nearly keeled over. I used to be able to do one take on a scene like that, then trot back to my mark, do another one, and do five more. But all it took was one sprint down the road and I was gasping like a gut-punched lunger. Breathing became so painful I had to double up.

The thought formed, as the first stars started passing before my eyes, that I had not really expended much physical energy since going to jail for the first time a million years ago. It's as if, in some way, I'd forgotten about my body for all that time. Maybe this was because of all the horrible things the paper said I'd done with it, and the horrible ways I'd done them. Did my belly think it was guilty?

For a second—it felt like a second, it might have been weeks—I blacked out, and suddenly one voice started echoing inside my head. Right behind my yellow eyeballs. What the voice kept blaring was that uncontrolled, roiling sea monster of a sentence from the first tabloid I saw after they locked me up. I can't even remember the paper. Probably the *Examiner.* What I remember are those words. The *image* they conveyed. The boot-in-the-balls shock of the fact that someone had seen fit to commit mythical slander about my life to print. You can't describe the sensation.

I am hated. People want to ruin me.

What these revelations bode for my immediate future was beyond scary. But before any of that could sink in, there was the voice itself. The voice I heard in my head—it was the voice of my father.

Didn't I always tell you, Roscoe? Didn't I? Listen to what you are . . .

And for a second, the shame and fear of the present was mercifully trumped with memories of past awfulness. Until Daddy began to read, in that high Hoosier whine of his, from the scabrous article I found in the jailhouse crapper.

"*Smothered by Fatty's copious man-breasts, Virginia struggled to inch her face sideways, trying for a final, desperate breath. But Arbuckle had other plans. Chuckling and spilling champagne over the girlish actress's exposed belly, the actor rolled his elephantine form on top of her, thrusting with an animalistic grunt, like a boar in rut, again and again. Until, her insides crushed, Virginia's feeble gasps and cries faded away to faint nothing.*"

The Daddy in my head took a deep, dramatic pause, then rode the story home.

"*She was helpless in the grasp of desires so perverted, so perhaps she can count herself blessed she did not live to feel herself soiled by a fat man's foulness.*"

I'm giving you that last, scalding sample of what lived behind my eyes. What I saw projected in the eyes of others. Just to show you how every word of sanctioned slander was emblazoned in my brain. I'm not as dumb as people think. I have a sizable vocabulary. There's just not much use for that brand of baggage when you do what I do. Not really . . .

But I was talking about slander. After one year. After five years. After 10. The burn of those words had not let up a single degree. I found ways not to visit them, but their heat was there. Like a boiler in the basement, going full-tilt even in summertime.

I can hear you groaning. Fatty Arbuckle, going philosophical? It's like the old Professor Pork Act, where the pig puts on a tux, then stands on two legs and does geometry.

After my little attack in the middle of *In the Dough*, I struggled wobbly to my feet and blinked. Jack Henley, the director, took one look at me and made the decision. "Let's call it a day."

I told Henley, "No dice, we keep going!" And so we kept shooting. The film was due that day, and by God, I'd make sure it was finished. See, this was my chance to get everything back. But—like you always hear people say—by the time I got what I wanted, I realized how little I really wanted it. And anyhow, what was anything a fat man accomplished worth? There seemed little doubt that I would become beloved again. But this time, I'd know it meant nothing. It was a bitter kind of happiness.

That same night, on the 28th—a week late—Addie and I celebrated our one-year anniversary. That very day, word had come down from on high, I'd be back making features next year. Warner was talking talkies. The contract was being drawn up. Maybe, I thought, everything would be returned to me, like the swallows to Capistrano. But what did that matter, once you knew the things were just going to fly away again?

Addie walked down Fifth Avenue and I held her hand and I looked up at the stars and I felt . . . nothing. But not in a bad way.

We went up to our rambling apartment. Gazed at the trees silhouetted by the streetlight. I felt so happy at that moment it was almost crummy. Because everything was so perfect. But I'd had perfect happiness before, more or less, and look what happened . . . The trouble with everything was how suddenly it could turn to nothing. Every Baby Ruth a toothache in a fancy wrapper. So this is what I did: I told Addie I loved her and wanted to hit the hay. She asked if she could undress me, and I said sure. We did that sometimes. Addie took off my clothes and ran me a bath. I called her my geisha girl, since I'd known a few of those in my *Mikado* days.

This is when Addie announced that she had something special she wanted to wear. But she insisted that she wait until after I came out of the bath before showing me. I told her, "Fine, dear." No longer even lamenting my lack of feeling. Life could be just as pleasant without feeling anything. I was going to be a star again. That was enough. Even if I wouldn't feel any differently, at least the world would be right again. And what was that worth?

I lay back in the tub. Closed my eyes. So this is what Job got in the end, I thought, with something like relief. Everything he lost came back—except the delusion that it was really his, and the belief that it mattered.

And then a voice I recognized, but couldn't, *wouldn't* let myself acknowledge, spoke right at me. Daddy again. Why wouldn't the old juicehead stay dead?

Well, bully, for you, Fat Boy. You got just what you wanted. Think that makes you special? Don't kid yourself, potato sack, it don't . . .

And in a flickering, like one frame of a two-reeler, I saw the old man standing there. Ragged as the clothes he was buried in, floating in front of the tub. Out of habit, I checked to see if he was holding a belt.

You know what you got? You got to keep your big rump roast out of the gas oven. That's what you got, Daddy said. And that's all you got.

I made the decision to get up and get the needle right there, and commenced to fix myself an arm cocktail on the spot. Same old heroin the folks at Bayer used to peddle. Okie had a pal in the warehouse. He'd slipped me enough for a weeks' supply.

I fired the whole tube and felt my toes uncurl. I never knew they were curled until I took a shot and I uncurled them. The bubble of dread in my heart whispered *P-O-P!* Red warmth flooded my eyes. The smallest breath of air became a solid thing, nearly too heavy to lift. But that was all right. I didn't need much air. Just enough to hoist my haunches out of the tub.

I toddled out of the bathroom, naked and dripping, and shuffled my last few steps to the window overlooking the park. Let my gaze rest on the dark under the trees.

Now I feel some peace. It's too much, getting everything back. The strain of maybe losing it again and again makes it ashes in my piehole. I would have lived with a crick in my neck from looking over my shoulder, waiting for Calamity Jane to ride up and shoot a message in my fat and mortal ass one more time.

No, sir. It's easier this way. Easier to gaze out the window, into trees and darkness. I ask you again, what was anything a fat man accomplished? A pile of leaves waiting for a wind.

I've been dodging the hook since I was 10. I'm out of somersaults.

Write this down.

St. Francis Hotel, Room 1221
San Francisco
2003

Bibliography

American Silent Film. William K. Everson. New York: Da Capo Press, 1978 (reprint).

American Silent Film: Discovering Marginalized Voices. Gregg Bachman and Thomas J. Slater, eds. Carbondale, Illinois: Southern Illinois University, 2002.

American Weekly. "Love, Laughter and Tears: The Hollywood Story." Adela Rogers St. Johns. Oct. 22, 1950.

A-Z of Silent Film Comedy: An Illustrated Companion. Glenn Mitchell. London: B. T. Batsford, 1998.

Behind the Mask of Innocence: Sex, Violence, Prejudice, Crime—Films of Social Conscience in the Silent Era. Kevin Brownlow. Berkeley: University of California Press, 1990.

California Babylon: A Guide to Sites of Scandal, Mayhem, and Celluloid in the Golden State. Kristan Lawson and Anneli Rufus. New York: St. Martin's Griffin, 2000.

Cocaine Fiends and Reefer Madness: An Illustrated History of Drugs in Movies. Michael Starks. New York: Cornwall Books, 1982.

Comedy Is a Man in Trouble: Slapstick in American Movies. Alan Dale. Minneapolis: University of Minnesota Press, 2000.

The Comic Mind: Comedy and the Movies. Gerald Mast. Indianapolis: Bobbs-Merrill, 1973.

The Day the Laughter Stopped. David A. Yallop. New York: St. Martin's Press, 1976.

An Evening's Entertainment: The Age of the Silent Feature Picture, 1915–1928. History of American Cinema, Vol. 3. Richard Koszarski. Berkeley: University of California Press, 1990.

Frame-Up! The Untold Story of Roscoe "Fatty" Arbuckle. Andy Edmonds. New York: William Morrow, 1991.

The Grove Book of Hollywood. Christopher Silvester, ed. New York: Grove Press, 1998.

Hearst over Hollywood: Power, Passion, and Propaganda in the Movies. Louis Pizzitola. New York: Columbia University Press, 2002.

Hep-Cats, Narcs, and Pipe Dreams: A History of America's Romance with Illegal Drugs. Jill Jonnes. New York: Scribner's, 1996.

Hollywood Babylon. Kenneth Anger. New York: Dell, 1975.

Hollywood Death and Scandal Sites. E. J. Fleming. Jefferson, North Carolina: McFarland & Company, 2000.

Hollywood Remembered: An Oral History of Its Golden Age. Paul Zollo. New York: Cooper Square Press, 2002.

Hollywood Studio. "The Early Years of Roscoe 'Fatty' Arbuckle." Frank Taylor. June 1971.

Inventing the Dream: California Through the Progressive Era. Kevin Starr. New York: Oxford University Press, 1985.

The Keystone Kid: Tales of Early Hollywood. Coy Watson Jr. Santa Monica: Santa Monica Press, 2001.

Letter to Adolph Zukor and Joseph Lasky. Arthur Hammerstein. Dec. 26, 1922. Academy of Motion Picture Arts and Sciences Library, Beverly Hills.

Letter to Adolph Zukor. William Hays. Dec. 1921. Academy of Motion Picture Arts and Sciences Library, Beverly Hills.

Letter to Adolph Zukor. William Hays. Dec. 25, 1921. Academy of Motion Picture Arts and Sciences Library, Beverly Hills.

Letter to Adolph Zukor. William Hays. Sept. 5, 1922. Academy of Motion Picture Arts and Sciences Library, Beverly Hills.

Letter to Joseph Lasky. Roscoe C. Arbuckle. Oct. 1, 1921. Academy of Motion Picture Arts and Sciences Library, Beverly Hills.

Mabel. Betty Harper Fussell. New York: Ticknor & Fields, 1982.

Motion Picture World. "'Fatty' Arbuckle Allied with Paramount." Jan. 27, 1917.

Moving Picture World. "Hays Suspends 'Fatty' Arbuckle Films." April 29, 1922.

National Board of Review of Motion Pictures. "The Return of Arbuckle to the Screen." Dec. 23, 1922. Academy of Motion Picture Arts and Sciences Library, Beverly Hills.

The New Biographical Dictionary of Film. David Thomson. New York: Alfred A. Knopf, 2002.

New York Sun. "Fatty Arbuckle Dies in Sleep." June 29, 1933.

New York Times. "Testifies Arbuckle Admitted Attack." Sept. 22, 1921.

New York Times. "Testify to Bruises on Virginia Rappe." Sept. 23, 1921.

New York Times. "Semnacher Tells of Arbuckle Party." Sept. 24, 1921.

New York Times. "Women Testify Today in Arbuckle Case." Sept. 26, 1921.

New York Times. "Charges Blackmail at Arbuckle Trial." Sept. 27, 1921.

New York Times. "Prosecution Rests in Arbuckle Case." Sept. 28, 1921.

New York Times. "Arbuckle on Bail for Manslaughter." Sept. 29, 1921.

New York Times. "Fatty Arbuckle Comes Back with Pardon from Hays." Dec. 20, 1922.

New York Times. "Fatty Gets Big Ovation at Pantages Debut." June 7, 1924.

"Nobody Loves a Fat Man." Minta Durfee Arbuckle. Unpublished, 1953.

The Parade's Gone By . . . Kevin Brownlow. 1968. Berkeley: University of California Press, 1996 (reprint).

"Personal Impressions of the Famous Trial." Rev. James L. Gordon. 1922.

Photoplay Magazine. "Heavyweight Athletics." K. Owen. April 1915.

Photoplay Magazine. "Love Confessions of a Fat Man." Roscoe Arbuckle, as told to Adela Rogers St. John.

Photoplay Magazine. "Speaking of Pictures." James R. Quirk. August 1925.

Roscoe "Fatty" Arbuckle: A Biography of the Silent Film Comedian, 1887–1933. Stuart Oderman. Jefferson, North Carolina: McFarland & Company, 1994.

The Silent Clowns. Walter Kerr. New York: Da Capo Press, 1990 (reprint).

Silent Stars. Jeanine Basinger. New York: Alfred A. Knopf, 2000.

This Is Hollywood: An Unusual Movieland Guide. Ken Schessler. Redlands, California: Ken Schessler Publishing, 1978.

The Timetables of History. Laurence Urdang, ed. New York: Simon & Schuster, 1981.

Jerry Stahl is the author of the bestselling memoir *Permanent Midnight* and the novels *Perv—A Love Story* and *Plainclothes Naked*. He has one daughter and lives in Los Angeles.

A NOTE ON THE TYPE

The text of this book is set in Linotype Sabon, named after the type founder, Jacques Sabon. It was designed by Jan Tschichold and jointly developed by Linotype, Monotype, and Stempel in response to a need for a typeface to be available in identical form for mechanical hot metal composition and hand composition using foundry type.

Tschichold based his design for Sabon roman on a font engraved by Garamond, and Sabon italic on a font by Granjon. It was first used in 1966 and has proved an enduring modern classic.